Grim and Bear It

Grim and Bear It

A Love Me Dead Romance

Heather Novak

TULE
PUBLISHING

Dedication

To Dana Nussio, for continuously shoving me out of my own way.

For Sarah Estep, who virtually held my hand through this entire book.

And as always, in loving memory of my mom.

Prologue

*Rule #1: Reapers are forbidden to remain in contact
with human persons from their human life.*

– The Reaper Code of Ethics, official handbook

Poppy

October

I KNEW SPYING on the love of my life without him know-ing was super creepy. In my defense, he couldn't see me—I'd been dead for twelve years. But I could see *him,* and if I had saliva, I'd be drooling. Jake was wearing faded, paint-stained jeans and a tight white T-shirt. He sat in a beat-up computer chair, pushing himself around with his non-injured leg as he used a long pole to paint the twelve-foot walls in Blackburn House's drawing room.

"Welcome back." Sebastian, Jake's ghost roommate who'd died in the mid-1800s, appeared next to me wearing his finest Victorian-era suit. I was a little jealous. The outfit I'd been wearing when I died was a bit embarrassing. But at least I got to cover it with a long purple cloak. "Enjoying the view?"

"Always. How's researching the venom going?" I

1

prompted. Sebastian and I had become close friends from my frequent visits, and he'd been keeping me up to date on Jake's latest case with SHAP, Supernatural Human Accountability Partnership.

"Tedious," he sighed, crossing his hands over his stomach. Sebastian worked as a ghost agent, often on the same cases as Jake. "But Jake's good at what he does and there have been minimal complications."

"Does he ever sleep?"

"You already know the answer to that. He has to care for everyone himself."

I watched Jake's back muscles flex with each pull of the roller and wondered what it would be like to wrap my arms around him and bury my face in his neck. Would he be warm and solid? Would he smell the same as he did in high school? Would his stubble feel scratchy against my skin? "That's probably my fault for dying on him."

"I'm not an expert on grim reapers, but I assume that you didn't have much of a choice in the matter."

I snorted. "You can't pick your ancestors."

Sebastian forced a smile but didn't reply, a specialty of his when something hit too close to home. A light laugh filled the air and I looked over to see Mina, Jake's former SHAP partner, wiping paint out of her blonde faux mohawk. Her girlfriend, Carma, was on the top of a very tall ladder with a dripping paintbrush in her hand.

I smiled as Carma blew Mina a kiss before scraping some paint off her brush. I was impressed at Carma's lack of fear of being eight feet off the ground. I was dead and would still hesitate to climb up that high.

"Will I see you next week for Mina's mother's nuptials?"

Before I had a chance to answer, Reggie—Sebastian's best friend and SHAP partner—poofed in at my other side. "Esqueleto, twice this month? Will you be at the wedding here next week? Mina's mom is getting married."

Sebastian crossed his arms. "I just inquired myself, but she has yet to respond."

I smiled at Reggie's nickname for me, skeleton. "Sí," I promised, switching to Spanish. I knew five languages, like most reapers. Being multilingual made communicating with souls easier. Sebastian wasn't fluent in Spanish, but in the year since Reggie's appearance, he'd learned the basics.

Since his death, Reggie couldn't speak to most of his family. When he found out I could speak Spanish, he had been thrilled, since most ghosts in Applechester, Michigan, only spoke English. While I had originally learned Mexican Spanish, I'd begun studying Reggie's Guatemalan dialect and was getting better with every visit.

I nodded about Mina's mom's wedding. "Me encantan las bodas." I loved weddings.

"Ya sabemos," they both said in unison, exasperated.

I waved my hand and clucked my tongue. *Whatever.* I glanced at Reggie. "How's Lola?" I asked in Spanish. "She stop trying to exorcise you yet?" Reggie lived with his brother Alan who had partial custody of Reggie's niece Lola, who was very afraid of ghosts.

He lifted a shoulder. "She searched 'how to talk to dead people' instead of 'how to perform an exorcism' last week."

"That's progress."

We sat in companionable silence for a moment, watching Jake cover a hideous orange with a pink so light it was almost white. It made the room look bigger and I bet the sunset would make the color glow.

"He should've used a primer. The orange will show through," I said.

Reggie waved away my concern. "Paint's changed a lot in twelve years. There's a primer mixed in. Promises complete coverage."

That would've been awesome to have when I was trying to repaint my childhood bedroom from magenta to mint green. Jake had helped me put on three coats before we gave up and bought a primer. I wondered what the new owners painted that room. Probably something boring like beige.

"It's weird that you come back to visit," Reggie said. "I can't go back."

I shrugged. "I tried to stay away, but I need to know he's alive and well. I can deal with the memories." Most of the time.

Sebastian tilted his head in question and I translated, before switching to English.

"Even if he can't see you?" Sebastian asked.

I pressed my hand to my chest. "I hope he never can." Humans only saw grim reapers when they were about to die. Jake seeing me would be the worst day of my unlife. Even worse than the day I died. "I hope he's moved on, but I also hope he thinks of me," I whispered.

I watched as Jake pushed himself to the back corner of the room, where an old bar used to reside. Now, it was little more than a discolored square of faded paint. Whenever our parents brought us here for Founders Festival tours or holiday open houses, we would always meet at the corner, where a large storage cabinet had hidden the rest of the room from view. Then we'd sneak off to the kitchens or to explore closed off rooms.

It had been the spot where he first took my hand when I was ten and he was twelve. Where he called me beautiful when I was twelve and he was fourteen. Where I waited for him at fifteen to show him my new holiday dress. Where he whispered, "kiss me," despite our parents forbidding a relationship between us, and I pressed my lips against his for the first time. Every room in this house held a memory of us, but that corner held the most.

He dipped his roller into the paint tray then lifted it, pausing in midair.

"Jake," I whispered, wishing for the five-millionth time he could see me, hear me, feel me, before desperately shoving the wish deep into the recesses of my dead heart.

He closed his eyes, shook his head, and continued painting.

Reggie leaned his head against my shoulder. "We can tell him about you, you know," he whispered. "You don't have to be a stranger like this."

I laid my head back on his for a moment, then straightened and stepped away. "It does have to be like this. If he could communicate with me, I…" I shook my head at the thought. "I couldn't… I wouldn't…"

I didn't need to finish the sentence. They knew. Sebastian looked out the large window, the crescent moon high in the sky. I recognized that haunted look in his eyes and wanted to ask but didn't. Pushing him to open up would just make him shut down and my friends were precious commodities. I was an introvert by nature, something dying hadn't changed.

"You're my date next week," Reggie claimed.

Sebastian blinked before focusing on him. "Incorrect, sir. She's my date. You have a boyfriend."

Reggie winked at him. "Just checking if you were paying attention."

I rolled my eyes. A sharp tug at the center of my chest silently warned me my break time was up. I blew them both a kiss and shot one last lingering look at Jake. "Miss you," I whispered. He didn't look over his shoulder as I disappeared.

Chapter One

Jake

One week later

I WAS CURSED, at least when it came to weddings. After the first one—my dad and stepmom Magnolia's wedding—my grandpa was diagnosed with dementia. After the second, coincidentally their vow renewal, my first love, Poppy, disappeared. The third was an almost wedding; my sister's fiancé died two weeks before.

As for the fourth? I was late and now had a bloodstain on my suit coat. Should've taken off the coat before trying to break up a venom handoff.

"Behind you!" My new partner, Paris, shouted before elbowing her assailant in the neck, then flipping him to his back. She had come from the research and development department, eager to dig into the oral vampire venom case. I was lucky that her twin brother also worked in the field and had cross-trained her. She'd passed her field work test immediately and was assigned as my new partner, since my former partner left.

I didn't have time to watch her cuff the guy before I turned around and used my cane to hit my attacker on the shoulder hard enough to bring him to his knees. I knocked him out with another stroke and rolled him, tucking my cane in my armpit as I zip-tied his wrists together. I should've brought the gray cane with the knife in it, instead of my civilian black, but I was supposed to be at a wedding.

This had been the biggest bust this month and we were getting closer to the top of the venom distribution food chain. As soon as this job was done, I was finished with field work. Another few weeks and I would get to mentor my niece, Daisy, and give my bones a much-needed rest.

The footsteps behind me might as well have been an air-horn. I swung around, fist connecting with a man's jaw. He crumpled and Paris dove down to finish restraining him. I stumbled forward and caught myself on her shoulder before righting myself with my cane.

"I've got an ice pack in my lunchbox. Grab it before you head out," she offered.

"Thanks." Two knee surgeries, shrapnel to my thigh and hip, and a touch of arthritis from repeat injuries had left me in chronic pain. Most days were tolerable, but the fighting days kicked my ass. I had a freezer full of ice packs and a heating pad in nearly every room of my place.

I sighed in relief as two SHAP vans rolled up followed by my sister's minivan. "You good?"

Paris gave me a thumbs-up.

"You don't want to come and say hi?" I teased. For whatever reason, Paris and my younger stepsister, Eliza, couldn't stand each other. I maintained if they just spent more time together, they'd get along.

"Don't forget the ice pack," she replied.

I shuffled to her car—she'd picked me up from my place—grabbed the pack and moved to Eliza's passenger door. With a groan, I hoisted myself in and slapped the ice on my leg, then buckled up. I was going to need to add heat to my hip later, but this would help for now.

"Well, at least there's no blood on your face," Eliza said before navigating out of the parking lot. "We'll sneak you in the back."

"Paris had my back, thankfully."

She just rolled her eyes. "Stop trying to make me like her. She better have your back, anyway."

I held up my hands in surrender. "You didn't tell Mina, right?"

"Cross my heart."

I nodded. "Good."

Mina, my best friend and former partner, had enough on her plate today. Mina was the maid of honor in her mom's second wedding, her girlfriend Carma the event planner, and Eliza, a bridesmaid. To add more stress to her plate, this was Carma's first event in her new bed and breakfast, Blackburn Mansion. Plus, Carma was meeting my stepmom today. Mina was so nervous, it almost made me nervous.

Mina was no longer part of SHAP, having been terminated for her relationship with her new girlfriend, who was our mark during our last case. The case I was still working at breaking open. The case that was a pain in my ass, as demonstrated by the bloodstain on my coat. I rubbed at the large spot on my sleeve and grumbled an expletive.

"SHAP cleaners will get that out," Eliza promised.

"We have fifteen minutes before pictures."

She grimaced. "Yeah, you're screwed." She made a hard right and then a left, pulling into the back parking lot of Blackburn House and bypassing the valet.

"I should be upset that the takedown was in Applech-ester, but today I'm glad," I admitted.

"Same. Mom would've lost her mind if we were late."

She was right. It didn't matter that I was thirty and Eliza was twenty-eight. My stepmom, Magnolia, lived by the three P code: punctuality, politeness, perseverance (and Jesus). My mom had died when I was a toddler and Magnolia had been the only mother I'd known. Out of respect for her...and because she still scared me a little, I always tried to be punctual.

I opened the van door and Sebastian appeared, touching the brim of his top hat. "Perfect timing. I shall distract Mina from the goings-on. The bathroom to the left of the kitchen is unoccupied."

I slid out of the seat, swallowing a groan. "Roger."

He disappeared.

Eliza tugged at my coat. "Come on, I'll help."

I brushed her off. "I've got it. Don't get blood on your dress. You're all pretty and shit." Her red hair had been pulled back in some fancy low bun and her blue dress matched her eyes, which for once weren't full of sadness.

"I can be pretty and help."

"Yes, but today is not that day. Go away before anyone gets suspicious."

With a roll of her eyes, she held the door open for me, then ran down the hall in the opposite direction, adjusting her hair as she moved. I moved to the bathroom Sebastian had recommended, concentrating on being inconspicuous.

My plan failed. Mina was one of the best SHAP field agents in North America. It wasn't hard for her to deduce why Eliza, Sebastian, and I disappeared at the same time. I had barely gotten the sleeve wet before Mina walked in, closing the door behind her and locking it.

"You thought I really wouldn't notice?"

I shrugged. "I'd hoped. You have enough on your plate."

She crossed her arms. "I'm only giving you a pass because this is Carma's first official event and she's stressed."

"I can't believe she offered to host."

Mina threw her hands up. "Right?! I had to redo all the invitations. But it is much better than city hall and a church basement."

"Agreed. And your mom's in love with her forever now."

Mina smiled in a way I'd only ever seen her do in relation to Carma. "Yeah. Me too."

My heart thudded hard once at the thought of Poppy, the girl who used to make me smile like that. There were so many memories of her in these walls, and I swore if I looked hard enough, I could almost see her. I had promised to love her forever and she'd promised me back. Turned out we were liars.

I cleared my throat. "You look magnificent," I told Mina. I didn't know a lot about dresses, but I did know the light blue fabric fit her perfectly.

"Thank you." Her fair cheeks turned pink and I almost started laughing. I didn't even know Mina knew how to blush until she met Carma. "You keep flexing your right hand. Did you punch someone? Need ice?"

I looked at my soon-to-be bruised knuckles. My white skin was tan from spending so much time outside over the summer, but even a tan couldn't hide the red splotches. I was sore, but nothing I hadn't dealt with a hundred times. "It's the coat I'm worried about." I turned off the water and squeezed out the sleeve, then laid it over the side of the sink. "I think the stain is actually worse."

"Not gonna get blood out with generic hand soap, buddy. Mom isn't gonna care if you're in a coat. Isaac isn't even wearing one and he's the groom."

I put my back against the wall, leaning on my cane to take the pressure off my left leg. I felt sixty years old today. "Magnolia will have thoughts."

Mina smirked. "She always does." She pursed her lips and tilted her head, her tell for when she was connecting the dots. "A venom deal in broad daylight? In Applechester? That's scary shit."

I just raised my gaze to hers and stayed silent. I couldn't tell her anything about the investigation. Mina didn't know how deep the illegal distribution ring of oral vampire venom ran, with Carma's mom merely a figurehead of the operation. We had taken down three groups in the last month alone.

While we hadn't spotted any more rogue vampires running around the city, it didn't mean we were in the clear. Mina's eyes widened for a moment, but she nodded. She could read my silence.

Two ghosts walked through the wall to the left of Mina. One was Sebastian, and the other was his best friend, Reggie. Reggie was a Guatemalan-American man in his early thirties, with tawny skin and dark hair.

"Gracias a Dios, I died wearing dress pants," Reggie said. "If I had to go to the wedding in jeans I would simply just die. Again."

"Eliza's dress is spotless, and Carma is repairing Eliza's hair," Sebastian added, turning to Mina. "Your mom's ready for family photographs."

I pinched the bridge of my nose. "What are we going to say happened to my suit coat?"

Mina walked over, unbuttoned my sleeves and rolled them twice up my forearms. Then she moved her fingers swiftly through my dark hair. "Nothing."

Reggie and Sebastian gasped in unison, as if what she said was against all rational thought. "Jake is going to break out in hives," Reggie whispered.

"Make sure you don't have any blood under your finger-nails and hurry up. Carma is in charge of the schedule today and if you stress her out, I will kill you with my high heel."

I looked at myself in the mirror and straightened my hair. It was a little longer than I usually wore it, mostly because I didn't have time to get a haircut. "You made me look like more of a mess."

She shook her head. "I made you look artfully casual. Totally different and looks intentional."

"Magnolia's still going to have thoughts."

"Would you rather her be annoyed at you for looking casual or for making a drug bust a half hour before the wedding?"

I winced. I had promised not to work today and Magnolia never forgot a promise. "Casual it is."

I looked over at the ghosts. "I know you both have thoughts."

Reggie sighed. "You're still unfairly attractive. Are you sure I'm not your type?"

I laughed. "I do prefer my partners to have a pulse." While I was pansexual and open to exploring a relationship with all gender identities, I had a preference for *living* people. "And ones that don't already have a boyfriend."

He held out his arm for Sebastian. "Let's go find Clint and get a good seat."

"Hey," I said as soon as the ghosts left, "you okay?" Mina had taken her mom's engagement hard.

She smiled. "I am really happy to welcome Isaac into the family officially. I know he's practically my age, but he and Mom are good for each other. As long as she's happy, I'm happy."

"Wow, Summers, I never thought I'd see the day you'd have as much emotional maturity as my eight-year-old niece. You've definitely graduated from wet toilet paper. Remind me to thank Carma."

"Do you think our moms will be mad if I broke your nose?"

"Wait until after the pictures, babe. You look smoking in that dress. Don't ruin it with my blood."

With a shake of her head, she walked over and wrapped her arms around my shoulders. "Love you, you weirdo."

"Love you, too. Now move it. We're late."

Chapter Two

Rule #4: Off-hours are to be spent in the reaper world and not in the human world.

— The Reaper Code of Ethics, official handbook

Poppy

I WAS BASICALLY the FedEx of death. DeadEx, if you will. My job seven days a week, nearly eighteen hours a day, was to ferry souls from the human world to the afterlife. I was a cog in the corporate afterlife. Well, technically I'd become a reaper at sixteen, so I'd never had a corporate job, but based solely on my memory of Dolly Parton's catchy song "9 to 5," this felt like the equivalent.

Except I didn't actually get any currency in exchange for my labor. Only chronic seasickness and moderate depression. And, if you asked my sister Sylvia, "too much snark." As if such a thing even existed.

Most grim reapers, especially my siblings, were obsessed with all things gruesome and deadly, but to me, it was just a dead-end job (pun intended). However, death was a family business, and I was one of four kids. Death was my birthright.

I was obsessed with weddings. More accurately, I was in

love with love. Death was fine, but so dark and common-place. Everyone died, and then it was my job to escort them—usually kicking and screaming—to the afterlife.

But love, true love, was rare. It was golden and glittery, like champagne. I could no longer consume food, but back in my human days, my friend Eliza and I had snuck a bottle of champagne into our cabin at summer camp. Our cabin-mate swore the fizzy drink tasted like love felt.

I'd only had three sips, but she'd been right. The bubbles on my tongue matched the way my heart burst whenever I was around Eliza's older brother, Jake. We weren't allowed to be together because of an almost two year age difference—both sets of parents had made that very clear—but Eliza was on our side and wanted me as her sister. Besides, I was supposed to have time to grow up, graduate, and start over with Jake somewhere else.

Time that I ended up not having. Not while alive, any-way. I had all the time in the world now that I was dead.

My great-grandma had been the last person called to be a reaper, and she had been in her late sixties. They hadn't called my grandparents yet, and anyway I had still been in high school. They rarely pulled kids, wanting us to grow up and live a little, get married, reproduce, and make more reapers. Nepotism at its finest.

I had been sixteen, full of dreams, and out of school for the summer. It had been sweaty days lying by the neighbor-hood pool with Eliza in matching pink bikinis, Jake beside us. It was the feel of wet skin on skin as I ignored the lifeguards and jumped on Jake's back, dunking him. It was sitting next to him in the passenger seat—at Eliza's insistence—while he drove us around. I was mesmerized by the easy way he handled the car. It was his tanned forearms, his long fingers wrapped around the wheel, the music playing with the windows down, the flash of his smile when I said something funny, his sunglasses reflecting my own smile back. It was his pinky finger wrapping around mine.

It was slipping out my window to the tree house as soon as our parents went to bed. It was curling into Jake's arms the moment he climbed in beside me, the butterflies in my stomach as we stared at each other, nearly nose to nose. It was whispered promises that in just a few more years, we'd both be over eighteen and could be together despite our parents' objections. It was the way he held my face in his hands as if I were precious, the way he'd ask, *kiss me?* It was those rare, secret moments, just before dawn, when our kisses grew more heated and he made me see stars behind my eyes with clever hands and soft lips.

It was long summer days looking online at colleges with Eliza, debating how we'd decorate our shared dorm room. It was whispered confessions that we didn't only like boys, and rainbow stickers on our cheeks during the town's Pride parade. It was that summer-camp-champagne-hazy plan to be neighbors when Jake and I finally grew up and got married.

And then August came.

"Poppy!" My older sister, Sylvia, whispered, interrupting my reminiscing. I jumped, still easily startled even though I was dead. "I was waiting for you! Why are you watching some wedding in Applechester?" She made a face. "And what's your obsession with this old house? It stopped being cool when we were like ten."

I sighed in exasperation. I only had six personal hours a day and I absolutely hated it when someone interrupted me. Even my siblings. I grabbed her arm and pulled her away from the ceremony, a reflex. No one could see or hear us. No one human, anyway. "Just let me watch them say their vows. Death isn't going anywhere."

"Ugh you're so gross."

"Says the woman who likes to watch people die."

"Says the woman watching a stranger's wedding. And on a Sunday. Who has a wedding on a Sunday?"

"Sundays are cheaper."

She crossed her arms and pouted, then pulled up the hood of her dark purple cloak, a reaper staple. I had covered my cuffs in sequins just to make it flashy. "Fine," she caved. "Get all mushy, just don't be late."

"I'm never late."

She rolled her eyes. She was ten years older than me and still found me—and my rule following—exasperating, even in death. With a huff, she waved and disappeared, likely going to enjoy watching the last moments before someone died.

I was glad she left before she got a good look around, because if she had, she'd know that I wasn't exactly following the rules. I brushed my hood down and inched closer to the ceremony just as the beautiful brunette woman in a simple ivory gown met the man at the end of the aisle. When the audience sat down, my old friends were standing there.

If I had a beating heart, it would've somersaulted. Jake was next to Eliza, wearing gray suit pants and a light blue tie, but no coat. His white shirt hugged his biceps, his hair just a little longer than he usually wore it. God, he looked even better than last week.

He shifted his weight so he leaned heavier on his cane. His jaw tightened for a brief moment, and I wished I could do something to ease his pain. My chest cavity ached with echoes of emotion as I watched Eliza wipe away a tear with her thumb while smiling, and Jake pull two gold bands from his pocket to give to Magnolia, his stepmom, who was officiating. They all looked happy. Good.

I scanned the crowd for Eliza's daughter, Daisy, who was sitting in the front row, leaning on the edge of her seat. She was so big now, maybe eight or nine. She smiled huge, her eyes wide as she watched the ceremony. She was the spitting image of her mom at the same age. I wished I could be her favorite aunt, tell her silly bedtime stories, take her to concerts when she got older, help celebrate all her milestones.

I wished, I wished, I wished...

Sebastian looked over his shoulder at me and touched the air where the brim of his top hat typically sat, although he'd taken it off for the ceremony. I nodded at him, and smiled at Reggie, who had his arm around Clint. I took a step back, preparing to disappear as soon as the couple walked back down the aisle. This time, I had to stay away for longer. I'd visited three times this month, and that was just too risky.

If I ever got caught, I would be permanently removed from duty. In the bad way. Sentencing ranged from working a desk job inside a reaper building, meaning no returning to the human world ever again, to being banished to Isle of Exile, where I would be removed from existence by a soul-hungry creature. Neither of those options seemed like a party.

To be fair, outside of Sylvia, it was unlikely someone would even bother to check on me. I was the "good kid." The one who always followed the rules and did as she was told, with the exception of my love for Jake. He had been mine since he was eight and I was six.

We had just moved in next door and he and Eliza came by to invite us to play in their treehouse. I'd nearly fallen down the ladder, but he had caught me. Twenty-two years later and my death had changed nothing. I was still in love with him.

I would give all of eternity to spend one more human day with them. Everything to hug Eliza. Everything to kiss Jake. Everything to redo my last living memory with them, when I'd chickened out on saying good-bye.

We'd been in this house, this same room, only twelve years ago. Jake had walked over to me and held out his hand and said, "Dance with me."

I had been powerless to do anything but slide my palm against his. He pulled me into him and slipped his arm around my waist, whispering the song lyrics against the top of my head. We weren't even standing close enough for it to be called a hug, yet sparks cascaded between my chest and stomach. I closed my eyes, memorizing the moment.

Tomorrow wouldn't come. Not for me. My dads had gotten *the call* and our time was up. At midnight tonight, just like Cinderella, my magical life ended. Tomorrow, I'd wake up as a reaper, joining the family business at sixteen.

I wish they hadn't told me, that they had let me be the

carefree, silly girl for one last night. The girl who would've shouted the lyrics to "Sweet Caroline" without pausing because she was fighting tears. Who wouldn't be staring at my best friends throughout the entire day, trying to memorize their laughs and smiles.

"What's wrong, love?" Jake asked, his lips so close to my ear, I could feel the heat of his breath.

"Nothing."

He squeezed my hand and twirled me, then brought me back in closer. "You're a terrible liar."

I bit my bottom lip, trying to keep it from trembling, but no amount of willpower kept a tear from leaking. Without saying a word, he maneuvered us to the side of the dance floor and out the patio doors. He dropped his arms and grabbed my hand, tugging us to the side of the patio. We were still in partial view, but a few carefully placed bushes lent us some privacy.

"Seriously, what's going on?"

I shook my head. I couldn't—and wouldn't—tell him. "Had a fight with my dads," I said instead. It wasn't a lie; I had screamed at them until my throat ached, then cried for hours. Only a cool cloth over my eyes and carefully applied makeup had covered up the swelling.

"Bad?"

I nodded. "Really bad." I tried to wipe the wet away with the back of my hands, but it kept coming. "We're…" *dying* "moving."

He sucked in a sharp breath and pulled me into his arms. "Eliza and I both have driver's licenses. We'll figure it out. Only a year and a half, love, and it's you and me, okay?"

Yes, please, yes. I just shook my head against his chest. "It's really far away."

"Poppy, you're breaking my heart," he whispered. "What can I do to help?"

I covered my face with my hands and sobbed.

He rubbed my back, swaying us back and forth. "I love you," he whispered. "We'll figure this out, okay?"

I didn't even bother to nod. There was nothing to figure out. I was going to be dead, and he wasn't going to be there. I don't know how long we stood like that—maybe a minute, maybe an hour—but we didn't move until Eliza called for us.

"We'll be right there!" Jake called. "Poppy just needed some air." He pulled back and brushed my hands away from my face, tilting my chin up. "You gotta stop crying unless you want twenty questions from Eliza."

"I don't know h-how."

He leaned toward me, his eyes never moving from mine. "Kiss me."

My stomach plummeted through my body, the ground, the center of the earth. "What? In public?" We only ever kissed in the dark, in secret moments or underneath blankets.

Of course, what did it matter? What were my parents going to do if they saw us? Punish me until I died? *Ha!*

"Kiss me," he repeated in a low voice. A command not a question.

In that moment, only two and a half hours before my time as a human was washed away, I couldn't think of a single thing I wanted to do *more* than kiss this man. I forgot all about my tears and wrapped my arms around his neck.

His nose bumped mine and I tilted my chin higher, brushing his lips with my own. It was an innocent embrace, him holding still as I pressed my mouth to his a second time, a third. A fourth. Tingles chased down my arms and chest, filling me with curls of heat.

When I pulled away, his lips chased mine for one more kiss, then another. My entire world narrowed down to that moment. Him and me, kissing under the stars on a warm summer evening. His arms held me tighter, and his tongue flicked over my lips, making me gasp. I deepened the kiss, trying to prolong the moment.

Jake wasn't my first kiss—that honor went to Mazy Kline at summer camp—but he was my favorite. And my last. And it was perfect. His tongue brushed my lower lip and then was gone, his head lifting and turning toward the party. "Someone's coming."

He let go of me, smoothed down my hair, and took a giant step away. My fingers went to my mouth, as if I could hold the feel of him there for eternity. I dropped my hand when Eliza bounced around the topiaries. "Uh, pretty sure Mom saw you—" She stopped short and looked between us. "What's wrong?"

"Had a fight with my dads. I'm fine now." I linked my arm through hers. "Let's go see if there's more cake."

She shot Jake a look, then hesitantly agreed. As we walked away, I looked back at Jake. *Thank you*, I mouthed. Somehow, inexplicably, his kiss had made me stop crying. He smiled at me and put his hands in his pockets.

My dads had forced us to leave the moment Eliza and I

had walked back in, confirming we had been caught. That kiss was the last moment I ever saw Jake when I was alive. It was amazing how much the memory still hurt twelve years later.

It was time to go. Being here today, in this house, with these people was too much. "Until next time, friends," I whispered, then turned around and headed down a hallway toward the kitchen. There was a creek behind the venue that would transport me to my next location. Flowing water always helped.

"This isn't a costume party."

Jake. Icy dread froze me in place. If I still had a stomach, it would have tumbled out of my body and through the center of the earth. "No," I breathed.

Something was happening in my chest. I didn't need to breathe, didn't have a heartbeat, but somehow I couldn't get enough air. I was suffocating. I sucked in a gasp, atmospheric dread crashing down on me.

No. No, no, no. Surely the universe wasn't this cruel, wouldn't make me take the soul of someone I cared for more than myself. I thought I had been hopeless the day I had crawled into my bed, knowing I wouldn't wake up again. This was worse.

"Who are you here for, Reaper?"

If he could see me, it meant he was on borrowed time. It meant I'd be back for him, even if he wasn't on my list today. It meant his days living were numbered, likely weeks at most. If I could cry, I would have burst into tears.

"You can see me?" I asked, my voice barely above a whisper. I hadn't dared to turn around.

He grabbed my wrist, and I sucked in a breath at the touch, at the heat of his skin against mine. He shouldn't be able to touch me, but he shouldn't be able to see me, either. He was so *warm*. He tugged me to face him, paused, then stumbled back.

"Poppy?" His voice cracked with emotion.

I took in his stricken face, his beautiful blue eyes, his parted lips. I could never come back here, never see him again. Even if they asked me to take his soul, I knew in that moment I couldn't do it. This was it. Our final good-bye.

"I'm sorry, Jake." I closed my eyes and disappeared.

Chapter Three

Jake

MY HEART THUNDERED so loud I could no longer hear the music. Every inch of my skin prickled with sweat. My lungs burned and I gasped for air. Holy shit, what had just happened?

Poppy? My Poppy was…a reaper? I reached down and picked up a purple sequin on the floor. I hadn't been hallucinating. She'd really been here.

I didn't scare easily. Didn't jump when the toaster popped, didn't panic when snow was forecasted. I'd been more angry than scared when Mina had crashed her truck and tried to die on me last spring.

Haunted houses and horror movies were mundane—a good thing, too, since I lived with a ghost—but staring at the space where Poppy had stood? Something inside me was irreparably broken. *Was this real life?* She looked exactly the same, except not.

She still had long, dark hair, gray eyes, and fair skin, but nothing that made her Poppy. Her smile was gone, the light behind her eyes extinguished. As if her face was only a mask.

I swallowed hard, knowing that's probably exactly what

it was. She'd been dead for twelve years. She didn't have a real human face anymore.

"Jesus," I whispered, rubbing the back of my neck. I leaned against the wall and took several gulps of air. Poppy was dead. Not only dead, but also a grim reaper.

And I could see her.

I could see her.

I counted out each inhale and exhale, trying to steady my breathing. Poppy had been the reason I'd joined SHAP. I had spent the last twelve years trying to piece clues together about her disappearance. I never found a trace. Not a death certificate, no social media presence, no school records, nothing.

I'd assumed she was in witness protection. How else could she just disappear completely? I'd never thought... I should've... I couldn't have. Access to grim reaper records were above my paygrade. I worked with the living. She worked for the dead.

I sucked in another sharp breath to clear the stinging in my throat and pinched at the bridge of my nose, trying to keep my eyes from watering. I needed to keep it together. I couldn't fall apart for several more hours.

"Uncle Jake!"

I startled as my eight-year-old niece, Daisy, ran at me and wrapped her hands around my waist. "You promised to come dance with me!"

"I did, didn't I?" I managed, then took a deep breath in through my nose and out through my mouth. "Uncle Jake doesn't break his promises. Let's go." I wanted to go clear my head, needed to take a minute or ten to figure out what the hell was going on, but I couldn't disappoint Daisy. There would be plenty of time after the wedding.

My niece bounced on the balls of her feet all the way to the dance floor and waved with both arms at the DJ. The DJ waved back. Only eight and already elaborately planning. I had my work cut out for me.

As I looked down at the smiling girl, I was struck by another realization—Eliza had named her daughter after a flower. Had that been because Eliza's mom, my stepmom, was named Magnolia? Or was that because Poppy's disappearance had left a deep scar on her, too?

"This one's a special request," the DJ announced, then the opening accordion to "The Chicken Dance" boomed over the speakers.

"Come on, Uncle Jake!" Daisy ordered.

"Did you know 'The Chicken Dance' used to be called 'The Duck Dance'?" I asked her, a trivia fact I had picked up on a sleepless night watching bad game shows.

She just shook her head at me while opening and closing her hands, simulating a chicken's beak. "You can't talk your way out of dancing."

I tucked my cane under my arm and moved my hands in the opposite direction. "Is this right?"

"No!" she giggled, turning my hands over. "Like this. Now we flap our arms."

"Kick our legs?"

She dissolved into more laughter as she showed me the correct moves. I hated this dance, but it was worth it to see her smile. I loved being an uncle. I couldn't wait until this investigation was done and I could concentrate on helping her grow into her powers.

If I was still alive. My stomach tightened and I gulped in a breath to keep my focus on Daisy. I looked up at the sound of cheering, spotting Eliza, Mina, and Carma recording us on their cells. Mina was like another sister, but one who didn't get to experience a true childhood. Who had used her gifts too soon, too young, and was still learning how to navigate the world as someone other than a cog in the SHAP machine.

I wouldn't let that happen to Daisy.

Daisy tugged on my sleeve, then jumped on my back. I clenched my jaw to not let out a string of expletives at the pain that shot through my leg at the extra weight. We'd done this dance move a dozen times, but usually I hadn't fought a bunch of drug dealers only hours before.

It had been back when I had more good days with my leg than bad ones, and the cane had been occasionally instead of frequently. Poppy's face flashed behind my eyes and I forgot my leg. If things were about to go wrong, I wanted this memory, wanted Daisy to have this memory.

Her knees dug into my ribs as she threw her hands up high above her head and laughed. I laughed along with her. This was worth the pain.

Then, as if to remind me I was breakable, my leg buckled. I lowered my cane and caught myself, throwing my other hand around my back to keep Daisy from falling.

Eliza rushed over, grabbed her daughter around the waist, and spun her around. "It's my turn to dance with Uncle Jake!"

I straightened, swallowing hard as the sharp pain dulled

to a throbbing.

"Daisy, come dance with me!" Mina called.

My niece scrambled to the ground and darted toward Mina. "Let's go get more cake."

Mina grimaced. She hated cake. "I heard there's also pie. Want to try some pie?"

Daisy grabbed her hand. "Both is good."

Eliza laughed and grabbed my free hand. "Let's sit down and grab some ice for your leg."

"Dance with me a second." Maybe I could give my sister one more happy memory of me, too. Just in case.

"You've overdone it. I can see it in your face."

"I can rest tomorrow," I promised.

She sighed and put her other hand on my shoulder. "We can stand still here for a few minutes."

"Can I ask you a question?"

She grinned. "Since when do you ask permission to butt into my life?"

"I'm feeling magnanimous tonight."

She rolled her eyes. "You can ask me anything. You know that."

"Did you name Daisy after a flower because of Poppy?"

She stilled, her gaze snapping to mine. "You still think about her?"

I nodded once. "Hard not to, here."

"Yeah." She looked around the room once, as if looking for her old friend. "I wish I knew… I keep combing social media, hoping she'll pop on. I just want to know if she's happy, you know? I looked through the SHAP database a few years ago, but nothing came up."

Grim reapers, despite being supernatural creatures, weren't always individually cataloged in the SHAP system. They didn't spend much time in the human world, and when they were here, they were just shepherding souls. Or attending weddings, apparently.

Eliza's eyes met mine. "To answer your question...yes. It had only been a few years since she'd disappeared and I dunno, I just thought it carried on the legacy of our friendship somehow. Plus, it made Mom happy, keeping with the flower theme." She laughed softly. "I'm ridiculous."

I lifted my arm and she twirled. "No, you're pretty awesome," I admitted when she returned. "I miss her, too."

"Maybe nothing bad will happen after this wedding. I mean, outside of the bloodstain."

"That's the dream." My voice was steady, despite the anxiety that poked at the top of my stomach. I wanted to tell her about Poppy, but then it would be real. Tomorrow. I'd tell her tomorrow.

As the song ended, I squeezed her hand. "Want to go find some more cake?"

She squeezed my shoulder then dropped her arms. "I thought you'd never ask."

So we ate cake, and I watched Eliza and Daisy dance the Macarena and Mina and Carma slow dance like they were the only ones in the room. And when we finally said goodnight to the bride and the groom, I believed for one moment everything was going to be okay. How could something bad infiltrate such a wonderful evening?

"There you are!" Magnolia called, rushing over as we opened the front door. "Family dinner next weekend."

Mina and Carma walked up from behind, and as if she had eyes in the back of her head—and I was pretty sure she did—Magnolia spun around and grabbed Carma's arm. "You, too, honey!"

Carma looked startled. "But I'm not family."

Magnolia gave her a pointed stare. "You love my god-daughter?"

"With my whole heart." Carma hadn't even paused.

"Then you're family. See you next Sunday." Magnolia blew us kisses and walked to her car.

"No offense, but she scares me," Carma whispered.

Eliza threw her head back and laughed. "She definitely should've worked for SHAP."

I winked at her. "Don't worry, we'll protect you." Poppy's terrified face flashed in front of my eyes and the words felt like a lie.

Carma wrapped her arm around Mina's waist. "Don't worry, my girl's got my back." Mina's cheeks turned pink as she leaned over and brushed a kiss on her girlfriend's lips.

I tried to memorize this moment, tried to internalize when things didn't go to plan, it still sometimes turned out okay. Despite the pain these two had gone through over the last few months, they'd found a new path with each other. Mina no longer had that soul-deep exhaustion weighing down every movement and Carma didn't look like she was two seconds away from bursting into tears.

If something happened to me, they'd be okay. Eliza and Daisy would have Dad and Magnolia. Sebastian materialized next to me and tilted his head to the side. I fell back two steps. "Everything okay?"

He put his top hat on his head. "Jacob, how were you talking with Poppy?"

I startled. *How did he even know Poppy?* I looked around, checking for people listening in. Magnolia had spies everywhere. "We'll talk at home."

"Yes, I suppose we will."

To: G_Fletcher@unbelievablebodies.inc
From: B.Somerset@cmail.com

Fletcher,

Your request to begin human experimentation with Vixen has been reviewed and approved as long as supply holds. Unfortunately, another liquid reserve was decimated by Agent Robinson and his team two hours ago and the labs are still working on replenishing. While it is a regrettable choice to directly interact with SHAP, I think it is time we send Agent Robinson a warning.

Please do so at your earliest convenience.

Somerset

Chapter Four

Rule #2: A reaper's most important duty is to protect a
vulnerable soul as it leaves the human body.

– The Reaper Code of Ethics, official handbook

Poppy

IT WAS BULLSHIT that I couldn't have an orgasm while dead—and believe me, I'd tried—but I could still feel my heart breaking. I couldn't feel temperature, but I could never escape the lack of warmth that came with being a reaper. Nothing had felt as amazing as Jake's hand on my skin in twelve years. He was so warm, so *human*.

I wanted to shout, yell, cry, be loud in some consequential way that was impossible when I was dead. I could scream for hours in the human world and no one would hear me. Except my sister and any lingering ghosts. Sylvia would probably shove her robe in my mouth after three seconds.

Maybe this was why I liked playing my violin so much. It let me be loud, took the feelings that somehow still clogged my chest and forced them into the world with every swipe of my bow. It was more productive—and more beautiful—than screaming.

Since the moment I'd woken up in the reaper world

twelve years ago, I'd been told I'd grow to love it. If I gave it a chance, I'd fall in love with the afterlife. I got to be with my family, help humans reach their eternal destinations, and spend the day on the water.

Everyone had been wrong.

With a sigh, I landed next to Sylvia. I never stopped being astounded at how potent the colors of the human world were, even at twilight. I missed colors.

I would give centuries of the eternity that lay ahead of me to hang out with Jake and Eliza tonight, dance with Daisy, eat cake until we got sick, laugh until our sides hurt. Instead, I was outside a brick ranch surrounded by grass up to my knees, waiting for six people's hearts to give out.

"Cutting it close," Sylvia mumbled as I moved to her side.

I didn't bother to respond. I had never been late to a soul collection. Didn't matter that for twelve years I'd done everything that was asked of me and more, I was still the youngest Grim daughter who still needed to have her hand held. It wasn't my fault I hadn't inherited whatever reaper gifts were supposed to be natural to me and that I needed a partner.

I hated this job.

With a nod to Sylvia, I began my pre-death inspection. Shifting silently through the grass, I circled the house while watching the way the air shifted. I followed the rays of the setting sun, searching for any disruptions, splinters, odd reflections, or shadows that shouldn't be there. I may not be able to take souls from bodies like I should, but I'd learned how to see what others often missed. I moved to a group of trees, whose shadows stretched long over the grass…shadows that looked bluer than they should. I took a step closer, pulling my sword from my cloak. The sun went behind a cloud, casting the entire field in a uniformly gray shadow.

I stilled, waiting for the cloud to move. Time was fluid when one was dead and I rarely counted seconds or minutes anymore, instead counting how many souls I had left to gather before the end of my shift. Moments like this, however, felt like eternity.

When the sun returned, the blue tinted shadow was gone. I looked across the field to Sylvia, who was watching me. Everything between me and her looked as it should, but something unseen, unknown still weighed heavy. She raised her scythe and pulled her hood up, signaling that our shift had officially started.

"What'd you find?" she asked when I returned to her side.

"Nothing."

"Do you believe it was nothing?"

I put my sword away and pulled out my violin. "The colors are too bright here."

"Hmm." She didn't believe me. I wasn't sure I did either. "Let's go."

I lifted my instrument to my chin, dragging the bow across the strings. Unlike the New Orleans reapers, who played upbeat bluesy-jazz to guide the spirits—my request for a transfer had been denied twice—I leaned into rich dark tones of a requiem. I needed music that matched my heartache. Humans couldn't hear me unless they had crossed over, ghost instruments being calibrated specifically for dead ears.

The notes unfurled around us, the air shimmering with the melody. Small flickers of light, like lost fireflies, poured from the sound hole and swept onto the wind, headed toward the cottage. These were real fairy lights. It was a trick I had picked up studying fairies, who were a nasty and invasive species. They used the lights their wings produced to lure freshly dead souls into their lair, where they'd swarm and devour.

After nearly losing a soul to a fairy, I stole its wings and used the lights to guide my souls to safety. The lights always pointed me toward the souls we'd be collecting, a cheat for my lack of reaper sight. Stealing wings to use for my own benefit was two-fold—I helped my sister, and fairies left us and our souls alone.

The lights circled in the air and went through the front door. I finished one song, then two, the familiar ache in my chest deepening, warning me the souls were coming. Souls were as unique as their human bodies. Some came somber, some in full *I need to speak to your manager* force, others danced on the breeze.

"Move," Sylvia ordered.

We walked through the front door and into a combination living room and kitchen, littered with folding chairs and five people slumped at unnatural angles. A man walked through the crowd checking vitals and making notes on a tablet. Sylvia stopped in front of a young woman who looked to be in her early twenties and waited for her senses to tell her when the soul was ready for removal.

It was like picking a ripe fruit. Too early, and the soul was sticky, trapped inside the body. It could tear or stretch on the way out, damaging the integrity. Too late and the soul would begin to rot and turn malicious.

Sylvia lifted a glowing golden string from the woman's chest and sliced it with her scythe. The fairy lights encircled the body and lifted the woman's soul up and set her on her feet. She stared at Sylvia, then me, as my fingers continued moving over the strings.

Realization dawned on her face as she turned and looked at her body, wrapping her arms tightly around her middle. She was wafer thin, her cheeks hollow, a wrap around her head. It was clear she had been fighting a losing battle before today.

She shook her head no and started begging for a second chance, but Sylvia just lifted her skeleton hand and pointed to me. I had left my human skin facade on, trying to make the souls more comfortable. It was easier to play the violin that way anyway.

Sylvia moved on to the next person, then the next, met with shock and surprise each time. "They promised it would work," one said to the other.

"It worked for my sister. There has to be some mistake," a second said.

"Excuse me!" a third called. "This isn't right. They promised—"

I played my music louder to cover their noise. I didn't have the mental energy to argue with them. It wouldn't do anything, and I couldn't change anything. My fingers missed a note at the realization that this was going to happen to Jake, and probably soon. One small slice and the soul and body were irrevocably separated.

Sylvia swung to face me. I didn't miss notes. I looked away and kept playing, refusing to acknowledge that anything was wrong.

The man who was checking the vitals circled back around to the young woman. "Shit." He moved to the next person, then the next, each one as lifeless as the last.

The man yelled to someone else as Sylvia moved to us. "Let's go!"

I moved into a quieter song and shook my head once. "Manifest said six."

"There are no other ripe souls here. Manifest must be wrong."

I frowned but didn't argue. The manifest was 99.99 percent accurate, but the information was still imputed by reapers, translated from the main source. In rare cases, a soul's trajectory could change so much that a person lived. I'd only seen it happen a handful of times in twelve years, but it wasn't impossible. Sometimes a soul ripened slowly with age, sometimes in a matter of seconds after an accident.

It was just…something wasn't right.

The man who had been checking the victims hurried through the kitchen and into another room, dim in the evening night. It was clear he was talking to someone else, gesturing wildly at the unseen person. I played a minor chord, moving the bow in long strokes to disperse more fairy lights.

With a long exhale, I directed the lights through the kitchen and to the doorway. They stopped before they crossed the threshold, dimming and falling into ash. That was an unmistakable warning. I abruptly stopped playing.

"Run!"

Sylvia and I herded the group out the door and across the field. While she and I could glide as if we were ice-skating, the new spirits didn't have their sea legs yet. They were still moving at human pace, which was not going to save us from whatever the hell was in that room.

Maybe a demon, maybe a soul eater. I wasn't sure and I didn't want to find out. Sylvia cried out, grabbed her chest, and stumbled. I rushed forward and caught her arm. "You okay?"

She looked over her shoulder and slowed, walking backward. "We've got company." She waved her scythe in the air. "Everyone, stay behind us."

I tucked my violin away and pulled out my sword, then turned. Our sixth soul was careening out of the house. It was a clump of a shadow, with jagged edges and no defining characteristics, followed by a demon who was more monster than man.

"Looks like there were six souls after all," Sylvia said. "This demon just beat us to it and had a little snack."

In a perfectly synchronized movement, Sylvia drove her weapon through the shadow as I drove mine into the demon. The shadow shriveled and fell to the ground, then Sylvia made a slash at the demon as I took a second blow. It tore open a portal in the earth and dove in before I could get in another slice. We staggered back, breathing heavily even though we didn't need breath.

"What the hell?" I whispered. *We lost a soul. How'd we lose a soul?* I asked her silently. We had a near perfect track record.

She just shook her head in disbelief.

Turning around, we saw four souls milling around in confusion and a fifth running toward the woods. With an expletive, Sylvia took off after him and caught up in seconds. When she reappeared, holding the man by the nape of his neck, she surveyed the group. "Anyone else have any stupid ideas?"

The other four shook their heads.

"Good. Let's get out of here. This place gives me the creeps."

Chapter Five

Jake

I STARED AT my laptop, the slideshow of pictures I'd digitized from childhood playing across the screen. Every single photo of Poppy was another cut, but I couldn't look away. My need to see her again overrode whatever self-preservation I had left.

I adjusted the ice pack on my knee, turned up the heating pad on my hip, then took a massive gulp of my iced tea, hoping it would wash away the bad taste in my mouth. *Poppy*. A reaper.

Poppy, who was pure sunshine and smiles. She'd laughed with her whole body, sang in my car at the top of her lungs, and rescued all the spiders and set them outside. She'd been vegetarian since she was ten.

How was she a reaper? Life, and apparently death, weren't fair.

Sebastian appeared next to me on my recliner sofa. "Are you ready to talk about it?"

"I'm fine."

He glanced down at my hands. I looked at my crochet project—an easy scarf that Amber said was both good practice and stress relief—and grimaced. It was becoming a triangle. "Dammit." I set down my hook and yarn and stretched my fingers. "I don't even know how to begin."

"Maybe begin with why you were conversing with a reaper."

"Poppy." I studied him. "How do you know Poppy?"

His gaze snapped to mine and held it. "We have mutual friends, you could say."

Did he mean me? Had Poppy been here before? "She used to live next door when we were kids. She was...mine. And she was Eliza's best friend."

"And you both observed her this evening?"

I tapped my finger on the keyboard. "No. No, I don't think so. No one seemed to notice her but me."

He stared at me for a long moment, not blinking as if he were seeing something I couldn't. "I see."

I narrowed my eyes at him. "What do you see?"

"I do not believe that seeing Poppy is a positive sign. In fact, she herself would say the same thing."

"It's so weird to me that you two know each other. How'd you meet?"

He lifted a shoulder. "Mutual hobbies. You're changing the subject."

"Seeing dead people isn't an unusual habit for me."

He leaned back on the couch, crossing his arms. "Hmm. Yes. But seeing reapers is."

"How do you know?"

He turned to look at the wall, then tilted his head to the side as if studying something. I followed his gaze but saw nothing. "Reapers aren't for the living, Jacob. They're for the dead. I am dead, ergo it is not unusual for me to see a reaper. You are living, and therefore I am extremely concerned at the new company you're keeping."

"I'll be fine."

"Forgive me for doubting you, Jacob." He tapped his finger against his lip. "I believe you should make a formal report."

I stopped the slideshow, pausing on a picture I had taken of the two of us on a walk. I smiled up at the camera, while Poppy's head was thrown back in laughter, the summer sun glowing between us. I slammed the laptop shut and swallowed. "If I report it, I'll be investigated. Reapers are considered a breech to security because they have access without restriction. I'd be removed from consideration as Daisy's mentor."

"Ah, I see." He stared past me. "I believe this may be a warning for you, Jacob. Please heed."

I dropped the laptop on the table. "We don't know that it is a warning."

"I've never known you to be this careless," he admitted, his voice cold.

My grief and anxiety turned into a ball of rage. "I used to think Mina was being dramatic when she threatened you with an exorcism, but you're so goddamn self-righteous all the time!"

"They really should pay me for being an off-hours therapist."

"You could just mind your own damn business."

He crossed his hands over his stomach. "I've been dead for well over a century. I've learned that if I don't bestow my wisdom, the people I care about will likely do something regrettable."

"Oh, I've done plenty of regrettable things. Like make a bet that I'd host a ghost agent."

Sebastian smiled. "I will admit, the new living arrangements took some adjusting." We sat in silence for a long moment, Sebastian watching me. "Are you having a staring competition?"

I moved the laptop to the coffee table. "Poppy was special to me."

"You were courting her?"

"Yes. No. Not officially. There was an eighteen-month age difference and our families forbade it." I finished the iced tea and set the glass on a coaster on my side table.

"How long has it been since you've seen her?"

"Twelve years." *Why hadn't she told me?*

Sebastian whistled. "That's a long time. And you've never had closure?"

"Closure isn't going to make this better."

Sebastian was quiet for a long moment, staring up at the ceiling. "After I died, when I was floating aimlessly around London wondering why I was inhabiting Earth, I went to visit my grave. I knew exactly when and how I died. I knew where I was buried. Somehow seeing it literally carved in stone helped me come to terms."

"I appreciate you sharing with me. But Poppy doesn't have a grave. At least not one that I've ever found."

"What happened when she disappeared?"

I made a fist, the knuckles on my right hand stinging. "She was like a ghost. She and her family left Dad and

Magnolia's vow renewal, and then we went straight to the airport hotel since we were leaving on a red-eye for our family celebration trip to Disney World. I tried to call her twice from the room, but there was no answer."

I ran a hand over my face. "I called her every chance I got, from every phone I came across. Right before we got on the plane, I tried again. The number had been disconnected and I knew in my gut she wouldn't be waiting for me."

Sebastian had straightened and turned fully toward me. "She was already gone." It wasn't a question.

I nodded. "By the time we got home, they had already had an estate sale and the house was completely empty. Everything had been painted white, and any memory of Poppy was gone." I laughed without humor. "We used to have a treehouse where we spent a lot of time together and I tore it out of the tree with my bare hands. I couldn't stand the sight of it."

"I can imagine."

My chest tightened, heat swelling and closing my throat. I swallowed hard. "We weren't allowed to talk about her," I whispered. "Dad and Magnolia said that if they wanted to move away without leaving a forwarding address, then we needed to respect their wishes. But Poppy would never do that. I've never found a single clue as to what happened to her until tonight."

Sebastian moved across the couch and sat next to me, his cold shoulder leaning through mine. "It pains me to hear how your grief was so easily dismissed. I am sorry."

"Thanks." I adjusted the ice on my knee. "What a day."

Sebastian reached for the remote and after two tries managed to put on highlights from a baseball game. "Mina preferred murder documentaries, but I suspect this is a better choice for tonight."

I nodded and stared at the screen, although I couldn't even remember who the teams were the moment I blinked.

"Are we going to disregard the fact that humans see reapers because they are about to perish?" he asked.

Yes. Because it couldn't be true. I had too much to do to keep my family safe. "You saw her, and she wasn't there to collect your soul."

"I'm not human."

I lifted one shoulder. "Maybe I'm not either. You've seen Daisy's powers. Supernatural blood runs strong in my family."

He was quiet for a moment. "I think it's safe to assume that if you were to be in mortal peril, it would be because of the investigation."

"It could also be a car accident, a fire, a heart attack. I can't give up my assignment because of speculation. Too much is at risk."

"Neither of us lack intelligence, Jacob. We both know that it's likely this investigation is ruffling more feathers than we're aware."

I stayed silent because he wasn't wrong. The closer we got to the top of the venom chain, the more dangerous things became.

"You could walk away," he continued. "Mina did. She's happier than I've ever seen her. Leave the investigation for someone else."

I didn't need to answer this time, either.

"But you won't," he said on a sigh.

"I made an oath."

"I wonder what Mina would say about this all."

I looked over at him. "I'm not sure why you're speculating as we're not going to tell her."

"Aren't we?" He smiled.

With a sigh, I turned on his favorite movie, *Titanic*. "You have problems."

He smiled at the bribe. "And your secret is safe with me. For now."

With a sigh, I turned off the heating pad and grabbed the ice pack, then pushed myself off the couch and out of earshot of Sebastian reciting the lines of the nineties movie. He and Reggie liked to reenact parts of the movie while using my furniture as props, but thankfully they typically waited until I wasn't home. After tossing the ice pack in the freezer, I shuffled down the short hall to my bedroom, where I hung up my tie and belt, put my shoes back in their storage box, placed my shirt in the hamper, and set my pants and suit coat in the dry-clean-only basket. Thankfully, SHAP had a cleaner who was great with bloodstains and wouldn't ask questions.

I limped into the bathroom and turned the shower on hot, then sat in my shower chair, letting the water rain down on me. I closed my eyes and tilted my head up. I'd miss showers when I died.

I wasn't an idiot. I knew that seeing Poppy meant I could be in mortal danger, but it didn't change anything. *Poppy.* At least I'd have a friend waiting for me on the other side.

After my shower, I did my stretching routine with my eyes closed, dropping the foam roller twice from sheer exhaustion. When I climbed into bed, I knew I'd be gone as soon as I hit the pillow. As I clicked off my bedside lamp, an email pinged on my phone.

Just leave it until morning, my brain pleaded, *just a few hours*. I could close my eyes and pretend I didn't hear the ding. A reminder ding sounded and I shouted an expletive. It was my work email tone, which meant it was something related to a case and not just a *we've been trying to reach you about your car's extended warranty* ad.

I swiped my phone off my nightstand, praying it was just a rescheduled meeting. Four pictures of me appeared on the screen, two from the wedding, one from the gym, and one of me through my kitchen window.

Jacob Robinson,

Congratulations on your successful capture today. Unfortunately, you have caused me major inconvenience. Stop the crusade against my business, and I'll stop my crusade against tearing your life apart. Continue and I'll make you wish you were dead.

Sincerely,
Yours

I ran my hand down my face and laid back on my pillow. I could ignore it. Could go right back to sleep and deal with it in the morning. My throat tightened with the thought of me climbing out of bed right now because some asshole couldn't wait a few hours to send me a death threat.

"Fuck me," I grumbled as I forwarded the email to the

SHAP technology team and flipped on the light. So much for sleeping tonight. I could sleep when I was dead, which apparently might be very soon.

Chapter Six

Rule #57: Reapers may only have authorized essentials in their personal space.

— The Reaper Code of Ethics, official handbook

Poppy

WE SHUFFLED THE group into the oversized gondola-style boat then pushed off the dock with Anya, who was like my second-ish cousin four times removed, at the helm.

"How are my favorite reapers?" she asked, her dark curls bouncing with her words. She wore her human face but left the rest of her body in skeleton form. Sylvia and I both grumbled a hello. "That good, eh? You can tell me the story later."

I slumped onto the bench in the back of the boat, glad my shift was officially over for another two hours. The River Styx was choppy tonight, which didn't bode well for my seasickness. Again, couldn't have an orgasm, but could get seasick. To make matters worse, I was the only reaper in the history of forever to get seasick and no one had a solution. This was crap.

"Are you okay?" Sylvia whispered.

"We lost a soul," I breathed. "We never lose souls."

She leaned close so no one could overhear. "That demon took that soul long before we got there. It wasn't ripe. There was nothing we could've done to stop him unless we had set up watch for hours."

I yanked my hood off and tugged my hands through my hair. "I know that logically, but it still hurt." I hit my chest once with my fist. "That's the third demon this week."

"I know." She looked out over the water. "Something weird is going on."

"Excuse me?" The young woman asked, turning to face me and Sylvia. "What's going to happen to us?"

"We're going to deliver you to the gates of the afterlife. Once we dock, you'll follow the brick path with the other souls and pass through the iron gate. They'll call you by name from the waiting area and you'll be informed of your options," I explained, my voice tight with nausea already.

"Like heaven?" An older man asked.

"Not sure. We aren't allowed past the gates. We're just the delivery service." I was seriously considering embroidering a DEADEX logo onto my cloak as a joke. I wondered if anyone would notice.

"How do we know this isn't a trick?" a third chimed in.

I took this moment to pull out a barf bag and dry heave. This always did wonders at shutting people up. When I finished, I wiped my hand over my mouth, a superfluous gesture. I couldn't actually throw up.

"Because I wouldn't suffer through seasickness several times a day to take ungrateful souls to the afterlife as a joke," I snapped.

Sylvia, despite loving conflict and mayhem, elbowed me. "What she means is you have a choice. You can trust us, reapers who put ourselves on the line to help souls cross over to the afterlife daily, or you can risk facing whatever else is out there. And trust me when I say most of what's out there has a taste for new souls."

The boat went silent, except for my dry heaves. I laid down on the bench and closed my eyes. Sylvia ran her boney fingers through my hair, trying to help me feel better. "Tell me about the wedding."

I must look really sick. She hated weddings. If only seasickness medications worked when one was dead.

I fisted my cloak in my hands. I was still in my human form to not scare the souls anymore, and mostly because I liked it better. "I…" My words bottlenecked, trying to keep from spilling out. As if saying them would breathe my fears to life.

How could I tell her?

"What?" she prompted.

I knew one day Jake and Eliza would die. All humans died, even those with supernatural genes. It was just that once my friends died, that was it. I would never, ever, ever see them again. Reapers existed only in an in-between, sandwiched between the human world and the afterlife.

For twelve years, it had been enough to know that they were alive and thriving. I checked the log after every shift, searching for their names. I could only rest once I knew they had survived another day.

My sister leaned closer. "Poppy?"

"I saw Jake."

She jerked her hand back. "What? On accident?"

I shook my head.

She leaned close to me, her voice full of quiet fury. "Are you shi—Poppy, if you got caught, you'd be permanently retired! I could be, too, if they suspected I had a hand in it. Good god, here I thought you never broke the rules and you're breaking one of the most serious ones! Tell me this doesn't get worse. How often—"

"Jake could see me back." My voice was barely above a whisper, but even I could hear the pain laced through it.

"Shit. This actually got worse."

I sucked in a shaky breath. "I can't do it, Sylvia. I can't take his soul."

She laid her head on my shoulder, which made it both better and worse. Better because I loved physical affection and being dead really hindered receiving it. Worse because Sylvia didn't like to touch other people, or other reapers, unless she was about to fight. Her touching me meant things were as bad as I had feared.

"I'll be by your side, okay?" she promised. "Whatever happens. I'll do it when the time comes."

"He was supposed to die when he was 101 with a dozen great-grandchildren and a lifetime of memories."

"I know." She sat up and brushed my hair back out of my face. "You know you can't go see him again, right?"

Her words cut through the fog of motion sickness and sank into my chest. "Yes." The word carried no sound but a lifetime of weight.

If I stuck to the rules and stayed away from Jake until his name came up on my list, and then I delivered him to the afterlife registration portal, then this wouldn't matter. Shouldn't matter. Couldn't matter.

We sat in silence until the boat docked. Sylvia took charge, ushering our lot off and into the registration line. I took a minute to sit on one of the large boulders that lined the shore, staring out over the misty water, trying to recharge and recenter.

My sister nudged me with her toe bone a few minutes later. "You wanna come watch a movie with me tonight? We can pick something you won't hate."

I shook my head. "Maybe tomorrow? I think I just want to read." I needed to lose myself in anything that wasn't reality. I needed a happily-ever-after.

"Alright, but if you change your mind…"

I smiled. "Thanks." I followed her back to our lodgings, a long brick building filled with studio apartments. We didn't need to sleep and couldn't eat, but reapers reported a higher quality of unlife when they had their own spaces. My dads even had a courtyard.

I was in the center of the building—not smart enough when I was sixteen to ask for something with windows—but that was okay. When I stepped into the small room with my worn recliner, scattered sheet music, and an entire wall of bookcases, the wiring in my shoulders loosened. It was a hodgepodge of things from the human world and magic, like my always-glowing twinkle lights that floated above my head without the need for electricity and a plush black rug that covered most of my floor. Reaching into my pocket, I took out the program from today's wedding and pinned it to my wall. It rested among dozens of wedding programs from events I had snuck off to watch.

I traced the Blackburn House lettering with my finger, the threads of colored paper pulp indicating that it was printed on recycled paper. The house had always been a staple in Jake and my relationship. Could that be all it was? Was my wishing so strong that it somehow defied the odds?

I set my violin on its stand, then hung my robe in a small closet before falling into my recliner. While my family always allowed their skeletons to show when they were home, I still wore my human form. I had died in my pajamas—unicorn leggings and a long pink T-shirt—which I was happy to see was back in style again. This pissed my family off to no end because they had worn black dress clothes. I had defiantly changed out of the outfit my dads had laid out for me, too angry to agree to their plan, the moment they had said goodnight.

Unfortunately, I hadn't remembered to put back on my socks or shoes. At least my fingernails and toenails had been manicured in a soft pink for the vow renewal. One perk about being dead: the nail polish never chipped.

I picked up the book on the side table next to me, running my thumbs over the pages. It was a frequent reread, but I still enjoyed falling into the story. On days like today, when I was shaken to my core, I needed the familiarity, the comfort of knowing exactly what would happen.

I opened the book and leaned back, trying to concentrate on the characters. Desperately ignoring the pulling in my chest that longed to check on Jake one more time. To beg him to stay safe. But if I saw him again, it would destroy me.

After rereading the same paragraph four times, I stood

and tossed the book down. I needed to scream, cry, throw something across the room—anything for a release. Instead, I grabbed my violin and headed out the door. I needed to go practice somewhere where no one but the lost reapers would hear.

Chapter Seven

Jake

As THE SUN crawled over the horizon, I tipped back the last of my coffee, which had a startling lack of cream and sugar. I was so desperate for caffeine, it didn't matter. Maybe this was how I died. Drowning in bad coffee.

"Robinson, you good?"

I nodded at Paris. Easier to lie without speaking. She waited at the front door of a brick ranch as I leaned on my cane hard and climbed to the front step with no rail. I bit down on an expletive. My leg hadn't recovered from yesterday and my normal regimen of pain relievers wasn't keeping up. I had five pills left of my in-case-of-a-pain-emergency stock, but I'd need a doctor appointment before I got a refill. I didn't know when the hell that was going to happen.

Anyway, combining the good meds with no sleep for thirty hours would definitely slow my reaction time. After an all-nighter with Paris trying to trace who sent the email with no luck, one of our ghost agents activated the communication tree and Sebastian had appeared in Paris's office an hour ago with this address. Who didn't love visiting a rundown house in the middle of nowhere at sunrise with several dead bodies waiting?

Paris opened the door and I limped through and into an open kitchen-dining room. Five human-presenting bodies were slumped over in folding chairs. There was no blood, no restraints, no needles, no signs of struggle. Whatever happened here was likely done willingly.

I navigated to a near-spotless kitchen space, where two white pills sat in a plastic cup next to a bottle of water. Paris was already at my side, removing a test kit from her shoulder bag. She slipped on gloves before inserting one of the pills into a handheld tester.

I approached the doorway to the empty bedroom beyond. A cold chill ran down my spine as soon as I crossed the threshold. Something bad had happened here. Something unnatural.

The bed was made with military precision and a small desk was completely clear. Maybe it was the order and cleanliness in juxtaposition to the bodies in the next room that threw me. No, it was something deeper. I squinted at the shadow in the corner, the one that didn't quite look right...

"Jake!" Paris called. "Got a result."

I blinked and looked around the room again. Sunlight streamed through the small window, casting out any remaining shadows. I shook my head. This lack of sleep was killing me. Still, I was going to have forensics bring in one of their witches. See if they could find a trace of what happened here. I texted forensics as I returned to the kitchen.

Paris handed me the handheld tester and I read the screen. "Positive for a chemical component of vampire venom and fentanyl? They're cutting venom with an opioid?" I looked up at her. "The venom is in powder form?"

She looked over the kitchen again. "It's a much more stable form than the suspension Thinner used, but far more labor intensive to make. SHAP had developed a method to make the venom into a powder right before I moved onto this case." She shook her head. "I'm...surprised? No...worried, that they've discovered the powder technique."

That chill ran down my spine again. "They're trying to make alternatives."

"Looks like. And this batch failed."

"But why? Why cut it with an opioid if they're trying to make hybrids? It makes it inherently more dangerous."

Paris shook her head. "If they were to mix in blood with the venom and the opioid, they could've saved every one of these people. Well, if turning them into vampires was the goal."

"So why slow the heart rate and respiratory system if they're not making vampires?"

"There's something we're missing. Why wouldn't they give them blood and stop a potential overdose? And based on initial visual examination of the bodies, I suspect an overdose."

I shook my head, taking in the scene with new eyes. I was prepared for this eventuality. As we researched Lucinda Nicks' suppliers, we unearthed groups illegally selling vampire venom. The more venom we took off the streets, the more desperate suppliers became. Desperate enough to try alternative versions and test them on unsuspecting people.

My gaze fell on a woman with a scarf wrapped around her head, her body frighteningly small. It was clear she had been sick before this and was likely promised she'd be cured. "I hate this case," I admitted.

Before this case, SHAP had been completely unaware that oral vampire venom existed. When Carma's mother, Lucinda Nicks, launched a weight-loss company called Thinner that helped people lose weight by turning them into half-vampire, half-human hybrids, it had sent the entire organization into high alert. How had this been going on for years without anyone at SHAP knowing?

Hybrids were extremely dangerous, as ingesting one drop of blood could turn them into a vampire, or worse, a feral creature. While most Thinner members were able to return to their human state after a blood transfusion, people like Carma, who had been on the program longer than six months, were forced to choose to be a hybrid or make the full change to vampire. Carma and her best friend Elena, had elected to stay hybrids.

Elena, who'd joined Thinner when Carma promised her that it would help with her Crohn's disease, went into remission the moment she'd started the program. I slipped on gloves and walked over to the woman with the headscarf, pushing the edge of it higher. Thin, patchy hair, no eyebrows, only a few eyelashes. She was most likely in chemo.

"Maybe this isn't about hybrids," I surmised, looking over at Paris. "Maybe it's about creating a universal cure-all."

Paris stared at me in an unnerving way, like she often did when processing information. "SHAP has been aggravated by our lack of success with a synthetic and they're not willing to do the testing with natural venom on humans. These people are."

I pointed at her. "A synthetic venom that didn't accidentally turn people into vampires would change the entire medical system as we know it." The only problem was no one had successfully produced an alternative.

A ray of sunlight pierced through a jumbled piece of curtain, landing on something shiny. Eyes narrowed, I moved to the front of the room and pulled a pair of tweezers from my bag. I crouched with a hiss, then picked up the small object, holding it up to inspect it.

A purple sequin.

Poppy had been here.

Twelve years of grief and confusion slammed into me all over again. She had been here, faced with watching them die. Did it bother her? Did she tolerate death and dying better now that she was older?

Why couldn't she have warned me? I might have been able to help these people. Even as I thought it, I knew it wasn't fair. She couldn't have done anything. These people had been desperate, and desperation made people try life-threatening and sometimes very stupid things.

How many times had our paths crossed without me knowing? Was this the first, and maybe I could've seen her all along? Or was it because I really was going to die soon? Did her being peripherally attached to this case mean it had something to do with how I was going to die, or was this coincidence?

"You okay?" Paris asked walking over. "You're staring into space."

I blinked and shook my head, trying to clear it. "Exhausted." I held up the tweezers. "Can you see it?"

She leaned closer. "See what? There's nothing in your tweezers."

"No purple sequin?"

She glanced between me and my hand. "No?"

I tucked everything into my pocket. "Good to know." Why could only I see the sequin? Was it because I could see Poppy?

"I...should I ask?"

Before I figured out an answer, forensics walked into the house and started documenting the scene.

"That was unbelievably fast," I marveled.

"We were already on our way," the lead explained. "Sebastian told us you'd need us."

Galinda, a witch that SHAP used on serious cases, followed the team inside and stilled just inside the doorway for a long moment. She walked through the bodies, pausing at each one. "They would've all died in the coming months, their souls were ready, but just barely." She continued to the back of the house, touching the door frame, then immediately pulling her hands away.

"Something evil happened here." She straightened her shoulders and marched into the room, determined. Less than a minute later, she burst back into the kitchen, gasping as if she had been underwater. "Demon."

She looked directly at me. "You need to warn your friend to be careful."

I frowned. "My friend?"

"The one who wears the purple sequins."

Paris's head snapped to face me. She narrowed her eyes.

"I, uh…" I cleared my throat. "We aren't really in contact."

"Get in contact," Galinda prompted. She studied me from head to toe, then tilted her head. "Hmmm. You may not have long to wait."

I didn't know what to say to that. Thankfully, my cell rang and with a mumbled excuse me, I stepped into a corner of the room and pulled it from my pocket. A picture of Eliza and Daisy wearing wolf ears from this summer's Founders Festival popped up on my display. "It's Jake."

"Ah, your serious work voice," Eliza said. "Quick, say '*you'll have the report by this afternoon*' so you sound busy and important."

I sighed in response.

"That kind of day, got it."

"What's up?"

"It may be nothing."

My stomach tightened. If she was calling me during work hours, it wasn't nothing. "What happened?"

"I dropped Daisy off for school and realized I forgot my ID badge and my coffee, and you know I need both. I ran home and the alarm was off. It's possible I forgot to set it. Daisy was in a mood today and I had to drag her out the door kicking and screaming."

I swallowed down the sharp stab of anxiety before I spoke. "How often do you forget to set it?"

There was a pause. "Not once since Ben died."

Two years. "Where are you?"

"In my kitchen. I did a sweep and used my watch and

checked my doorbell camera and nothing showed up. If someone was here, they're gone now."

"Are you sure?"

"I know how to do a sweep, Jake. I might not be a top five field agent, but I'm good at my job." The sound of a keypad beeping and a door closing filled the silence. "Anyway, I'm headed to the office. You heard me activate the alarm."

"Yes. Good. And I know you're good at your job, but I'm allowed to worry about my little sis."

"Yeah, okay."

"Be careful."

"I will. You coming over later?"

It took me a beat to catch up. Today was Monday. Ever since Daisy came into her powers, I tried to have Monday dinner with Eliza and Daisy, then help Daisy with her human and supernatural homework. "Yeah. I'll see you at five."

"Try to get a nap in. You sound like hell."

"Love you too." I hung up and ran my hand down my face. "Let's finish documenting this scene. I need to take a nap on lunch."

"Shouldn't have said that out loud," Paris sighed. "You've jinxed it."

On cue, my cell rang again. This time, it was my boss, Jim. "Dammit." It was going to be one of those days.

Chapter Eight

Rule #13: Reapers are to stay in inhabited areas of the city unless otherwise indicated by a formal work order.

— The Reaper Code of Ethics, official handbook

Poppy

THE ISLE OF Grim, our little slice of afterlife, looked like a coastal fishing town in Maine, only with all the color leached out. It wasn't so much that everything was all one color, more so that everything was muted. Except for our cloaks.

The switch to purple cloaks was recent, in the last few decades. While the black cloak was iconic, test audiences responded better to the color purple. Since the switch, there had been a thirteen percent decrease in souls trying to escape the afterlife. With how many ghosts were currently occupying Earth, it was a marked improvement.

It was rare to see a reaper in human form and without their cloak, but I didn't bother worrying about either tonight as I walked to the industrial side of the island. Away from the residences and boat docks, the milliners who made the cloaks, the city council, a general store that carried home goods imported from the human world, and a library clustered to make a small downtown area. Nearby, a boat and fishing rental hut sat waiting for the morning shift to wrap up. Reapers could rent a speedboat and go waterskiing or a rowboat for fishing.

Not that there were many fish here. Mostly mermaids and some soul suckers you didn't want to lose a fight with. Still, every day there were at least a dozen older reapers sitting on the water, poles cast, reclining in their boats.

Behind the rental place, there was a small path carved through ancient trees. The leaves were limp, and there was no breeze to make them rustle. The moment I crossed over into the forest, I felt absolutely secluded. My shoulders relaxed and my jaw unclenched. *Peace.*

It was only about a half mile, but this part of the island jutted off and narrowed down to a small, wooden boat dock. In the last twelve years, this dock had only been used as a loading station for reapers who were permanently retired, which was a nice way of saying *removed from existence.* The water around the wooden posts shimmered, a clear indication of where the protective spell ended and the open water began.

If I squinted hard enough, I could see a lighthouse through the fog that had long since lost its glow. The small island just out of view was where reapers who disobeyed the reaper code and caused grievous harm were sent until their permanent demise. Without protection against any of the afterlife creatures, rumor had it the average banishment only lasted a few years.

I didn't know anyone who had been banished, but my grandmother said her dear cousin had been. She hadn't shared the details of her cousin's case but admitted that she wished she could send a message, letting her know she wasn't forgotten. Her words had stuck with me.

Whenever I couldn't rest, when my head was spinning or if my heart was in need of mending, I came to this little wooden boat dock, sat down on the edge, and started playing. I didn't know if anyone could hear me across the water, but I hoped so. If they heard it, maybe they'd know someone was thinking of them. It wasn't that I thought people who did bad things shouldn't be reprimanded. The reaper code was in place for a reason—to protect both us and the human world.

I didn't play for my great-great-uncle, who had sold souls to demons in exchange for alcohol, and besides he was probably long dead. I played for the reapers who'd made a serious mistake on a bad day and had no chance to rectify it. And trust me, we all had bad days.

Pandemics, wars, terrorist attacks, hate crimes could all happen without warning. Sometimes even with warning, we could barely keep up. No reaper had a perfect track record. Souls ran away sometimes, choosing to stay on Earth where it was familiar. But reapers had a three-soul limit. Lose more than that, and you were evaluated by city council. They could choose to retrain a reaper, reassign them, or banish them.

Outside of the soul today—which would likely be expunged from our records since it happened prior to our shift—I'd only ever lost one soul on my first day. I hadn't followed the code, pouted and shouted and refused to participate. It had cost a stranger their afterlife. That was the last time, outside of visiting Jake and Eliza, that I had ever broken a serious rule.

For a long time after I'd lost that soul, I felt like I deserved to be punished. Maybe I still felt that way. Maybe that's why I played to an island that no one ever thought about.

I started off with an upbeat polka, then moved into a more somber sonata. I didn't pause between songs, letting one morph into the other, swaying with the music. The fairy lights danced over the water, carving a path through the fog and toward the lighthouse. It gave me hope that the notes reached their destination, too.

There was no sunrise or sunset here, making it impossible to tell the time by looking at the sky. I didn't know how long I sat there, trying to channel my feelings about seeing Jake into dissonant chords and long strokes of my bow, until a small tug at my chest warned me I needed to get ready for my next shift.

With one final song, a blues tune, I let the last note echo and the final fairy lights blink out. I would need to restring my bow with more wings soon, but it had absolutely been worth it. When I stood to go, the water in front of the dock moved with the force of something underneath. A large shadow swam away. If nothing else, at least whatever that was had enjoyed the show.

Each step leaving the forest was harder to make. I needed more time to recuperate. Sure, I didn't get physically fatigued on account of being dead, but I was emotionally fatigued. I longed to cry when I got back to my room and slipped back on my cloak.

Sylvia stuck her head in my door. "You ready?"

I plastered on a fake smile. "Always."

"Then let's go collect some souls."

I trudged behind my sister as I followed her to the docks, greeting and waving at the appropriate times when I crossed paths with my dads, my older brother, my cousin, and my grandparents. I was so tired of being motion sick, and I sent up a quick prayer to whatever was listening that they make this trip an easy one. My prayers were not answered.

As I dry heaved into yet another empty bag, Sylvia gripped my shoulder. "I think maybe I'll take this first group back by myself. I can only listen to you yak so many times in a row before I want to carve my own ears off and I don't even have ears anymore."

A small thrill of excitement laced with dread shot through me. If she took the first group back herself, that would leave me with a little extra break time. Alone.

I knew I shouldn't go visit him. I knew I needed to leave well enough alone. But I had to know if Jake could still see me. I mean, yesterday could've been a fluke, right? It would be irresponsible for me not to check. Before another wave of nausea washed over me, I gave my sister a thumbs-up.

Chapter Nine

Jake

THE PROBLEM WITH having a nosy ghost roommate and a sister who was also a SHAP employee was that keeping a secret was a pipe dream. When I walked into Eliza's house, she took one look at me and crossed her arms.

"Have you slept at all since the wedding?" she chided.

"Of course." I'd had a nap at lunch earlier today.

"Then why are you slurring your words?"

"I am doing no such thing." I was over-enunciating, but my point stood. "I'm doing a check."

She waved me away. "Of course you are."

"You're my baby sister. Deal with it." I activated my watch, then checked every access point. Eliza was right, of course. Nothing was out of place, no broken latches, no locks cut off from behind.

The watch showed no supernatural creatures—except Daisy—and no trace of residue. Despite the reading, the pit in my stomach didn't dislodge. I opened the master bedroom closet and looked over the rows of clothes and shelving. A stack of photo frames in a shoebox sat on the ground near the back of the closet and I used my cane to pull them toward me.

I leaned down and grabbed the first two frames. Dust floated up with the movement and I sneezed. Blinking away my watery eyes, I looked at the photos. The first was Eliza with a group of friends from high school. The second was at her baby shower, a novelty size bow stuck to her head while she held up a box of diapers and a teddy bear. I smiled, trying to fathom how Daisy had ever been small enough to be inside another person.

I set the two frames aside and grabbed a third, my smile fading as I flipped it over. Ben, Eliza, and Daisy stared back at me. The photo was just blurry enough to not merit hanging on the wall, clearly taken in low light with an old cell, but the joy on their faces in the extreme close-up shot was apparent. I ran my thumb over the glass, surprised to find it dust free.

Did Eliza still sit in her closet when she was sad? Pull out old pictures and cry until she could lock her emotions away? Or were the first two pictures responsible for keeping this one clean?

"When you said you were going to check the house, I didn't think you also meant my closet," Eliza said, coming into the room.

I blinked up at her. "Being thorough."

"Being nosy."

"Reminiscent."

"Brooding." She took the picture from my hand and looked down, the corner of her lip curving upward. "Daisy learned to ride a bike that day." She glanced up at me and hugged the photo against her middle. "I still miss him."

"Me, too," I admitted. "Did you ever write to him?" I had always wondered if she'd used her gift to send him a final letter or open the communication for him to write to Daisy.

If I could write letters to the dead, would I have written to Poppy? Even if it cost me one year of my life? Well, if I had known she was dead.

Eliza let her hair fall in front of her face as she put the photo back in the box and toed it into the closet, then shut her doors. "He wasn't the letter-writing sort."

"And that stops you?"

"You're nosy." She gestured around. "Did you find anything?"

I shook my head. "Maybe you did just forget to set the alarm." I still didn't believe that.

"So, exactly what I said. If only you bothered listening to me."

I walked over to her and gave her a quick hug. "I will never stop wanting to protect my favorite girls. Deal with it."

She rolled her eyes when I pulled away. "Dinner will be ready in thirty. Daisy's working on her spelling homework. We need to get through the '*how to keep my powers a secret*' chapter in the SHAP handbook this week, but I can do it with her tomorrow."

"You're annoying."

"Love you, too, loser." She turned and I followed her into the kitchen and found Daisy drawing words in the air with her pointer finger. The word shone in the air, then disappeared.

We were definitely going to need to study that SHAP

chapter tonight. "Hey munchkin. What're you doing?"

She reached out and gave me a half-hearted hug around my middle before looking back down at her tablet. "I remember the words better if I make them light up."

Okay, sound logic. "You can make them light up at home, but you won't be able to during the test."

She frowned. "Oh, yeah."

"Can you imagine them lighting up in your head only?"

She squeezed her eyes shut and bobbed her head as if she were using her whole body to write the words, then opened them and checked her book. "Yep!"

"Okay, good. Do that." She may look a little silly, but if it worked, it worked. "You ready to run through your list?"

She sighed as if it were a major inconvenience. "Do we have to?"

"The faster we finish your spelling, the faster we get to study magic."

She practically shoved the tablet at me. "Okay!"

It only took ten minutes to get through the rest of her homework; closing her eyes and imagining writing the word seemed to work. The moment we were done, she closed her tablet, then ran to her room to grab her SHAP laptop. A twinge of sadness caught me off guard. She was still a kid and already training for a career.

When I was eight, we had one household computer that we were only allowed to touch if we had a report due, and even then, the first choice was taking us to the library to use the public ones. Daisy had a kid's cellphone that would call four people—Eliza, me, Dad, and Magnolia, a tablet for school, and a laptop for SHAP business. She was already an adult in too many ways.

She opened her laptop and waited for it to boot. She was excited about all the training now, but how long before she became resentful? Sure, she had amazing powers, but at what cost?

I wished I could take them away from her until she was older. Wish I had told Eliza to wait another year or two before registering her as a witch with SHAP. But as she tapped her fingers on the table, little pink, gold, and green sparks popped out. No, she couldn't have waited longer.

She logged into the portal and brought up the chapter with corresponding quiz. "Are you ready?"

I leaned back in my chair, straightening my leg, taking care not to make any noise of discomfort, then nodded. "Read it out loud."

She began reading, sounding out the words that she stumbled over. "We all want to share secrets with our best friends but remember that your magic is a secret you can't share. If you want to tell someone, they have to be on your sharing list. Your mentor will help you make a sharing list."

She frowned, then looked at me. "Does this mean I can't tell anyone who's not on my list?"

I nodded. "That's exactly what it means."

Her eyes got wide. "Really?"

I nodded again. "Really, munchkin."

"Like forever?"

She looked shocked. I didn't blame her. This was a lot on a kid's shoulders. Their brains didn't understand the bigger picture yet. "You can make the list bigger when you get older, but you'll always have a sharing list."

"But then how will people know? I want everyone to know. Magic is so cool! Maybe I could start a magic show online. I bet I'd get like…a thousand views." She bounced in her chair, excited.

"Hey, hey," I covered her little hand with mine. "Daisy, you can't share anything about your magic to anyone not on the list. That includes online, too. No one else can know. If the wrong people find out, it would be dangerous for you and your mom."

I smoothed my hand over the top of her hair as she deflated in front of me. "But you can talk to me and your mom and your grandparents and your Aunts Mina and Carma as much as you want."

"But I can't tell Ashlynn or Brayden?"

I looked over at Eliza who was watching us from across the kitchen counter, her knife paused above a pile of vegetables. I knew from our conversations about school that Ashlynn and Brayden—twins—were her best friends at school. "No, you can't tell them. At least not for a long time."

"This is stupid." She kicked the table.

"Daisy," Eliza reprimanded, "no kicking the furniture. What can you kick instead?"

"I DON'T KNOW!" she shouted, crossing her arms in a huff.

"How about you go kick the soccer ball around the back yard?"

"Fine!" She pushed herself away from the table and stomped over to the sliding door. She shoved her feet into shoes, grabbed her soccer ball from the toy basket, and stormed outside.

When she was out of earshot, Eliza put the knife down and covered her face with her hands. "Shit."

I pushed myself up and limped over to her, rubbing her back. "Was not expecting that reaction."

"I should've warned you. She'd asked a few times when she could tell them. They got a new puppy and won't stop talking about it. She wants something cool to tell them, too."

"Well then, I guess you're gonna have to get a puppy."

She gave a watery laugh and put her head into the crook of her arm on the counter. "What am I doing? I should've waited to register her."

"No. You were right."

She straightened and wiped her eyes with the back of her hands. "You sure?"

I nodded. "Positive. She's practically leaking magic. If she can't get it under control, we're going to have to talk about homeschooling or applying for the SHAP boarding school."

Eliza sniffed and shook her head. "I want her life to be normal for as long as possible."

"Me, too. And you know as long as I'm around, I'll do whatever it takes to help. Including homeschooling math." I made a dramatic face.

She elbowed me. "Shut up. You love math."

"More than most things in life."

She shook her head and returned to cutting. "Stir the sauce, please?"

We tag-teamed dinner and finished it quickly, then Eliza grabbed plates to set the table. "Usually this is Daisy's job, but I'll still have to get her to finish that chapter after she calms down. Might as well save my energy arguing for that instead."

"I'll get her cleaned up." I opened the back door and looked around the yard, not seeing her. "Hey Munchkin! Time for dinner."

No answer.

"Daisy!" I used my serious voice. Nothing. *Don't panic. She's eight and upset. She's probably fine.* I cleared the anxiety from my throat and shuffled onto the small patio. "Daisy Grace Robinson! Come here now, please!"

For two agonizing heartbeats, there was silence. What if the email threat had found its way here? What if something had happened to her?

I held my breath, listening so hard it nearly hurt. Suddenly, there was a rustling of bushes at the edge of the property and a soccer ball shot into the yard, followed by Daisy. I nearly shouted in relief.

"Sorry, Uncle Jake! I kicked the ball too hard." Her cheeks were pink with exertion and she was smiling.

"Dinner," I managed, my heart close to exploding. I sucked in a deep breath. "Then lessons."

She kicked the ball toward me, but then paused. "Do I have to?"

"Would you rather do the dishes and I'll do your lesson?"

She rolled her eyes with her entire body. "Nooooo." She walked over until she was standing in front of me.

"If you get an 85 percent or above on your quiz, I'll take you for ice cream this weekend."

She stuck her pinky out. "Pinky promise?"

I held out my pinky. "Absolutely."

"Double scoop? *With* sprinkles?"

"Do I look like some kind of monster? Of course with sprinkles." We wrapped our pinkies around each other and shook on it. I moved out of her way and she dashed inside, leaving her ball outside the door.

I leaned down to scoop it up. Something purple fluttered at the corner of my vision. I shot up, spinning around, flinching at the sharp pain in my leg. The soccer ball rolled across the patio. "Poppy?"

Silence.

"If you're here, we need to talk." I looked around again, finding nothing. "I know you were at the same crime scene I was assigned. Found a purple sequin."

She didn't respond. I turned around to open the door when the soccer ball rolled to a stop at my feet. She was here. "Whatever was there wasn't human," I relayed.

"I know," she whispered, her voice no louder than a breeze. "Watch your back."

"You too," I whispered, before grabbing the ball and carrying it inside.

Chapter Ten

*Rule #17: Interfering in human matters is dangerous
and irresponsible. Reapers must stay separate and distant
at all times until a soul is in their possession.*

— The Reaper Code of Ethics, official handbook

Poppy

HIDING BEHIND THE kitchen counter, I felt like Edward
in *Twilight* when he was watching Bella sleep, except I
was watching Jake, Eliza, and Daisy eat while the adults read
whatever was on a laptop out loud. Daisy seemed uninterested, her attention focused on mutilating noodles, but still
answered any questions sent her way. Eliza sagged in relief
when she closed the computer, then focused back on her
plate. She mouthed "thank you" to Jake, who nodded once
in response.

The moment she was relieved of the assignment, Daisy
finished shoving food into her mouth and haphazardly wiped
her face with a napkin. "Can I go watch TV?"

Eliza reached over with her own napkin and cleaned
away some errant sauce on her daughter's cheek. "Half an
hour. Then bath time."

"Okay." She ran around me, all but threw her plate into

the sink, and ran to the other room. Her hurried steps stopped, and she ran back. "Uncle Jake?"

"Yeah, Munchkin?"

"Who's Poppy? Is it Mommy's Poppy?"

Eliza dropped her fork on a gasp. I took a step back. No, there was no way she could see me. Right? I looked between her and me, trying to figure out what was going on.

"Daisy," Jake said in a serious voice. "Can you see Poppy?"

She looked at him like he'd asked her if she could see a unicorn. "No."

"Then why did you ask about Poppy?"

She shrugged. "She popped into my brain." With no concern for how completely in shock Eliza and Jake were, she spun back around and ran to the living room.

Jake put his fork down and ran a hand over his face. "Shit."

Eliza's mouth opened and closed once before she managed to ask, "Why is my daughter asking about Poppy out of the blue?"

"Because...I know what happened to her." He said each word as if it were a separate sentence. Because. I. Know. What. Happened. To. Her.

"Jake." She grabbed his forearm. "It's not good news," she surmised. Her voice was barely loud enough for me to hear.

He shook his head. "She's a grim reaper."

Eliza stood so fast her chair nearly tipped backward. Jake reached out and caught it. "She's a... You saw..."

"Yeah."

"When? Where? Jake are you—?"

"Breathe." He pulled the chair back over to her and she sat down, heavy, then he handed her a glass of water. "She was at Blackburn House. She wasn't there for me."

"How do you know?"

"Because she ran the moment I saw her."

"None of this makes sense."

I wanted to walk over and see her and touch her and hug her, but I knew it was a futile effort. Wasn't it? I didn't consciously decide to move, but I was somehow putting one foot in front of the other, rounding the end of the counter and standing behind the chair Daisy had vacated.

"Ah," Jake said. "You're still here."

Eliza grabbed Jake's shoulder and stared at the chair, but her eyes went *through* me. "Poppy?"

The emotion in her voice frayed the edges of my heart. "Hey, Eliza."

"She says 'hey, Eliza,'" Jake relayed.

"I can't see you," she sighed.

"You're not supposed to," I returned. Jake shot me a look but didn't translate. "I don't know why you can see me," I admitted.

"She doesn't know why I can see her," Jake explained.

Eliza looked at her brother, then back to the chair. "You're not here to take him from me?"

"No," I promised, even though it wasn't one I could make. Jake shared my response. "I just...wanted to see you."

She laughed. "There's so much to say, I don't know where to start."

"We'll catch up in several decades. I promise to be the

one who'll come get you."

As Jake shared, Eliza smiled. "I could always write you a letter."

Jake and I said *no* simultaneously. "Don't you dare waste a year of your life on me," I warned. I couldn't live with myself if she did that. "You have a beautiful daughter."

"She'd love you," she admitted.

"I'd love her." I pulled my hand back. I moved my gaze to Jake's and his eyes bore into mine. Desperation, anxiety, and longing tore through me. I wanted to hold his face between my hands, press my lips to his, listen to his heartbeat echoing in his chest. "I need to go," I whispered, more to myself than him.

"Will I see you again?" Jake asked.

"I hope not for a very long time." For a moment, neither of us moved. We just stared into each other's eyes. "Goodbye."

Chapter Eleven

Jake

ELIZA JUST STARED at the spot Poppy left behind. She sucked in a shaky breath. "Is she…"

"She's gone," I confirmed.

She shook her head. "I can't believe I never guessed. Her last name is Grim."

"Figured it was fairytale related."

"Turns out, quite the opposite."

I laughed once without humor. "Yeah."

Eliza turned her entire body to face me. "Jake, you need to stay away from her."

I jerked back. "Don't have control of that."

"How many times have you seen her?"

"Why's it matter?"

She hit the table with her palm. "We may not have personally known any reapers until now, but we've been at SHAP for a decade. People only see reapers when they're about to die, Jake."

"If I'm about to die, avoiding Poppy isn't going to help," I countered. "She's not the one who's going to kill me."

"Dammit, Jake," she hit the table again. "Take this seriously!"

"We cannot predict or stop death. We know that better than most. Poppy would tell me if I was in danger. She said I wasn't on her list and I trust her."

"How many times have you seen her then?" she asked again.

"Two and a half."

She narrowed her eyes and shook her head in confusion. "A half?"

"She dropped something at my last crime scene. I found it on the floor. I didn't see her, just something of hers."

"And the other two?"

"Beth and Isaac's wedding and tonight."

She tapped my upper arm with the back of her hand. "You saw her yesterday and you didn't tell me?"

"To avoid you overreacting." I flinched even as I said it. Foot in mouth.

"Why is it that men always say women overreact when they used to have duels and start wars?"

"You read too many historical romances. And you are overreacting."

She held up her hand. "First of all, no such thing. I'm allowed to experience my emotions. Second of all, you want to talk about overreacting, Mr. Searching My Closet?"

"Calm down—"

"Calm down? Really?" She growled. "Men make me—*argh!*"

"Good thing you also like women," I teased, trying to break the tension.

She just glared at me. "You know the rules. Reapers are a

class-D supernatural."

I threw my hands up. "I don't think she's hanging around to compromise any top-secret investigations. She's not moving in with me. SHAP's class system doesn't apply to this situation."

She leaned closer. "Someone catches wind you're friends with a reaper and reports it? You're out as Daisy's mentor. They'll never let you do it in any official capacity."

I knew she was right, but it didn't make her warning any easier to take. "I'd never let that happen."

"Poppy deals in death, Jacob Michael Robinson. She's not the sixteen-year-old girl we used to know, okay? Don't let your nostalgia blind you."

"You're turning into your mother, Eliza Barbie Robinson."

She play-shoved my shoulder. "Go away. You're annoying and need sleep. In fact, you could just stay here. I'll sleep with Daisy and you can have my bed."

"I have a ghost who'll worry if I don't make it home. I'll be okay." I pushed myself up from the table, my body slowly unfolding. I wished I could just replace my entire leg. Didn't matter with what—Legos were fine.

"Skip Magnolia's choir concert tomorrow and rest," Eliza ordered.

I swore. I had completely forgotten. "I promised Magnolia I'd be there. She's singing a solo."

"I'll record it. I have a fancy-ass phone." She tapped her phone on the table.

"I promised."

"You know, things like boundaries exist."

"Family first." I picked up my plate from the table. "I'll sleep tonight. I'll be okay."

She grabbed my plate and set it back on the table. "I'll clean up. Go away." She stood and wrapped me in a hug. "Text when you get home."

I kissed the top of her head. "Will do." I walked over to the doorway between the kitchen and the living room. "See you tomorrow."

Daisy ran at me and hugged me around my middle, then ran back to the television without turning her head away from the screen. Impressive. As I turned to leave, my phone buzzed.

I shouldn't have said I'd sleep tonight out loud. The universe was always listening. With a practiced smile, I followed Eliza to the door and made it to my car before reading a text from Mina.

Mina: *Belphegor is stuck in the elevator shaft trying to fix it again. U around?*

God, the Countryside Village Apartments had a shit landlord. It was why I lived in a condo across town. I sat heavily in my car and leaned my head back on the headrest. One slow blink, then a second. It would be so easy to go home and let the slow blinks turn into no blinks. One long sleep and I'd feel like a person again.

Mina: *OMG. George just grabbed his toolbox. Reggie's trying to stall him.*

I tossed the phone onto the dash in frustration. George Andrews was one of Mina's neighbors, well into his retirement, who wanted to fix everything. His failing eyesight and lack of flexibility, however, had caused him to get seriously injured the last time he had attempted a repair. Belphegor, a close friend of the Andrews and the only demon allowed in Applechester, had taken pains to repair everything possible before George could hurt himself anymore.

He wouldn't give up if Belphegor was in trouble. "Dammit!" I knew it wasn't Mina's fault, but I was so tired and so tired of being in pain, that I'd blame a pebble if it got into my shoe.

Jake: *Be there in 20.*

It was going to be a long night.

EVERYTHING HURT WORSE when I didn't sleep enough, but I couldn't sleep when my pain was bad anyway. A terrible cycle usually solved by the good pain meds I kept in my nightstand. I had popped one of the few remaining pills, but with only four hours between the moment my head hit the pillow to when my alarm went off, it wasn't enough time to recover.

If seeing Poppy really meant I was going to die soon, I didn't want to waste a single moment sleeping anyway. I sat on the edge of my bed for a long time, slow blinks and big breaths racking my body. My eyes watered from exhaustion and my head felt like it was floating.

Sebastian knocked and leaned through the door. "Forgive me for overstepping, but you haven't rested in days."

I grunted. I didn't have the energy to respond aloud. Full day of work, then Magnolia's concert, then hopefully sleep.

"Jacob, you need more rest."

"I just woke up from resting," I defended, my words like marbles in my mouth. Had I even remembered to brush my teeth last night? I lifted my hand to wipe my mouth and sucked in a sharp breath through my nose at the pain in my arm.

I looked down at my forearm, where medical tape and gauze covered a scrape. *Ah*, I'd forgotten. It had taken a few hours to get Belphegor out of the elevator. My arm and Belphegor's sweater sleeve had paid the price.

Luckily Mina had a first aid kit for me, and Amber Andrews, George's spouse, who'd originally knitted Belphegor's sweater, knew how to fix the hole in his sleeve. Then she insisted on helping me fix my triangle scarf while Belphegor and Mina got into a heated argument over whether knitting or crocheting was easier. As neither of them crafted, my ears were ringing for no reason. I hadn't made it to my bed until almost three this morning.

Sebastian crossed his arms and leaned against the door. "Jake, I'm sure if you take a sick day—"

"Duty comes first, end of story."

"You need to come first."

"I always keep my word." We both looked over at the letter from my mom that was framed and hung on my wall. Every SHAP agent had a box with their will and letters to be given to loved ones in case of their death. My dad was in human resources at a human company, but my mom had been a SHAP agent like her parents.

I made it a point to call my grandma every few weeks, especially since she had so many stories of my mom. It was nice to get to know Mom through the memories. Combined with the letter Mom left me, I had gotten to know the woman who had given her life to save someone else.

I could recite her note by memory, a list of life lessons she couldn't personally teach. SPEAK UP WHEN SOMETHING'S WRONG. CLEAN UP AFTER YOURSELF. IF YOU CAN HELP, DO IT. ALWAYS KEEP YOUR WORD. SOMETIMES FAMILY ISN'T BLOOD BUT LOVE...

I hadn't spoken up loud enough when Poppy had confessed she was moving. I'd known something bigger was wrong, but I was too afraid to bring it up to my parents. I hadn't wanted to ruin their day.

Would me saying something have changed her future? Could I have prevented her death? Would we have at least been allowed to say good-bye?

My phone vibrated with a text.

Eliza: You didn't text me when you got home

Jake: Had to work. You were sleeping

Eliza: I'm going to kick your left knee if you show up to the concert

I sighed, locked my cell, and pushed myself off the bed with a groan. I felt like rusted metal on a cold day. Coffee, then shower.

After filling my coffee pot, I limped to the shower and turned it on, and stopped to stare at myself in the mirror. I looked—and felt—like I hadn't slept in a week. Was this what would kill me? Pure exhaustion?

I glanced at the sink, which had a glob of toothpaste in the bowl and some beard trimming near the faucet. That was unacceptable. I reached into the lower cabinet and pulled out my homemade cleaning solution, sprayed down the sink and the toilet, and wiped it clean with a microfiber cloth. The floor really needed a cleaning, but there was no way I could manage that today.

My phone alarm went off, reminding me I had to leave in fifteen minutes. "Hey, Sebastian?" I shouted.

"Yes?" he responded, putting his head through the door.

"If I'm not out in five minutes, make sure I didn't fall asleep."

Chapter Twelve

Rule #7: Reaper manifests are confidential and not to be shared.

— *The Reaper Code of Ethics, official handbook*

Poppy

JAKE STILL WASN'T on my list. I was terrified every new human day that he'd appear, but even more scared that he'd end up assigned to someone else. Just because I was the closest to him didn't mean I got priority. If I had a busy schedule, it was possible another reaper in the area would get him, although it would likely be someone closely related to me. He could end up on *anyone's* list and I wouldn't know.

I didn't have a stomach anymore, but it still felt like I had swallowed a large boulder. Waiting for someone to maybe die was the worst thing I'd ever experienced. Would Jake have been my reaper partner if I had told him the truth? Would he have chosen to come with me and leave Eliza and his family? Would his company have made being a reaper more bearable or would I still feel this trapped and out of place? Was I the only one who felt like they didn't belong?

The moment I was born, even by a surrogate, I was a Grim. Adult reapers were allowed to bring their spouses or a committed partner or partners as long as they were approved by the reaper council. Once born of, adopted by, or committed to a reaper, an outsider became part of the family business.

This was ridiculous to think about. Despite time being completely fluid, marked only by boat rides and playing the violin at a rundown pier, I couldn't rewind the events of the past. I couldn't make this make sense. And anyway, there was no other choice. I was a reaper, end of story.

Just like I couldn't figure out why, despite promising to stay away, I was sitting in the back of an empty church watching Jake listen to a community choir concert. On paper, a reaper in church was incongruous, but in reality we were neutral creatures. We didn't steal souls, we guided them. We didn't work for any specific afterlife location—we were like an afterlife waiting room—and our allegiance was to protecting our cargo.

If I tried really hard, I could convince myself that I was protecting Jake's soul, even if it wasn't ripe yet. So I stayed, and I watched as his long blinks turned into closed eyes, and his head dipped. Eliza elbowed him and he jerked awake, looking around.

I didn't need to see his face to know he was exhausted. I could tell by the way the air moved around him, the way he held his shoulders. It may have been years, but I still knew him.

A shadow moved along the outside of the stained-glass window, disrupting the early evening sunlight. Probably just someone walking by, or maybe an animal. I looked back over at Jake whose head was dipping again. I wish I could just walk over there and tell him to get up and go home. He always gave everyone everything before he gave to himself.

He still hadn't learned boundaries. At least, not when it came to committing his time. Not that I had room to talk, but my time wasn't my own.

I was glad I no longer slept. The nightmares would be the worst. I'd seen too much as a reaper, the worst of humanity and of soul eaters. I couldn't even sit in church and not be suspicious of a shadow.

It passed by again.

A third pass. More blue than gray. A fourth pass.

If I had a heart, it would be beating in my throat. I scrambled to my feet and around the back side of the pew, watching the sunny spot where the shadow had been. I wanted to go get my sister, but if she knew that I was here, she'd hand me my ass.

I heard the rustling of someone walking down the aisle and spun to see an aggravated Jake coming toward me, punctuating his silent frustration with each thump of his cane. From the look on his face, I knew he was going to react poorly to me spying on him again. He opened his mouth to speak, but I held up a hand.

"I think there's something out there."

The exhaustion fell from his face and he slipped into Agent Robinson right in front of me. "Let's go," he mouthed.

The moment we were in the foyer and out of earshot of his family, Jake turned to face me. "Why are you here?"

I just pressed my finger to my lips and slid through the door. Jake followed as we crept around the side of the building toward the wall of stained-glass windows. When we reached the corner, I peered around the edge. A large rabbit startled and looked up from the plant it was eating right in front of the window.

Jake pressed against my back and looked over the top of my head. "Ah, yes. A threatening rabbit."

The weight of his body pressed against mine made me forget how to use words. I closed my eyes for a moment, soaking in the feeling. He was so warm. I wanted to turn around, to bury my head between his neck and shoulder, to get lost in the strength of his arms.

He stepped away and I pressed my hand to the brick to keep steady. God, I was so touch starved. How did no one else in my immediate family feel this way? We were never huge huggers. Sure, my parents hugged me whenever I needed, but I loved casual touch. Craved it.

Eliza, Jake, and I were always touching. Hands, heads, legs, feet. If we were hanging out, we always were within touching distance. Even twelve years later, I missed it every day.

Jake sighed and leaned against the wall. "Poppy, I can't be seen talking to you, especially by any supernaturals. If it gets back to SHAP, I'll lose my clearance. I'll be removed as Daisy's future mentor." He looked over at me. "I'm sorry."

"I understand," I whispered, trying not to show how deep his words cut. I studied his face, trying to memorize every curve. "You weren't actually supposed to see me today."

"No?"

"I was just…checking on you. You're the one who left

early."

He rubbed the back of his neck. "Yeah, I fell asleep too many times and Magnolia ordered me home."

"Don't get pneumonia on me, again," I warned, recalling when he didn't sleep much before finals and ended up sicker than he'd ever been.

He sighed. "Yeah, I know. I promise I won't." He looked out across the parking lot. "I'm so tired." The words were spoken so softly, I wasn't sure he'd meant to say them out loud. I was sure he didn't mean only physically.

I tilted my head. "I'll walk you to your car."

I FELL INTO step with Jake as we walked away from the church and toward the parking lot. He slipped his hand into mine, and the entire world stilled at his touch. God, unlife was just unfair.

I squeezed and sucked in a breath. "I miss this."

"Holding hands?"

I nodded. "Also, just touching someone so warm. Human skin is so soft and full of life." I looked down at our hands. "I'm the only reaper I know who prefers to wear their human glamour, even off duty. It just feels more like me."

He squeezed my hand and I almost tripped. "Is there anything you like about it?"

I pressed my lips together for a moment, avoiding eye contact. "Is it that obvious?"

"Poppy, you cried for two days over Binx, who I'll remind you was a fictional cat, after watching *Hocus Pocus,* and then refused to ever watch it again."

"I'll admit, that's on brand for me." I hesitated as we stepped up to his car. "I mean I get to hang out with my family, and that's pretty cool."

He lifted his eyebrows. "Is that it?"

I shook my head. "There's something else." Showing him would require me to release his hand and I hesitated, but he made the decision for me by pulling his away and tucking it into his pocket. My chest hollowed out at the loss, but I covered it by reaching into my cloak.

He sucked in a sharp breath through his nose when he saw the violin. "How?"

"I was allowed to bring one thing with me, so I chose the most precious." The instrument had been my sixteenth birthday present from Jake. When he'd given it to me at my party, our families had lost it saying it was too expensive and that we were too young to be exchanging such big gifts.

Ultimately neither set of parents could bring themselves to take it away from me. Jake had found it in a thrift store and worked extra shifts for weeks until he could afford to have it repaired and restrung. I was also able to return the rental I had for the school orchestra, which made my frugal parents happy. Jake and I swore up and down that we weren't secretly in a relationship—we didn't need the labels to know how much we loved each other—and once the party ended, everyone was mostly appeased.

I slept with it in my bed for the next month and practiced until my fingers bled.

"I thought it was lost forever." Jake reached out and touched the edge of the body, over a decade of unspoken words filling the space between us. "Can you play me something?"

I nodded, the corners of my mouth softening into a smile. "Most humans can't hear it, but I suppose since you can see me, it's worth a try." I lifted the instrument to my shoulder and closed my eyes. I pulled the bow over the strings, the air around us shimmering with fairy lights and the emotional sounds of Tchaikovsky.

I played for him and only him, leaning into the music. Moving with it. There was no self-consciousness, no worry that I'd mess up. The exact notes didn't matter.

It was the memories, the emotions, the way music could say everything I couldn't. The crescendos and the decrescendos, the accidental flats and the changing time signatures, giddy eighth notes and the long heartbreaking pleas trapped in fermatas.

When I finished and lowered the violin, Jake was leaning against his car, staring into me. His eyes shone in the setting sun and he was silent for a long moment, letting the last note fade into the fall breeze. "You're still so talented," he breathed.

Thank god I couldn't blush. I tucked the instrument away. "I use it every day."

He smiled. "Good."

We stood there in silence, knowing that the next words needed to be a good-bye, trying to delay the inevitable. "So…"

He straightened. "So." He opened his arms. "A proper good-bye this time." His voice caught on the last word, and it frayed my non-beating heart.

I stepped into him, tucking my forehead against his shoulder and closing my eyes. His arms wrapped around me tight, his cheek leaning against the top of my head. My imagination had not done a Jake hug justice. He was completely wrapped around me and for the most perfect of moments, I felt *human*. I was so warm. The spiraling internal clock inside of me quieted and my thoughts slowed and eased away.

Before I even had a chance to daydream about stopping time and never letting go, dread—no, something infinitely colder—shot through me. I pushed out of Jake's arms and threw him behind me as an out-of-control car careened around a line of parked vehicles and straight toward us, a demon I'd recently sliced in half in the front seat. *Oh hell no.* It was not getting revenge today. I dropped my human glamour, my skeleton being the safest and strongest form, and pulled out my sword.

With two strikes of my weapon, the car stopped dead in front of me, the engine literally cut in half. The crumpled metal spat smoke and fluid in one last visceral attack, then fell silent. A final thrust with my sword through the windshield, and that demon was in pieces again, escaping through a self-repairing tear in the earth. I was breathing heavy, despite not needing oxygen, because I was freaked out.

Holy macaroni.

Jake had almost died in front of me.

Worse, he saw me change into full reaper skeleton. I pulled my sword out of the wreckage, replaced my human skin, then forced myself to look at the man whose life I just saved.

"Holy shit," Jake whispered. "You just Edward Cullen-ed me. With a really badass sword."

"I"—I blinked at him—"guess I did? It's been a while since I've watched the movie." Eliza and I had made him take us to the movies three times in one week to see *Twilight*. To his credit he'd gone every time.

His face went serious, then blank as he surveyed the scene, Agent Jacob Robinson slipping firmly in place. "This is why you've been coming around, isn't it?"

I took a step toward him, but the crease between his brows deepened and I took it as a warning. "Partially."

"Because I really am on your list?"

"No! No. At least, not yet." I shook my head to clear it.

"I'm not following."

"I think you might be in danger and I'm trying to protect you."

"Why now? Why this case?"

I shook my head. "I don't know. I don't have all the"—I flailed my hands near my head—"fancy reaper intuitions that are supposed to help me figure this stuff out. All I know is that you can see me, and I don't know why."

"Have you come to visit before? Have there been other times I haven't seen you?"

I pressed my lips together. *So many times.* I couldn't tell him. Not yet. I just nodded instead.

"How long have you been checking on me, Poppy?" His voice was low but demanding.

I looked at his feet when I answered. "Every few weeks…for twelve years."

He sucked in a breath, reached out, and brushed his

knuckle under my chin, then lifted my face until I met his eyes. "Why didn't you ever let me know?"

"I wanted you to live your best life."

"And now?"

"I'm scared," I whispered.

"Why?"

"Because once you die, that's it. You go to the afterlife and I carry on being a reaper and I can never ever see you again, and I don't know how to exist without you, okay?!" I slapped my hand over my mouth.

I don't know how to exist without you? Oh my god. *Ground, please swallow me up.* The ground ignored my pleading.

Jake's eyes went molten, but the moment we heard a car door close, he blinked and turned into professional Jake. "I need to call this in." He nodded to the wreckage behind me. "Can we meet later and talk?"

I didn't even bother to pretend I wasn't going to be there. "Yeah. I get a break around midnight your time."

"Can you find me?"

I smiled but it was forced. "Always."

Chapter Thirteen

Jake

I'D CHANGED THREE times. What did one wear for a serious, secret meeting with the former love of their life who was also a grim reaper? I ended up in gray joggers and a white T-shirt. They were more comfortable on my sore leg than jeans but they weren't pajama bottoms, and white T-shirts matched everything.

Sebastian leaned against my doorframe, arms crossed, judging me. I narrowed my eyes at him. "Were you this annoying when you lived with Mina?"

"More, likely. She was so emotionally naïve she didn't figure out she was falling into love until it was too late. You know exactly what you're doing." He glanced at the wall above my bed, then back at me.

I ran my hand through my hair to make it sit right. "A runaway car almost turned me into a pancake today. She has insider info. That's all this is."

After Poppy disappeared, I phoned in the accident to SHAP. I had given the credit to Belphegor, saying he stopped the car with a pole he had found in the parking lot. I was going to need to brief him next time I saw him. While having him on the paperwork wasn't ideal, he had made himself invaluable during the initial investigation of the Thinner case, and SHAP had been lenient on his presence in Applechester. It would be far worse to have a reaper on the report.

"I am always deeply impressed by the excuses humans are able to create when it comes to matters of the heart."

I shot him a look. "I'm not Mina. I'm not going to let you be in my business."

He laughed. "I find it humorous that you think Mina didn't put up a harder fight than you. When you're my age, you'll understand."

I grunted in response, not bothering with the energy to fight him. "You can't be here when she shows up. It'll make you liable."

"Contain your concern. I'm departing momentarily." He gave me a long look. "I know trying to dissuade you is futile, as I know you and Poppy carry great affection for one another, but please proceed with the utmost caution." With a tip of his top hat, he disappeared.

As I moved into the living room, my phone chimed with my Mina and Carma group chat text.

Mina: *Why's Sebastian interrupting movie night with Reggie? He said you have a clandestine meeting*

Carma: *Is this Sebastian code for date?*

I knew this chat was going to bite me in the ass.

Jake: *Not a date. A work thing*

Mina: *At 11:45PM? Alone?*

Carma: Mina, weren't our first like 7 dates "work things"???

Jake: I'm blocking you both

Mina: I'll tell Magnolia

Jake: If you do, I'll tell her you proposed

Mina: JAKE!

Carma: Remember how I said I always wanted a little brother? I take it back

Jake: I give good birthday presents

Carma: *thinking emoji*

Mina: Careful what you wish for. This one comes with a side of revenge

Mina: For real be careful tonight

Jake: Of course Mom

Carma: I love you guys

Mina: *barf emoji*

Jake: *barf emoji*

Carma: *eye roll emoji*

I nearly dropped my phone when a knock sounded on the wall. I looked up to find Poppy standing near the front door. My heart thudded hard against my ribcage.

"Can I come in?" She smiled sheepishly. "More in, anyway."

"Yeah, of course." I gestured to the couch. I sat down and straightened my leg out with a deep breath. It hurt a little less than yesterday, which was a slight improvement.

Poppy pulled her hood down and tugged at the fabric. "Mind if I take this off?" I shook my head. "You have to promise not to laugh. Remember, I was sixteen and trying to rebel."

I lifted my eyebrows in a silent question. "Promise."

She pulled out her violin and set it on the table, then laid her sword on the floor next to the couch. She shrugged out of her cloak, revealing her bright pink T-shirt and unicorn leggings. I pressed my lips together and put my hand over my mouth to hide my smile.

She glanced up at me as she laid the cloak over the arm of the couch and crossed her arms. "You promised."

I cleared my throat. "I'm not laughing. I'm going to sneeze."

She shook her head and slumped onto the couch next to me. "Fine, just hurry up."

I threw my head back and let out a belly laugh. "How pissed were your dads?"

"So pissed. They had gotten us all matching black out-fits. They just made the mistake of not waiting until I was totally asleep before leaving my room."

I thumbed wetness away from the corner of my eye. "Only you would rebel against your family by wearing a pink shirt and unicorns." I had seen her in this outfit before, but twenty-eight-year-old Poppy wore it differently than her younger self. Her shirt was tighter around her chest and hips, and the leggings were no longer baggy around her fuller thighs.

She lifted a shoulder. "It's comfy, and the reaper magic keeps them in good shape." She lifted her arm. "See? No pit stains."

I laughed even harder. That was such a Poppy thing to

say.

She pulled at the leggings on her lower thigh. "No saggy knees either."

"Reaper magic keeps your clothes nice, but you can't change them?" I asked, once I caught my breath.

"I know, right? Apparently, that's the limit." She laugh-sighed and shook her head. "Oh well, there are worse outfits to be stuck in for all eternity. Like the distant cousins who died during a costume party dressed as a horse. One was the front and one was the butt."

I groaned. "I c-can't l-laugh at that." I sucked in a steadying breath. "I'll die wearing a clown costume or something."

She nodded. "We have at least three clowns, actually."

"That's terrifying."

"You're telling me. One is from 1812, and clowns back then were freaky."

I pulled out my phone and searched *clowns in 1800s*, then promptly closed the browser. "Well, I'll never sleep again."

She nodded. "To be honest, I haven't slept since I saw them either." She winked at me. "That's a joke. Because I can't sleep."

"Ha, ha." I smiled and rested back against the cushions. "I really miss you."

"Same." She looked around the room, taking in the gray walls, patterned curtains, and matching armchairs with throw pillows. "Magnolia was here."

"Literally before the moving truck showed up. I walked in to find the place painted and half furnished."

"Do you like it?"

I bounced my head. "Better than anything I would've done by myself."

She sat up and faced me. "Can I look around?"

I gestured with my hand to the kitchen. "Have at it."

She slid off the couch and walked toward the kitchen, and I smiled at her bare feet with pink toenails. Her floor length robe had covered them, but her leggings stopped just above her ankles. The thought of Poppy walking around collecting souls in bare feet, probably because she forgot to put shoes on when she changed her outfit, was bittersweet. It was so very Poppy, and so very much proof that she had been too young to carry this much of a burden.

She stuck her head out of the kitchen doorway. "Why's your kitchen so clean?"

"Because I don't like mess," I answered, shuffling toward her.

"You would not like my room in the barracks. It has stacks of books and sheet music everywhere."

I shook my head. "Of course it does."

"Let me guess," she said, opening the oven door, "I could eat off any surface in this house?" She leaned in to inspect the oven. "Have you ever even turned this on?"

I rolled my eyes. "Two days ago."

"Sure." With a cheeky smile, she closed the oven, then slid past me and moved down the hall, pausing to open my hall closet. "Even your fitted sheets are folded in perfect squares!"

"They aren't hard."

"You would say that. My arms are too short."

"Do you fold many fitted sheets as a reaper?"

"I ruled it out as a hobby my first week. I mostly stick to small throws and towels." She stuck her tongue out at me and I laughed deep.

My hand pressed to my stomach as the tension eased, a feeling I hadn't experienced in a long time. Was it the laughter? Or was it just being near Poppy?

She moved across the hall and into the combination guest bathroom-laundry room. "There is not a speck of lint anywhere." I could hear her remove the lint trap on the dryer. "Did you clean this with a toothbrush? Why are you like this? You didn't used to be. At least not this bad."

I didn't answer. I didn't have a way to explain my need to control everything I could. That real life was messy and emotional and the more organized and clean my space was, the safer I felt. I couldn't tell her it all started when she disappeared.

"Just habit," I answered, dismissing her questions. "We should probably talk about why you're here."

She leaned against the doorframe. "With your bedroom right there and completely unseen? Not a chance."

She scooted by me, so close her clothes brushed my skin, and moved toward the darkened doorway. As she reached for the light switch, realization dawned as to why I should've exercised more caution before letting her explore. "Poppy, wait—"

The light flipped on. She gasped. I covered my eyes with my hand for a moment, feeling like a silly teenager who just got caught writing a note to his crush. Except I wasn't a teenager anymore, and this wasn't a note.

It was an extravagantly large acrylic painting above my bed that depicted a field of poppies. The petals of the flowers were textured, giving the painting a three-dimensional look. Rows and rows of poppies made a half moon around one large flower in the center. In a room of cool grays and whites, the petals' vibrant red was the only bright color.

She stood in the doorway, one leg tucked behind the other, her arms around her middle, except her right hand, which was pressed to her mouth. Emotion clogged my throat as I watched the woman who had changed every aspect of my life bear witness to how much she still affected me. I never dreamed this day would or could happen and had never stopped to be self-conscious.

Somehow this felt like saying "I love you" all over again. As if I was still sixteen, awkward and unsure about every-thing in my life except her. Teenage Jake had gotten a bouquet of fake poppies from the fabric store and squeezed them tightly as I paced the small treehouse, keeping my head bent low to not bang it on the low ceiling. The moment she'd gotten to the top of the ladder, I just blurted it out without any pretense. Thankfully, she laughed, told me she loved me back, and kissed me.

Now, present-day Poppy unfolded her body and walked on the balls of her feet into the room, approaching the painting like she would a frightened animal. I felt like that animal. She skirted in between the bed and the side table and stood in front of the canvas.

I had found the painting when I was on a mission in Grand Rapids. It was in the window display for a small gallery and stopped me dead in my tracks. After staring at it for an hour, I purchased it and carried it with me from hotel room to hotel room for forty-three days, until I finished the mission. It was the most expensive thing in the condo that wasn't an appliance.

Poppy reached up and traced a petal with a delicate finger. She studied her finger, as if searching it for answers.

I moved into the room behind her, leaning on the edge of my bed. "You aren't the only one who can't figure out how to move on." My voice was barely louder than my heartbeat. "It was supposed to be you and me."

She turned to face me. "Do you think we would've made it?"

I rubbed the back of my neck. "I used to stay up all night wondering why our parents were so against us being together." I scrunched my nose. "Which makes a lot more sense now. I mean, I know my dad was worried about our age difference, but my guess is your folks were worried about you being a reaper."

She nodded, looking down at her feet. "They always had serious talks with my siblings' partners, but they were all adults then. I think they weren't sure how to explain it to another kid and that kid's family."

I looked up at the painting, then at her, the juxtaposition making my chest warm. They were both breathtaking. "For what it's worth, I would've come with you," I whispered.

She shook her head. "You would've had to give up everything, Jake. You wouldn't even know Daisy. Eliza wouldn't have her older brother."

"Do you remember the night we saw the shooting star?" She bit her bottom lip and nodded. "Do you remember what we wished for?" We had been wrapped around each other, whispering dreams about the future, kissing each other every few minutes until the sun came up.

"We wished for forever."

"I'd still make the same wish today," I admitted. I didn't want to leave my sister and definitely not my niece. The thought tore my heart in half. But Poppy was my person, the other half of my heart, the soul who understood mine without words.

She unlocked and ran over to me, wrapping her arms around my shoulders and burying her face in my neck. I put my forehead on her shoulder and held her against me. She was cold, as if she'd come inside from a winter day with no coat on. I smoothed my hand over her long hair, trying to calm the way her arms trembled.

"I know I need to stay away from you," she whispered, "but I don't know how. My heart may have stopped beating, but it never stopped loving you."

"I don't know how to do this either." I lifted my head and raised both my hands to cradle the side of her face. "Twelve years later and we still have bad timing."

"And I have the unfortunate problem of being dead." She said it with a smile, but her voice was thick with emotion.

"Death doesn't stop love."

"Don't I know it."

I slid my hands into her silky hair, and then she slid hers over mine, our fingers entwining. "Kiss me, Poppy."

Her eyes widened, then moved to my mouth. She pressed her forehead against mine and bit her bottom lip. "I can't," she breathed and pulled my hands away from her face. "I'm barely hanging on as it is. If I kiss you…" She pressed her lips together then took a deep breath. "If I kiss you, and something happens to you, I don't know how I'd go back to just being a reaper. Honestly, I'd probably jump into the River Styx and swim to the Isle of Exile and call it a day."

"What's the Isle of Exile?"

She shook her head and gave me a sad smile. "Long story." She took a step back, allowing the real world to fill in the space between us. "We should talk, Jake. Try to figure out what's going on."

I pressed a fist to my chest for a moment, the ache greater than the pain in my leg. "I'll meet you back in the living room."

She nodded and turned on her heel, pausing for a moment to take one last look at the painting before walking out.

Chapter Fourteen

Rule #28: Nonplatonic relationships with other supernatural creatures are highly discouraged.

— The Reaper Code of Ethics, official handbook

Poppy

I HAD NEVER experienced a breakup, unless you counted dying. Was this what it felt like? A mini-death? Drawing that line with Jake, telling him no, and walking out of his room hurt so bad I almost couldn't remember how to move one foot in front of the other.

Without looking at him following behind me, I put my cloak on, tucking my violin and sword back into the magical pockets. I was here to help him solve a case in reaper capacity and it was time I started acting like it before I hurt us both. I just needed to forget about the painting over his bed, the way his hands felt on my body, how close his lips had been to mine, and his shaking voice when he asked me to kiss him.

I turned to face him, each of us standing on opposite sides of the room. My gaze rested more on his feet than on his face. "We were scheduled to take six souls from that house. A demon had gotten to one before we even arrived."

He nodded. "Back to demons again, then."

"What are you working on? Does anything coincide?"

"Digging into the illegal sale of vampire venom. Trying to find the accomplices of someone who was turning humans into hybrid vampires without their consent. The demons threatened that if we didn't get it under control, they were going to make a move. But we have it under control. All remaining vampire-human hybrids are registered with SHAP."

A ding echoed through the living room and Jake glanced at the laptop on the coffee table. "Who's emailing this late?" He walked to the couch and sat, then popped open his computer and pulled up his email. He sucked in a sharp breath.

I leaned over to read the screen, the threat clear even from across the room.

"Jake…"

He leaned back and sighed, "I've gotten threats since my first day on the job, Poppy. It's nothing."

"You need to stay off this case. Transfer. Quit. Find something else to do."

"You know I can't do that." He looked up at me.

I shook my head even as I knew I wouldn't say no to him. "Jake…"

"I don't want these people to hurt anyone else."

I stuck my hands through my hair and blew out a breath. "If I hear or see anything, I'll get in contact."

He nodded. "Thanks."

I spent one last moment looking at him, memorizing him, then nodded. "Stay safe, Jake." I walked out of his condo and back to the place where I was safe, lonely, and had forever to think about the kiss I was walking away from.

Chapter Fifteen

Jake

DESPITE HAVING A full five hours to sleep, I spent most of it lying on my back, looking up at the poppy painting. She had stood in this very room, touched that painting, pressed her body into mine. She fit in my life again in an instant, as if twelve years were twelve minutes, and we'd just been separated by walls instead of worlds.

A text message lit up my phone. It was Paris.

Paris: *Call me when you've read the autopsy.*

I checked the time and groaned. Already six and only exhaustion to show for my efforts. I opened my email, read the report, hit Paris's number, and put the phone on speaker.

"Good morning," she greeted, chipper and well rested.

Jealous. "Morning."

There was a beat of silence. "Did you sleep at all?"

I didn't bother to respond. "All died from fentanyl overdose."

"All with terminal or degenerative illnesses."

I rubbed the sleep from my eyes, trying to get my foggy brain to make the connection. "Why fentanyl? Are they mercy killings or are they trying to cure people? It doesn't make sense. Why use it to dilute stock they're not selling? Why risk overdosing test subjects?"

She paused to think over the comment, a trait that I appreciated, yet it tested my patience. "That remains the question of the day. Speaking of, does any of this apply to the near-accident yesterday?"

I winced. "I should have told you. I'm sorry, I was exhausted."

"Jake, I know we haven't worked together very long, and I know I'm likely not your ideal partner, all things considered, but I need you to communicate better with me."

The memory of me giving Mina almost the same speech—she had been completely out of her element falling in love with Carma—was a kick to the stomach. I had yelled at her for not keeping up on the case, for not communicating, for being too much in her own head, and here I was doing the same thing and not thinking twice.

"I'm sorry," I admitted. "Truly. I'm struggling with something personal and didn't realize how much it was affecting my work."

"I appreciate you saying that. I just worry—oh, text from Jim."

My phone buzzed with a text. I opened it to read the address of a new crime scene. "Who's driving?"

"I'll pick you up in ten with coffee."

DESPITE BEING IN a small storage unit instead of a house, the scene was almost identical to the place we'd been to earlier in the week. All different ages and body types, all slumped over in chairs. A cardboard box as a makeshift table with powder residue.

I checked the pulse on the young man closest to me. "He's still breathing! Paris, call for medics. We gotta check the rest." I pulled the guy to the ground, swearing at the pain as I knelt and began performing CPR.

Paris spoke quickly into the phone stuck between her shoulder and ear, feeling for pulses with both hands. She crouched in front of a young woman, slapping her face on both sides and trying to shake her awake. "Come on, come on, wake up for me."

The woman opened her eyes. "Was supposed to..."

"Was supposed to what? Come on, talk to me. What'd you take?" Paris pleaded, then into the phone. "We need medics! We have two victims still alive." She returned her attention to the woman. "Why are you here? What did they promise?"

"...heal us. He promised." She slumped forward. Paris caught her and laid her down on the floor, then hit speaker on her phone.

"What was going to heal you?" Paris begged, leaning her head close to the woman's nose and mouth. "No!" She started doing compressions.

Was supposed to heal us. The phrase repeated over and over in my head as I kept up my compressions, stopping to push breath into the man's lungs. My arms hurt and my leg was on fire, but if we could just keep these two alive until we got some answers, it would be worth it.

The air changed around us, smelling sweeter, and the ambient noise grew quieter. I knew Poppy was here before I saw the flash of purple, before I heard the somber sound of her violin. Her hand touched my shoulder and I stopped compressions, looking up at her, and leaned into her touch for just a moment.

"He's on the manifest," Poppy explained quietly. She gestured to the woman Paris was working on. "So is she."

"Can you ask what happened, what they took?"

"Not gonna help!" Paris shouted.

"Talking to my ghost friend," I explained, purposefully avoiding the word reaper so she didn't panic.

Poppy glared at the center of the room. "I know!" she snapped at the air, before turning back to me. "Sylvia says we have to go."

I looked up to where Poppy had indicated. "Sylvia's here? Why can't I see her if I can see you?"

Poppy looked behind her then back to me. "I don't know, but I'll take it as reassurance I'm not here for your soul. You and Sylvia don't have the same connection that we do." She looked back over her shoulder. "Do they make chill pills for reapers because you need one."

"Sylvia," I tried, "I know I was never your favorite, but please help us figure out what's going on."

"This is why she didn't like you," Poppy explained. "Why, because he wants to help people?" she retorted back. She paused then crossed her arms. "Fine, yes. Please."

I couldn't hear Sylvia's side of the conversation, but I could guess. Poppy and Sylvia were opposites. She thought I had a stick up my ass, and I thought she was the personification of an internet troll.

"They say it was supposed to fix them," Poppy explained. "Like the Thinner shakes. They said it was a supplement called Vixen." She stilled; her head snapped to the right. She tucked away her violin and brought out her sword. "Get out of here. Now."

"Paris, get to the car!" I ordered.

She paused doing compressions on the woman, looked at my face, and then ran over with hands extended. "Hands, now."

I shook my head. I was going to be too slow. "Right behind you. Go!"

She shoved her hands beneath my arms and started dragging me back. "Not leaving you."

"Get out of here!" No way my leg would be able to support my weight after kneeling on concrete. It would take several minutes of straightening, massaging, and swearing before I could stand, let alone run.

Poppy bent low and wrapped her free arm around my legs and lifted me off the ground, while keeping the sword in front of her. I straightened my leg as they carried me, grunting at the spasm of pain from my hip to my ankle.

"Should I ask why you're floating?" Paris grunted.

"Later," I said.

"Coming!" Poppy yelled, just as we reached the passenger side of Paris's car. Poppy set me down, then ran back toward the unit.

Paris opened the door and I hopped on my good leg, then dove inside the car. My partner slid across the hood and climbed into the driver's seat. When I looked out of the windshield, I saw Poppy in a standoff with two demons and a ragged shadow.

Poppy brought her sword down on one of the demons' head, slicing it in two before it pulled itself together and disappeared. The weird shadow fell next, presumably due to Sylvia. But the second demon had disappeared. I turned around in my seat, looking out every window trying to find it.

"Jake!" Paris warned.

I turned to face her, then followed her gaze behind me. A dumpster was rolling toward my side of the car alarmingly fast. Paris turned on the car and threw it into reverse, flooring the accelerator. She honked the horn before she cut hard to the left, turning us down another row and nearly plowing into an unloading U-Haul.

The dumpster rolled past the opening followed by a streak of purple, and the crunching of metal. Paris and I jumped out of the car and stared down the aisle. Poppy stood over the remnants of a demon. The dumpster had hit an empty security booth, which was now collapsing in on itself.

I ran a hand down my face and shook my head in disbelief. That dumpster weighed more than Paris's car. At the speed it had been moving, it would have done some serious damage, especially to me.

Poppy met my gaze across the space, the truth settling between us. This wasn't an accident. She'd been right. That email wasn't an empty threat.

Paris turned to face me. "I think it's time you and I had a talk. We can start with who—or what—you can see that I can't."

Chapter Sixteen

Rule #32: Information shared between a human soul and a reaper is confidential. Reapers are forbidden to be involved with human investigations, as a matter of security.

— *The Reaper Code of Ethics, official handbook*

Poppy

SYLVIA HAD BEEN quiet since I returned to the storage unit and put my sword away. She sat in stoic silence while I tried to pry more information from the passengers, but it was an echo of what they'd said at the storage unit.

"How'd you find out about the trial?" I asked.

A middle-aged man ran his palm over the short beard on his chin. "Mine was an ad on social media. Kept popping up. Promised it could reverse cancer. Thought it was worth a try since nothing else was working."

"I got a message from an old classmate," a woman in her early thirties explained. "Hadn't talk to her since we graduated, but she saw my post about stopping chemo. Sent me the link. Some woman named Fletcher called me to confirm."

The stories were all the same. They were targeted based on social media posts and reached out to a company called

Unbelievable Bodies to be vetted for a clinical trial of a new supplement called Vixen. Once selected, all they had to do was pay a thousand dollars to participate.

I held myself together until we stepped off the boat, then I ran to the shore and dry heaved so hard I fell to my knees. The greed and selfishness of the people behind the trials was overwhelming. Except that I couldn't throw up, couldn't cry, couldn't scream. I hated this job, hated this scrap of a life I had been saddled with against my will, hated how terrible humans were to each other.

Sylvia stood behind me until my body had settled, then helped me off my knees and followed me back to the barracks. "I want to be alone," I called back. Before I walked through the door, she grabbed my arm and pushed me around the side of the building. "What's your problem?" I asked, pulling my arm free.

"My problem?" She stepped close and lowered her voice to a whisper-yell. "Care to explain why Jake wasn't surprised to see you?"

"He's already seen me once, remember? Anyway, he works for SHAP. He's used to weird and unexpected."

She shook her head. "Nuh-uh, don't buy that for one second. You had that silent communication thing going on. You used to do that shit when you were younger, and it was creepy."

"We know each other—"

"Stop lying to me, Poppy! How many times have you seen him?"

I tried to back up, but the stone wall was against my back. "I don't know. A few."

"A few? Try again."

"No."

"I'll tell our dads—"

"I've been watching him and Eliza since we died, okay?" I was done pretending I was fine. It was as if everything that had been holding me together was now pulling me apart at the seams and if I didn't get it off my chest, I'd burst into a million pieces. "Every few weeks, I check on them. When Jake figured out he could see me, he asked for help on the case."

She took a step back as if I'd slapped her. "For twelve years? You've been watching them for *twelve years*?" She looked around, as if there were answers hidden just out of sight. "Jesus Christ, Poppy, no wonder you can't let go."

I turned to the side, not looking at her, but out to the gray expanse of the horizon. "I know. I'm supposed to only care about other reapers."

"Because space and time are supposed to help you move on. Do you think I haven't thought about my friends? My ex-boyfriend? That I don't miss them? Of course I do. I wish I had found a partner who wanted to do this with me, like Daniel." Our older brother's wife had jumped at the chance to join him in a forever adventure.

"Max didn't want to be a reaper?" I asked, shocked. She hadn't talked about him since we died. All I remembered was Daddy saying he thought Max was going to propose, then Sylvia coming home in tears the next day. I never saw Max again.

"When he proposed, I said yes, and I was so happy." She looked out over the water with her arms wrapped around her middle. "But when I told him what marrying me would mean—the opportunity to join the family business might come at any time—he decided it was too hard, too unknown. He would rather live on his terms. So I walked away."

If Jake had known and then decided he couldn't be a reaper, would I have walked away? Would I have been strong enough? *For what it's worth, I would've come with you.* No, he wouldn't have gone back on his word. Hell, his job was literally tearing him apart and he still refused to back down. Poor boundaries aside, Jake was loyal to a fault, and he loved with his whole heart.

My sister hadn't known unconditional love like I had with Jake, and my heart broke for her. "I'm so sorry," I breathed. "Didn't it make you mad? That this reaper crap got in the way of true love?"

She shook her head, then looked back to me. "No, Max made me mad. He wanted to exchange vows saying we'd love each other through anything, but he didn't even want to try. I'm proud to be here, Poppy. Proud of our family, proud of being a reaper."

She walked over and leaned against the stone, our shoulders touching. "When you look out at that water, how does it make you feel?"

I laughed once without humor. "Cold. Lonely. Trapped."

She wrapped her arm around mine. "I feel peace. Pride. Out of all the creatures, all the people that have ever existed, our family is the one that's accepted the task of helping souls cross over safely. We have to give up a few years of human life and—I'll admit, some things that made life fun—but in exchange, we get so much more in return."

She squeezed my arm. "Do you feel any of it? Any pride in what you do?"

It's a good thing I couldn't cry, because I would've started and never stopped. Her words opened a chasm inside of me. I wished I could feel the same way, that feeling of doing what I was born to do, like I belonged. "I don't know," I admitted. "Sometimes, I guess?"

"How long have you felt like this?"

"Twelve years," I whispered. "If you had the choice, to go back and live a regular human life with Max or have the timeline play out exactly as it did, what would you choose?"

She paused for a long moment. "I'm exactly where I'm supposed to be, where I need to be. I wouldn't change it."

I nodded and smiled at her. "I'm glad." It wasn't a lie. I was so happy that my sister was content. It was all I ever wanted for her.

"What about you?"

"I love being here with you and the family," I hedged.

"But?"

"I would change everything," I admitted, pressing my fist against my chest to keep the words from cracking me open. "There's this huge piece of me missing, this emptiness that's only filled when I'm in the human world. I want to watch the sunrise, play the violin to the stars, swim in the ocean, smell the damp earth as I walk through a forest when it's just rained."

She looked at me as if I had just broken her heart. "I knew you'd watched *The Little Mermaid* too much as a kid," she teased, but her voice cracked at the end and betrayed her feelings.

I play-hit her arm. "It's not the same."

"Because Jake is smarter than Prince Eric?"

"Truth." I sighed. "But this doesn't have only to do with Jake. I mean, he's part of it but...I don't want to be in the human world only for him. I want to be there because it makes me happy and he makes me happy, too." I lifted a shoulder. "But, even if I could ever go back, so many humans are so full of hate, and I think learning that hurts the most."

She leaned her head on my shoulder. "I'm sorry, Poppy."

"I don't know how to do this," I whispered. "Every day having to take the souls of people who died from someone else's selfishness, worrying about if Jake or Eliza or their family will appear next on my list. There's no break, no end in sight. How am I supposed to survive it when I'm already dead?"

She squeezed my arm tighter. "You don't have to do it alone. You have me."

"Thanks." I rested my head against hers for a moment, then straightened. I blew out a sharp breath. "It would've helped if Jake hadn't grown up hot."

Sylvia snorted. "He did get better with age. Rude." She sighed. "Have you thought about maybe dating any of the super distant cousins? Technically, we're not blood related to all of these people. Some were adopted, some are stepfamily, some are like three hundred years old..."

I lifted my head and looked up at her. "Strangely enough, I haven't felt the urge to date any family I'm legally related to while trapped forever on a death island. Imagine the breakup."

"That's fair." She squeezed my arm again. "Maybe it's time to submit a reassignment application? I don't want to lose you as my partner, but you're burned out. I think taking a decade or so off from reaper duty would help you. You won't be tempted to go visit, and even if you were, you couldn't."

I knew she was right. I should apply for reassignment to island duty at city hall or something. The thought nearly broke me.

"What's with the girl talk?" Sylvia and I looked up to find Daniel standing a few feet away. "You coming to family dinner?"

While we couldn't eat, we all had arranged our scheduled so once a month, all of our immediate family spent three hours together talking about our weeks. While usually a highlight in this monotonous existence, I would've given anything to just be alone with my thoughts tonight.

"Just a sister chat," Sylvia said. "Of course we'll be at dinner. It's your birthday, loser."

"Wouldn't miss it," I promised.

Chapter Seventeen

Jake

DESPITE SITTING IN a back corner booth at Café Eleonora, I could feel eyes on us. I knew Mina jumping ship was still a source of constant gossip, and Paris replacing her meant people were wondering what would happen next. Didn't help that Paris and I sat on the same side of the booth—neither of us comfortable with our backs to the front door—as we nursed our drinks. I picked the bite-sized brownie off the top of my whipped cream and popped it in my mouth, a perfect treat after the sandwich I'd just inhaled.

Unlike Mina, Paris didn't sneer at or judge my sugar addiction, just toyed with the wooden stick she used to mix honey into her tea. It was bittersweet. I missed working with my best friend, but I was glad Paris kept to herself. My head was a mess right now.

A wave of guilt washed over me at treating Paris like a stranger. I grabbed the second brownie bite and offered it to her as a silent peace offering. She looked up at me, then down at my hand and shook her head. "Probably for the best," I admitted, popping it in my mouth. After I'd swallowed, I added, "Sugar is going to be my downfall."

I paused, my cup halfway to my mouth, then checked my watch. "Have you eaten today? It's nearly two."

"I'm fine. I had an apple." Her stomach betrayed her by grumbling. She sighed and looked up at the ceiling, as if asking for patience. "I forgot to bring my lunch. I'll eat when I get home."

"What do you want? I'll buy you lunch."

"I'm fine, thank you."

"Paris—"

"I have food allergies and intolerances. A lot of them. I prefer to make my own meals."

I angled to face her. "Why didn't you tell me? We don't have to stay here."

She touched my forearm. "I'm fine. Let's talk and finish our drinks, then we'll go."

"Okay." I shifted in the booth, looking down at my cup as if it had answers. "When I was eighteen, my girlfriend Poppy and her entire immediate family disappeared. My dad and stepmom told us they had moved without a forwarding address, but I heard them talking about it a few nights later when I couldn't sleep. Magnolia had said that what happened to them was a tragedy and my dad replied, '*if only we could've done something to prevent it.*'"

I tapped on the table. "I'd known in my gut Poppy hadn't *just* moved and I wanted answers. When I confronted my folks, they both denied knowing anything more. So, I joined SHAP the next week despite my dad's reservations. My mom and her parents had started at my age, too. I figured maybe with SHAP's resources at my fingertips, I'd discover what really happened." I picked at the edge of my paper cup. "And maybe I could keep whatever happened to her and her family from happening to someone else."

Paris stared out the front window, looking like she wasn't paying attention, but I knew it meant she was listening extra hard. "And did you figure out what happened to her?"

I nodded. "On Sunday I learned she's a grim reaper."

Paris didn't react immediately, instead sitting with the information for a long moment. If Eliza were here, she'd complain that Paris wasn't interested, that she was just listening to be polite and not engage. This is where my sister and I disagreed. Uninterested Paris would change the subject. Quiet Paris was what made her a great SHAP agent.

Like me, she'd started in the research and technology department, then worked her way up to active fieldwork. She was a natural, despite this being only her first active agent job. I wasn't sure if I could've handled the body count of this case while being a newbie.

She glanced over at me and nodded, whatever expression on my face confirming her suspicions. "Why can you see her, and I can't?"

I hesitated with answering this time, taking a long sip of chocolate-peppermint coffee. There was something very comforting about the taste, and everything was better with caffeine. Especially since I wasn't sleeping.

"She said she's checked up on me before, but recently was the first time I'd seen her. She says I'm not on her list of souls to collect. Maybe we can only see each other because of"—I took another sip and cleared the emotion from my throat—"the nature of our relationship."

"Soul mates?"

I leaned back in the booth. "I don't know, it sounds ridiculous. I'm not even sure I believe in the concept of soul mates."

"You live with a ghost."

I laughed, more breath than sound. "Somehow that's easier to believe than I can only see Poppy because we're soul mates." I crossed my arms over my chest. "I knew she was my person the moment we met. Nothing has changed about that in twelve years. So why can I only see her now?"

Paris studied me for a moment, her shrewd gaze too knowing to be comfortable. "If we remove the soul mate equation, then why can you see her?"

I ran a hand over my face. "Means this is my last mission."

She nodded once, already knowing that I wouldn't walk away. That's what made her a great agent. "We better make it count."

I drained the rest of my coffee. "We're stopping at your house so you can grab some food and some inside info." I stood, using my cane and the table to help push me up, then waited for her to follow.

"Inside info?"

"There's a neighbor of yours who may be able to help put some pieces together, if we're lucky." I gave her a long look.

Realization dawned and she hurried to her feet. "No one can know," she whispered. "They'll throw out the case."

"I'm aware. But we're just going for your lunch, remember?"

PARIS LIVED ON the first floor of Countryside Village Apartments, which housed mostly SHAP agents and ghosts. A former hotel-turned-hospital-turned-apartments, it still had early nineteenth-century charm with modern conveniences (or inconveniences, if one was referring to the perpetually broken elevator). As expected, Reggie was in the lounge area to the right of the foyer, cuddled up with his partner Clint as they played a game of chess.

Reggie's eyes widened and he gestured up, indicating Mina's apartment. I nodded once, pointing toward the door Paris was opening with her key. He whispered to Clint, then disappeared.

Even though the exchange had been silent, I looked around. A shadow moved underneath Doris Manalin's door across the hall. I clenched my jaw. That woman was a nuisance.

Paris held the door open for me and locked it behind her, staring through her peephole. "No doubt Doris will slip a pamphlet preaching about purity culture under my door tomorrow. Might even make an offhand remark about my new gentleman caller." She stepped away from her door and shook her head. "I would move, but I hate moving more than I hate her meddling."

I laughed. "Mina and you should compare notes. She really is after the young women in this building." I cringed. "Speaking of Mina, I haven't told her about Poppy."

Paris dropped her keys into a bowl on a small half table next to the door. "I won't be the one to break the confidence."

"I will tell her," I defended, a sharp sting of guilt shooting across my chest.

Paris nodded and walked to the kitchen. "You don't need to explain your personal decisions to me. As long as they don't threaten my safety." She pulled a bowl from her fridge and grabbed a fork from her utensil drawer. "Can I offer you anything?"

"I'm good."

When the knock came, Paris hurried to the door, opening it to reveal Mina and a nosy Reggie. "Hi, I'm Mina, your upstairs neighbor?"

Technically, Reggie's brother Alan was the apartment right below Mina, but Paris was only one door over.

"Yes, hi! What can I help you with?" Paris returned.

"My toilet was running and I wanted to make sure it wasn't leaking into your place. I don't think you're directly below my bathroom, but I wanted to double check."

I pressed my lips together to keep from laughing. Mina would never come check on a neighbor. She'd send Reggie to do it.

"Thanks for checking," Paris returned. "Come in; we'll take a look."

Mina stepped in and Paris closed the door on Reggie, who just walked through it anyway.

"Nice cover," I said.

Mina smirked at me and shook her head. "I had like two seconds to come up with something." This time, I did laugh. Mina turned to Reggie. "Don't you have a hot man to make out with?"

"And miss whatever's happening here? Not a chance, Mi Minita. Anyway, I don't sleep. I can hang with Clint when all the drama is over."

Mina rolled her eyes and looked at Paris. "Never house a ghost agent. They're an invasive species. This one's not even mine!"

Reggie put a hand on his hip. "Says the woman who—"

"Going to interrupt you before this goes further," I said, looking between them. "Reggie, if you want plausible deniability, leave."

He huffed, then waved, walking through the door.

"Let's check that bathroom," Paris said, motioning for us to follow her to the back of the apartment to her bedroom. She closed the door and turned on a white noise machine on her nightstand. "I don't trust that Doris doesn't have some listening device at my front door right now."

"Maybe it's a good thing the elevator is always broken," Mina said. "Harder to sneak up on me."

I leaned against the wall, looking at Mina. "We're digging, finding a lot of suppliers. Getting them off the streets."

She held up a hand and looked between Paris and me. "You're aware that telling me anything could get this case dismissed?"

I nodded. "We need your help."

"I put everything in the case report." I stared at her for a long moment, our argument silent and short. She sighed and crossed her arms, a sign of her acquiescence.

"You watch a lot of true crime," I explained. "Let's say you had a batch of…special cocaine. And you wanted to do a trial run and see how people reacted."

She narrowed her eyes. "Okay…"

"Would you cut it with fentanyl and why?"

She frowned. "If I wanted to test how people reacted to *'special cocaine,'* why would I cut it with fentanyl? That would defeat the purpose of the test."

Paris and I exchanged a look. Exactly what we had said. "A solid point."

"But," she continued, "the people running these trials? They're low level. Just doing the grunt work. They're probably not the ones messing with the product. Something's happening in distribution or higher."

"It still doesn't make sense. It's like we're playing two different games at two different stadiums with one ball," I grumbled.

Paris looked between us. "Maybe that's it." She pointed at me with her fork. "Whoever is making the drugs isn't the one testing them. Maybe there are two games going on here."

Mina stared at her for a beat. "Okay, fuck the pretense. So you've got oral venom laced with fentanyl. The two most popular uses for oral venom are to make hybrids and as an overall 'health tonic.' What's curious is why they're calling it Vixen."

"It's a sexy, alluring word," Paris explained. "Both a promise and a tease. Great marketing."

"If someone found a way to make a cure-all without turning people into vampires, they'd change the entire world," I said. "They could sell it to the highest bidder."

"Countries would go to war for that kind of technology," Paris added.

Mina nodded and pointed at her. "Yes. Good call. But until someone develops a synthetic, it doesn't matter. Can't risk turning people into vampires."

"And the fentanyl?" I reminded.

"My unprofessional opinion?" Mina asked. I nodded. "Sabotage. Someone on the inside has their own plan."

"I bet whoever is sabotaging the trials is behind the threats to you. By locking up the suppliers, you shook up their plan," Paris suggested.

I winced. I hadn't told Mina about that either. "Mina—"

"Oh, you have three seconds to explain before I call Magnolia and tell her," Mina warned.

"Don't call Magnolia, she'll flip."

"I know. So talk."

I glanced at Paris, who managed to look sheepish and amused at the same time. She shoved another forkful of food in her mouth and pretended to look out the window. Too bad her curtains were still closed.

"I've gotten a few threatening emails warning me off the Vixen search is all," I explained.

Mina blinked at me. "And?"

"What makes you think there's an *and*?"

She raised both eyebrows at me. "Because you're basically my brother. Let's go, Jake." She pulled out her cell, her thumb hovering over the screen.

"Eliza thinks someone was in her house the other day."

Mina twirled her hand in the air, motioning me to continue.

"And there are some demons who tried to kill me."

"There it is." She just shook her head. "And you got

pissy with me for not telling you about Carma, who was just trying to get me naked and not kill me."

Paris pressed the back of her hand to her mouth to cover a smile. She cleared her throat. "They tried to crush my car with a dumpster today."

"You have to put your family in a safe house," Mina warned. "And we need to send ghosts with you. Call my dad. If you don't, I will."

I opened my mouth to argue, but what could I say? That having ghosts around Poppy may be counterproductive because we couldn't be seen publicly together? If she ended up in a report, it could jeopardize too many things.

"We don't know that someone was in Eliza's house. We don't have any proof that they're after them. So far, it's only me," I explained. "Without solid, substantial proof, Jim's hands are tied."

Mina tugged at her fauxhawk and grunted. "Fine. But literally, the first warning."

"Of course. I'm stubborn, not stupid."

Mina shot a look to Paris. "The first warning."

Paris nodded. "You have my word."

Chapter Eighteen

Rule #36: It's important to have fun and reconnect with your reaper family in your off time.

— *The Reaper Code of Ethics, official handbook*

Poppy

FOR BEING DEAD, we were loud. Our dads had built a long picnic table at the back of their cabin, then strung it with twinkle lights, just like we'd had at home. Except the grass here was brown and the sky was perpetually gray and never quite dark enough to make the lights glow. Still, it was the closest to home I felt on this death island.

Despite not having skin or muscles, reapers still aged and my family made it a point to celebrate birthdays. While I couldn't get osteoporosis or arthritis, I allowed my human glamour to age along with me. Every year on our birthday, we got a survey asking if we wanted to update our look. I was one of the few people in my family who always said yes. Granted, I was still the youngest of the brood. Maybe in ten years I'd feel differently.

It didn't matter that I was twenty-eight, I was still the baby girl when I walked in. My dad Joe picked me up and swung me around, then passed me onto my daddy Neil, who kissed the top of my head and tucked the hair that had come loose from my braid behind my ear. My grandparents and great-grandparents waved from a smattering of chairs at the edge of the patio. My siblings and cousins called greetings. Everyone wore their human form to dinner, and if I squinted hard enough, we looked like a normal family.

Since there were no bugs to worry about, Dads had left their back door open and an old record player filled the backyard with Cab Calloway. The table was set with the same empty bottles and dishes that had been dusted off for the last twelve years, and we took our usual seats. I played with my fork, running my fingers over the tines, trying to remember my favorite Sunday meal from back when I could eat. Probably roasted potatoes and carrots. Comfort food, they called it.

Sylvia took the seat next to me, a cautious smile on her face. "We okay?"

I nodded. "We never weren't okay." I straightened my shoulders and set down my fork. "So, long list this week? I swear mine doubled overnight."

She shrugged. "No longer than usual."

"You didn't have that weird glitch thing on your fourth page?"

"Nope." She waved to Daniel and his wife, Caroline, as they took spots across from us. "If you're glitching, make sure to go visit tech."

Caroline nodded. "I had an issue with my manifest last week. They had me in and out like that." She snapped her fingers in emphasis. "Good thing too. Had a bus accident I didn't want to miss."

Daniel laughed. "Oh yeah, it was gruesome, let me tell you. Best birthday present ever."

Caroline looked up at him with hearts in her eyes. "That was a great night." She kissed him.

I looked down at the table. The illusion that we were just some normal family always dissipated before I let my guard down too far. Why did everything have to be about death and dying?

"Oh it was," Caroline said, not picking up my mood.

I cleared my throat and forced myself to look at my brother and smile. "Happy birthday, Daniel!"

Sylvia threw a napkin ring at him. "Yeah, happy birthday, Assface. How's it feel to be forty?"

"You can find out in two years," he teased.

Our cousin Anya and her partner Nel plopped down on my other side. "Hey strangers. What're we talking about?"

"Daniel's advanced age and the bus accident," Sylvia explained.

"Watch it, I'm six months older," she warned, then sat down. "Happy birthday, man. Which accident?"

"The 202," Daniel explained.

Nel whistled. "Heard like seventeen people died. How many reapers were on it?"

Oh god, I couldn't sit and listen to this. With a smile, I excused myself, waving at another brother talking to another cousin, and wandered into the house. I couldn't smell anything, but if I closed my eyes, I could almost make out my dad's citrus aftershave and the scent of sun-warmed leather couches. I could almost hear daddy singing along to the radio while he cleaned the kitchen, and the tags jingling on our dog CJ's collar.

The cabin was smaller than our old house, since we all had our own places to live now. But the media center still sat across from the old leather couches, and the shelves were cluttered with dust-free photos of our before lives. I picked up CJ's collar, clicking the tags together.

The sound hurt to hear tonight, a wordless wish that things could be different. I knew that I needed to stop thinking about what life could be and just observe what my unlife was. I could never go back. I put the collar down and slumped into the couch. Before Jake could see me, I had managed to get by, to shove everything unpleasant down and just exist.

Now, this existence was unbearable. I was at once suffocating and spinning out of control. I wanted to jump into the river and just keep swimming until I never had to climb into another boat or help another soul.

"What's on your mind, Poppy?" Daddy asked, sitting down next to me.

I shrugged. "Do you ever wonder what life would be like now if we weren't reapers?"

He put his arm around me, something he hadn't done since the last time I was questioning everything, about six years ago. I stilled for a moment, resting my head on his shoulder. "Does this have anything to do with you seeing Jake again?" I stiffened. "Sylvia told me about your run-in the other day."

I pressed my lips together, hoping he couldn't read on my face that it wasn't the first time. "Yes, I think so."

"Must have been quite a shock to see him again after so

long."

I nodded. "Definitely."

He was silent for a long moment. "The night we got the call, your father and I had the biggest fight of our marriage."

"Really?"

He nodded against the top of my head. "Really. I didn't think it was right to force a sixteen-year-old to give up a life she barely got to live. I offered to stay behind with you for a few more years. Let you graduate high school, have another few summers with your friends. I wanted you to live a little before you had to die."

I straightened up and searched his face. "What happened?"

"Joe appealed to the board, but ultimately their decision was final."

"Oh."

He squeezed. "I wish I'd fought harder, but I'm not sure it would've done any good. Death isn't something we can plan for, no matter how hard we try."

"I know."

"You okay?"

I shrugged. "Yeah. Just my annual unlife crisis."

He chuckled then sobered. "I know Jake was more than just a friend."

"I...how?"

He raised his eyebrows. "Because I'm your father and I have eyes. The way you two looked at each other didn't fool anyone. And I also found your journal."

I gasped. "You read my journal?!"

"Well maybe if you had a more creative hiding place

than under your pillow, I wouldn't have found it. Who do you think changed your sheets, hmm? The sheet fairy?"

I crossed my arms. "That was private."

He shook his head. "I knew you thought he hung the moon and stars even before you confirmed it yourself. You had heart eyes whenever you looked at him."

My mouth hung open.

He reached out and lifted my chin. "Stop being so offended. You wear your heart on your sleeve. It's why you're my favorite. But it's also probably why this life is harder on you than anyone else."

I smiled and put my head back on his shoulder. "Liar. You're not supposed to have favorites."

"Says who?"

I made a hand motion. "Them."

"Who's them?"

"I dunno. The people who say these things about parenting."

He laughed a deep belly laugh. "Yeah, but grim reapers are a different breed."

"Truth."

We sat in silence for a long moment. "You okay now?"

I forced a smile. "Yeah. Thanks."

He stood and nodded. "Better go check on your brothers. If things go according to schedule, we're due for another birthday brawl."

"I miss when birthdays were cake and ice cream instead of brawls."

"Me too, kiddo." He leaned down and kissed the top of my head. We both winced at the sound of a dish shattering.

"Not the Wedgewood!" he called. "They're a nightmare to replace."

Shouts filtered in from the backyard and Daddy pulled off his robe and tossed it on the couch, his black slacks and oxford shirt easier to fight in than a cloak. Less to grab on to and pull. He took off running and my gaze rested on the inner pocket of that cloak, where he kept his manifest.

I scooted closer and wiggled his list out of his pocket just enough to see the names. I scrolled the first page, then the second. A quick look around confirmed no one had noticed me in the chaos. Third page, fourth, and finally, the fifth.

I released a long breath. Jake wasn't on his list. I looked up to find the fight had turned from an actual brawl to a show. My brothers were performing with exaggerated movements and a lot of bouncing.

Cloaks were piled on the ground. Would be a shame if someone stepped on them. Better go and pick them up. Sort them into a pile.

I scooted back outside, hanging the cloaks on the back of the chairs. Dad glanced at me and smiled but turned back to watch the show. I was just doing my usual task, after all. Being helpful.

While all our family on Dad's side were reapers, we weren't all *travelers*—the reapers who carried the souls to the afterlife. Dad, like his mother and the past four generations before them, was part of the grim reaper Counsel and wore a deep burgundy cloak. They were the ones who wrote the rule book, who listened to cases when reapers were charged with breaking the rules, who kept our world in order. Daniel was slated to be the next member of the family to join the

Counsel, but I knew Dad thought I'd be really good at it, too. Honestly, the thought of spending my days in a small room deciding how to run an entire community did not appeal.

My aunt and uncle worked in city services and had burnt-orange cloaks. They made sure the residential areas were maintained, the common areas were in good repair, and adjusted landscaping or architecture as required.

My oldest brother, Craig, had a deep-blue cloak, indicating that he maintained and monitored the boats and piers for soul distribution. While we were here because of some sort of physics I didn't quite understand, our little afterlife didn't magically fix itself. After my first required decade as a reaper, I had attempted to move into another area, something with less death and gore. Something that would help me with my obsession of checking on Jake. I didn't pass the test to get into the technology sector—I was computer smart but not Dead-Geek-Squad level—and city services didn't appeal.

I had considered applying for a front desk job, where I directed souls through the gates, but that would mean never leaving this gray monotony. So I leaned into the big perk of being a traveler, which was getting to spend a little time in the human world. This had made my attachment to being human and to Jake much worse.

And now here I was, illegally pilfering manifests from people I loved and trusted for a human man. Maybe I had watched *The Little Mermaid* too much as a kid. I didn't even feel guilty about what I was doing. I wasn't given a choice, like Daddy was, like Caroline was, like Nel was. I was just forced into this life and I wasn't going to let it take away another thing I loved.

I took my time hanging the purple capes, slipping out the lists and tucking them into my pocket. Then, I moved back into the house and scurried to my dads' bedroom, where I liked to hide when dinners were too noisy. Scrolling two manifests at a time, I scanned. Nothing, nothing, nothing.

I was halfway through Sylvia's list when I heard someone walking around the house. I shoved everything back into my pocket and pretended to be resting at the foot of the bed. The footsteps retreated.

That was too close. Sylvia would tell me if Jake was on her manifest, right? Especially because we were partners. We had nearly identical lists, but sometimes she had a few extra souls that she could handle alone. I stood and shook out my hands. I was going to have to figure it out another way.

I scooted out of the room and back outside, where I slipped around the table, making sure to drop the correct list into the corresponding cape. Sylvia's had hand-drawn flames on the case (she was an amazing artist), while Caroline's was brand new, and Daniel's was dinged around the edges. Nel's had a large rainbow sticker.

"Why are you creeping around?" Sylvia asked.

I jumped. "Just lost in thought."

"You're walking around, feeling up cloaks, because you're lost in thought?"

I nodded. "It's been a weird day."

"Yes, it has." She grabbed her cloak and slipped it on.

I pointed over my shoulder. "I'm going to head out. I'll see you in a few hours."

"Wait," Sylvia called. She padded her robe until she found what she was looking for. She pulled out her manifest, then looked from it to me. "Why was this in the wrong pocket?"

Shit. I almost slapped my face with my palm, but thankfully refrained. "Oh, it fell out when I moved the cloak. I just tucked it back in."

She narrowed her eyes. "Hmm."

"Night, everyone!" I said with a wave, and hurried away from the backyard, a chorus of good-byes following me. I should feel guilt for betraying my family's trust, or maybe even fear over Sylvia's suspicion, but I didn't. I needed to think about how to access the reaper's main death manifest instead.

Chapter Nineteen

Jake

I KNOCKED ON Eliza's door before using my key and stepping inside. "Hello?"

"Kitchen!" My sister called.

I walked through the dining room to find her kneading bread dough. *Oh no.* While Eliza loved cooking, she only baked when she was stressed. Bread meant she was really struggling.

"What's going on?" I asked, taking a seat at the table and balancing the handle of my cane on the top.

She glanced over at Daisy's door, blew hair out of her face, and leaned toward me. "Daisy got in trouble at school twice this week. Once for 'telling lies' that she's a witch, and a second time for shoving an older kid who said she was a bastard because she didn't have a dad."

"Good for her for standing up for herself."

"She broke the kid's shoulder." Eliza shook her head. "She must have used some kind of magic. It's like it's manifesting when she's angry and she can't control it." She stopped kneading and looked over at me. "I think we're going to have to apply for someone to help in the interim while you finish your case."

I swallowed hard, trying to shove down the anger and frustration. It was supposed to be me. Lucinda was supposed to plead guilty; I was supposed to move on and help Daisy. "I'll help you find someone, okay?"

"You're so busy."

"Not too busy to help you through this." I reached over and squeezed her forearm. "You're not alone, okay?"

She sucked in a deep, watery breath. "I just don't know what I'm doing wrong. I'm trying so hard." She picked the bread up and smacked the dough on the floured counter.

"You're not doing anything wrong. Your high-spirited daughter has big feelings and magic isn't helping. We'll figure it out, yeah?"

She wiped her eye with her shoulder and nodded. "Yeah."

I stood and walked over to her, squeezing her shoulders. "How about I take her out for ice cream and give you some alone time?"

"That would be amazing, thank you."

I walked over to Daisy's bedroom. "Does my favorite niece want ice cream?" I asked loudly, knocking on the door. No answer. "Munchkin, can I come in?"

I shot a look to Eliza who narrowed her eyes on the door. "Daisy, can you come out here please?"

One second. Two. Three. Five. Ten. Silence.

I turned the knob, meeting the resistance of a lock. I reached for the top of the doorframe where Eliza kept an emergency key. "Daisy, I'm unlocking the door and coming in," I warned. I turned the handle and pushed open the door.

My heart plummeted through the earth. The room was empty. The window on the side of the house was open, her floral curtain billowing in the breeze. Eliza pushed past me, opening Daisy's closet and checking under the bed to make sure she wasn't hiding.

I yanked my phone out of my jeans, dialing SHAP. "Agent Robinson. I need to report a missing child. Potential kidnapping. Daisy Robinson."

SHAP DIDN'T WASTE time launching a search, especially on an agent's child with powers. Mina's dad and Territory Director, Jim Summers, arrived first, Paris second. Magnolia and my dad definitely broke speed limits to get here from work, and Mina and Carma—no doubt notified by Jim—followed.

"Can't be here," Jim ordered when Mina walked in.

"Dad, I can't not be here!" she defended.

He shook his head and walked over to his daughter, putting his hands on her shoulders. "If this has to do with the case, and it's documented that you're here—"

"Yeah, okay. I get it. It's fucking stupid, but I get it." Mina looked at me, her eyes shiny. "Call me the moment you know something, yeah?"

I tapped my chest. "Promise."

"I'll have Sebastian activate the ghost search."

Eliza ran over to Mina and hugged her, then Carma. Mina held the sides of Eliza's face. "We're going to find her.

Try not to kill Paris before you do."

Eliza laughed through a sob and nodded. "I'll try."

Despite their mutual dislike, Jim and Magnolia were looking over a paper map spread out on the kitchen table, dividing up the town into sections, while Dad made calls to alert the search party leads of their coordinates. "We only have two hours until dark. Let's get feet on the ground," Dad ordered. "Check in at this number or with Jim."

I moved back to Daisy's bedroom, where Paris was dusting the window frame inside and out to look for magical residue that didn't belong. She was leaning through the window, pulling samples off the frame. She looked over her shoulder at me when I walked in, then eased herself back and put the swab sample into her handheld machine.

"Your niece has very strong magic," she told me. "It's hard to decipher all of it, although it seems to have similar structure."

I leaned against the door frame. "Yeah, makes sense. It's like it's growing faster than she is."

"That's why you're going to help her." It wasn't a question. Paris knew it was important to me. The machine beeped with a result and her brow pinched. She looked back at the window, then around the room, before looking back at the machine. "This room is chaos," she grumbled. "Gotta take a new sample."

Eliza, who had just approached the doorway, crossed her arms. "Yes, please worry about how messy my daughter's room is instead of doing your damn job."

I flinched. "Eliza, that's not what she meant—"

Eliza put up her hand. "I don't want to hear it." She

glared at Paris. "Finish and leave me alone." She stomped away.

Paris's cheeks burned bright red, her eyes fixated on the machine. "I didn't mean…it's just…"

"I know," I promised. "She's just struggling right now, and her daughter is missing. It has nothing to do with you."

Paris smiled ruefully. "Neither of us believe that." She straightened her shoulders and turned back to the window, pulling another swab from her crossbody bag.

I left the room to find Eliza scrubbing a pan that had probably been clean an hour ago. "She just pisses me off so much," she said, obviously complaining about Paris. "She thinks she's better than everyone and on top of that, she's judging my housekeeping skills? Let's see her keep a perfectly clean house with a full-time job and a kid who can throw temper tantrums while hovering three feet in the air." The pan slipped out of her hands and into the sink.

Eliza leaned against the counter and started sobbing. I turned off the water, handed her a towel, then wrapped my arms around her shoulders. "Nothing's going to happen to Daisy," I promised, even though I had no business doing so.

"What if Poppy was here for her?" she whispered. "What if my last words to my daughter were '*go to your room*'? She was so upset and scared and I just—"

"*Shhh, shhh.* No way Poppy would let something happen to Daisy and not warn us." I looked around the room to double check, but didn't see any purple. "You'll have plenty of time to give her stories to tell in therapy."

As Eliza cried, her shoulders shaking with gut-wrenching sobs, everything that had been threatening to tear me apart during this investigation—the lack of sleep, the constant pain, the bittersweet heartbreak at seeing Poppy again, the fact that I put my niece in danger just by doing my job, the heartache that Eliza kept getting beaten down by life— clawed at my chest, making my own breath ragged. Unlike Eliza, I didn't want to cry. I wanted to break shit.

As if she could sense it, Magnolia touched my shoulder. I shifted Eliza to her arms and took a deep breath, trying to compose myself. It did nothing to abate the fire in my chest.

"Robinson, your computer here?" Jim asked.

"No, it's at home," I managed through a tight jaw.

"Go get it and come back. Paris will run the scene until then." He looked over at me and then moved his gaze to the front door. It must have been obvious I was about to lose it. "Do you want backup?"

I shook my head. "Nope."

Chapter Twenty

Rule #3: Under no circumstances is a reaper to make purposeful physical contact with a human who is not their charge.

– The Reaper Code of Ethics, official handbook

Poppy

I KNEW I needed to stay away from Jake, but something ached in my chest. The wish to see him grew into an urge, then a demand. So when break time came, I lied to my sister, and told her I was going to watch another wedding. She promptly made barfing noises and left me alone.

I went to find Jake.

I stilled in shock when I walked into his apartment, the perfectly clean and organized space now chaos. Chairs were turned over, pillows thrown across the room, half the bookcase's contents littered the floor. I let out an involuntary gasp as a baking sheet sailed across the kitchen and hit the wall.

"JAKE!" I called, rushing over to him.

He turned to face me, his eyes wide, then he pointed at me. "Don't you dare take Daisy. You can have me, but you can't have her."

I held up my hands. "I'm not here for either of you. What's going on? What happened to Daisy?"

"She's gone." He shoved his fingers into his hair, tugging at the scalp. I could see his heart breaking as a tear leaked out of the corner of his eye. "Just gone. And it's my fault."

He shoved a drinking glass off the counter, not caring about the shards of glass that exploded across the tile. "They took her and it's my fault."

"We're going to find her!" I promised, even though I shouldn't. There was no way I could help conduct a search for a human child in the hour I had free. But there was no way I could leave him either. I had to do this for him and Eliza.

"How much more does Eliza have to lose?" He shouted. "She lost you, then Ben, and now her daughter?! HOW MUCH MORE, POPPY?"

His words hit me in the gut. He was right. While he may be able to see me, Eliza couldn't. I held the grief over the loss of our friendship every day.

"Jake!" My voice cracked at the pain in his eyes. This man had taken a vow to protect people and he wasn't able to protect his own family. It was tearing him apart. My own heart broke watching him.

He was breathing heavy, his hands shaking, his gaze wildly searching for something else to destroy. He shoved a water bottle across the counter and took a stepped forward. His cane hit a chunk of glass and slipped, throwing him off balance. His leg buckled and I caught him as he went down.

"I've got you," I promised.

I helped him limp to the couch and he sank down on the

edge, a broken gasp of pain and grief escaping from his chest. I knelt in front of him, grabbing both sides of his cheeks and tilted his head up to look at me. His blue eyes had storms behind them, glistening with unshed emotions.

I needed to pull him back, to ground him. "Kiss me."

He blinked, confused. "What?"

"Kiss. Me."

He focused on my mouth and his hands dug into my hair. Then his lips crashed into mine. This wasn't the soft, gentle coaxing of an overly cautious teenager. This was heartbreaking desperation.

My entire body electrified. Every inch of skin warmed, as if I were human and standing under the sun on a warm summer day. I felt *alive*. My eyes flew open at the sensation, only to find him watching me.

He pulled back, lips parted, eyes searching mine. The air between us was thick like summer afternoon storm clouds. "Poppy…" My name was both an exultation and a plea.

I brought my lips back to his, and he inhaled sharply through his nose and closed his eyes. The moment I lowered my lids, I was drowning. I wasn't calming the storm, he was dragging me in. Oh god, I didn't know if I was going to survive this.

Good thing I was already dead.

He pulled me against him, my knees going to either side of his legs. We were mouth to mouth, chest to chest. One of his hands cradled the back of my head, keeping me in place. The other arm was wrapped around my waist, his fingers pressing into my side. I had desperately missed being held like this, like I was the only thing in the universe that mattered to someone else.

Good god, this kiss was going to destroy me, ruin me for the rest of eternity. There was nothing in the reaper world that felt as good as Jake's mouth on mine. It was ice cream on hot summer days by the pool, it was snuggling under a blanket together in front of a fire pit on a cool fall evening, it was every secret glance and shared smile and brush of hands. It was the exact reason I knew I shouldn't have kissed him.

Maybe we could just stay like this forever, ignore the rest of the universe. Let nothing penetrate this bubble around us. I wouldn't have to ferry any more souls and he…he needed to go save his niece.

Our kisses softened and small fissures in my heart deepened into canyons as our time ran out. As open mouths turned into lip touches, turned into forehead presses.

"Thank you," he whispered.

I bumped his nose with mine. "We are really good at that."

He smiled. "Yeah. We are." His arms moved until they were around my waist. He kissed the tip of my nose. "Who knew kissing could stop a panic attack?"

"It's like we figured it out before or something."

He released a breathy laugh, then leaned back but kept his arms around me. "God, I've missed kissing you."

"That feeling is definitely mutual."

He reached up and pushed a piece of hair behind my ear and took a deep breath. "I wish…"

He didn't need to complete the thought. I wished, too. I grabbed his hand at my face and kissed his palm, before easing back and breaking his hold. I stood and smoothed down my robe, the small space between us feeling infinite and cold.

The sun on my skin had disappeared and left me in a hailstorm. My heart was very firmly still *not* beating in my chest and no matter how much I wished for it otherwise, that meant kissing him again would be an even worse idea. I took a cleansing breath. "I'm going to clean up the glass in the kitchen. You check in or do whatever you need to do."

"Poppy—"

I raised my hands to stop him. "I can't talk about it because I don't get to keep you. I only get our memories."

He nodded and swallowed hard. "Okay." His cell rang, piercing the awkwardness of the moment. He immediately answered. "Robinson."

He stood, grabbing his cane and pulling his keys from his jeans. "Where?" He paused. "Be there in ten." He hung up and turned to me. "They found her."

Chapter Twenty-One

Jake

I DIDN'T KNOW it was possible for a human to go through so many emotions over the course of three hours and not have their heart explode. I gripped Poppy's hand tight as I navigated my car toward Countryside Village Apartments. Apparently, Belphegor had spotted Daisy trying to buy ice cream with Monopoly money. Recognizing Daisy from her visits to Mina's, he managed to get her ice cream—I didn't want to know how—and carried her back to the apartments.

"She's okay," Poppy reassured me, kissing my knuckles.

My chest warmed at the feel of her lips. "I know. But she might not have been. What if the people threatening me had found her?"

She squeezed my hand back. "They didn't and she's safe. Is there someplace else she can stay while you finish the case?"

I gripped the wheel harder with my left hand. "They're not going to like it."

"Better to be annoyed than in danger."

"Yeah." I released Poppy's hand to turn into the apartments. I didn't bother with a parking spot but pulled parallel to the sidewalk.

I pushed out of my car and rushed inside, Poppy matching me step for step. With the elevator still broken, I started negotiating the stairs with a grunt. The slip this afternoon had cost me, and my leg was throbbing.

"I got you," Poppy said, lifting me into her arms. "Remember? I have magical dead person strength."

I wrapped an arm over her shoulder as she took the stairs two at a time. "If Doris Manalin is spying on me, she's going to see me floating."

"I don't know who Doris is, but yes. It will look awesome."

Belphegor was waiting at the top of the stairs wearing a new orange and brown sweater, pacing outside of Mina's apartment. He was hard to look at, somehow blurred around the edges. "Amber wanted to bring some cookies and…"

"The elevator is still broken," we said together. "The landlord really doesn't give a shit about disabled people," I grumbled as Poppy set me down. It was one of the big reasons I didn't live here.

"Are we gonna talk about the creeper in purple?" Belphegor asked, his raccoon-tail-eyebrows raised.

"Poppy, Belphegor, Belphegor, Poppy. She's a friend."

"A reaper is your friend?" He grunted. "Don't want to hear any bitching about me being the scary one when you hang out with a reaper broad." He turned to Poppy. "No offense."

"It's cool, I am creepy." She turned to face him. "Speaking of creepy, can you tell me why your friends are snacking on live souls? I haven't had to fight a demon in years and now you're all up in my business."

He held up his hands in surrender. "Don't blame me for their bullshit. I haven't tasted a human in a decade." He smoothed his talons down his sweater. "These sweaters feel better than people taste."

Poppy made a face, but then bobbed her head. "It's a great sweater. But can you tell your buddies to lay off before I have to chop any more in half? It's a whole thing."

He guffawed. "You're the broad who cut up Amon?" His long tail thumped against the floor, as if in joy. "Good. He deserved it." He turned to me. "I warned Mina to get this hybrid shit under control, or the demons would come."

"I've got it under control," I argued.

"Apparently not as under control as you think."

I bit back a retort and took a deep breath. "Thanks, for Daisy."

He nodded.

I brushed past Belphegor and opened Mina's door to find barely controlled chaos. Jim and Dad were on the phone while Magnolia and Eliza snuggled an ice-cream-stained Daisy on the couch. Amber sat in the armchair with cookies on her lap, leaning over to talk to Daisy. Carma was fiddling with the coffee machine in the kitchen and Mina was talking to Paris on the other side of the room.

"Daisy," I breathed, the sound making the room still. She looked up at me with big blue eyes that matched Eliza's. She slid out of her mom and grandma's arms and ran over to me. Despite the pain, I crouched down and picked her up and her arms went around my neck.

"I'm sorry, Uncle Jake," she said, her voice shaking.

"As long as you're okay, Munchkin. Just don't do that again, okay? You can call me, and I'll come get you. Or call Aunt Mina or grandma or grandpa, yeah?"

"Promise." She sniffed. "I didn't want you to be mad at me."

I pulled back to look at her. "I would never be mad at you about your powers, you got that? And as soon as I'm done with this one last job, I'm going to help you figure everything out, okay?"

She nodded.

"Would it be okay if I have someone else come help you for a little bit until I'm done?"

She hesitated. "I don't know."

"Could you try for me?"

She studied my face carefully, then nodded. "Okay."

"That's my girl." I kissed her head and set her down. She ran back to the couch and jumped onto her mom's lap.

"Pardon me, Jake," Sebastian said. "I didn't realize you'd be bringing your Poppy."

My Poppy. Yes, she was. The memory of her lips against mine made my chest warm as I looked back at her. "Yeah."

"Is there a reason she's present? Not that I'm not thrilled to see her."

I turned to face him. "Because she was with me when I got the call, and she cares about Eliza and Daisy."

"And you still say I shouldn't be concerned that you're getting threatening emails and spending time with a reaper?"

I narrowed my eyes. He said it loud enough for a nearby Mina to hear. Mina, never one to let anything go, turned to me. "Do you care to explain what I just heard?"

"Nope," I said. "No, I do not."

She turned to Paris. "Talk."

"I...think it's best if you two talk in private," Paris said. "I can't break my word to Jake."

"Hey, Jake, can you come check out the ceiling fan in my room?" Mina said, loud enough for everyone to hear. "It's doing that thing again."

I motioned for her to lead the way, then followed her into her bedroom. "How long until it takes them to figure out you don't have a ceiling fan?" I asked, closing the door behind her.

"About two minutes, so start talking."

"I don't know where to start."

"The reaper is a good place."

"It's Poppy."

Mina rubbed the heel of her hand over her breastbone. "Holy shit."

"Yeah." When Mina and I became partners, I told her about Poppy. She even helped me look for clues as to what happened, but we had gotten nowhere.

"She's a reaper?"

"Explains a lot, doesn't it?"

She shook her head in disbelief. "It's why we couldn't find anything on her. Why every trace of her was gone. God, Jake, are you okay?"

"Fine."

"Bullshit."

I looked at my friend who was for all intents and purposes my older sister. "No. I don't know."

"Jake, seeing a reaper isn't good, childhood love or not."

163

"I know. But she swears I'm not on her list or whatever."
Mina tilted her head. "For now."

"For now." I studied my feet. "She kissed me today. Well, I kissed her. We kissed each other and…"

"And?"

"Just…fuck."

"Ah." She walked over and gave me an awkward hug. "What can I do?"

"You're voluntarily hugging me? It's that bad, huh?"

She pinched the skin on my inner upper arm before stepping away. "Yeah, well, Carma's made me soft." As she said it, her entire face lit up. Carma was the best thing that had happened to her, even if Mina's life had been turned inside out while they were falling in love.

"Okay, now about the threats."

"They're only against me. SHAP won't put my family in a safe house until there's a direct threat." I rubbed the back of my neck. "But Eliza needs help until we can get Daisy's powers under control and Daisy is just as overwhelmed."

She looked at me as if I were missing the most obvious thing in the world. "Have Eliza and Daisy go stay with your dad and Magnolia. You know Daisy wouldn't cross the line at her grandparents and Eliza will have help."

"And I can add cameras to their security system."

"No, I can. You have enough to deal with. Finish your case. Watch your back."

I nodded. "Thanks." I put my hand on the doorknob as I turned to leave, then hesitated. "You didn't give me shit about Poppy."

"Your first love is a grim reaper. This doesn't have a happy ending, bro. And I don't know how to make it any better."

Another nod. "Yeah." I opened the door and walked back into the living room to find only my family, Jim, and Carma. Amber, Belphegor, the ghosts, and Poppy were gone.

I didn't have to wonder where they went for long. A violin version of "My Heart Will Go On" rose up from the apartment below. I looked over my shoulder at Mina. "I can't tell if the boys pulling Poppy into their Titanic obsession is a good thing or a bad thing."

"This may solve your entire problem. They may chase Poppy off," she mused softly.

I hit her shin playfully with my cane, smiling, then froze as realization dawned. I grabbed her arm and pulled her into the bathroom. "That's Poppy playing," I whispered, remembering her practicing the song over and over again when we were kids. She was more skilled now, but I could tell her playing anywhere. "You shouldn't be able to hear her."

Chapter Twenty-Two

*Rule #48: For your safety, and the safety of all creatures,
reapers are required to keep a low profile. At no time
should they be in large crowds of humans and/or
supernaturals. More exposure creates higher risk.*

— The Reaper Code of Ethics, official handbook

Poppy

"DON'T LOOK AT me like that!" I defended, watching
my two ghost friends stare at me with matching
expressions of concern. "I didn't *mean* to kiss him."

"You tripped and your lips collided?" Reggie offered.

I threw my hands in the air. "I've been in love with the
man my entire life. My willpower is only so strong."

Sebastian shook his head. "You're not alive."

Reggie uncrossed his arms and sighed. "This only ends in
heartbreak." He gripped my shoulders. "Esqueleto, you're
just causing yourself more pain."

"Yo sé," I admitted. I knew I was.

We had shifted to Reggie's brother's apartment, below
Mina's, which had pictures of a very alive-looking Reggie on
the wall.

"I'm concerned that you interacting with Jake will be

166

extremely detrimental to you both," Sebastian admitted. "I hold you in the highest esteem, Poppy, but this entire situation is distressing."

"I don't know what to do about it," I admitted. "He's still not on my manifest, but I just can't walk away."

"This is all giving me a headache," Reggie said, and flopped down onto the couch. Well, more like through the cushion.

I rolled my eyes. "Sos un fantasma, no tenes cabeza. No te puede doler."

"Solo es un decir," he sighed. "And maybe there's a simple explanation."

Sebastian perched on the edge of the couch, spine straight and shoulders back. "Which is?"

"His belief system changed. Like Lola's."

"What do you mean?" I prompted.

Reggie picked up a photo of him and a little girl with the same dark hair and smiling eyes. "Mi sobrina, Lola. She interacted with me for the first time two days ago."

I reached out and gripped his shoulder. "Reggie! Why wasn't that the first thing you told me?"

"We were busy," he defended. "Alan's been telling her stories about me and kept promising she had nothing to be afraid of. She told me once she stopped trying to avoid me, she could see me clearly. Then, when she was working on my kite for Día de Todos los Santos, she looked over at me and asked if I wanted to help. A change in perspective was all it took."

Sebastian smiled. "I'm so pleased for you."

I put my hands to my mouth. "Reggie, that's great! Is

that celebration like Día de los Muertos?"

He nodded. "Sí, but in Guatemala, we call it Día de To-dos los Santos. On November first, we honor our deceased loved ones by making kites and flying them over their graves while praying. We'd leave flowers at the cemetery, and share a meal called fiambre."

HE GESTURED WITH his arms as he spoke. "Poppy, you should see the kites there! Some of them are as tall as a house. More beautiful than you can imagine. I wish you could see the tejido—the weaving."

He sighed. "Applechester doesn't celebrate, but since my family moved here, we still fly kites down at the park every November first."

"That sounds amazing." I wondered if I had any family to miss me on Earth, would they have had any traditions to keep my memory alive? I guessed the good thing about being stuck with one's family in death is I didn't have to miss them.

"If you're around this year, come fly a kite with me," Reggie said.

My smile faltered. Would I still be here in three weeks? Would Jake still be alive?

"Ah," Sebastian surmised. "While Jake is not present on your manifest, it appears you still have concerns."

I rubbed my face with my hands. "The fear of losing Jake...it's like dying all over again. How does it still hurt so much? Like, I'm a legit bag of bones." I asked, my voice cracking with emotion. I dropped my human glamour for a moment, allowing them to see my true form.

My family didn't understand why I had so many emotions, and despite Sylvia trying the hardest to get me, it just wasn't in her nature. It's probably why Reggie and Sebastian were such good friends. They were undead, like me, and still full of feelings, at least when watching their favorite movies. Death wasn't simple, no matter how the humans spun it.

Reggie gripped my skeleton hand, and I pulled my glamour back on. "I died last August, but I think I feel things more deeply now. I didn't have a reaper waiting for me, which turned out to be a good thing."

"Staffing issues," I reasoned. "Hence the reaper at sixteen part."

"Makes sense." He shrugged. "My heart may not still beat, but it can break all the same. Ignore Sebastian though. He's been emotionally unavailable for centuries."

"A century and a half, if you please. I'm not so old," Sebastian grumbled.

Reggie rolled his eyes. "I'm not *afraid* to have feelings anymore. This is like a second chance for me." He stuck his hands in his pockets. "Even though last year was really hard."

I nodded, remembering the stories. "I still can't believe Alan's ex-wife." She'd made him get a physical and mental evaluation before letting Lola stay over because his ex didn't believe in ghosts. I tried to convince Reggie to go haunt the ex, but he didn't want to cause Lola more anxiety.

"Death complicates everything," he continued, "but it doesn't stop us from being who we are. It may actually make us more ourselves."

"Basically, what you're really saying is that we still don't know why Jake can see me and I'm just going to be an unstable pile of emotions forever?"

"Me rindo," Reggie said. "I tried."

"I do observe your point, Reggie," Sebastian began, "but Jake hasn't been able to see Poppy in twelve years, no matter how desperate he became. I think it would be safe to assume whatever change happened is because of something that changed in you, Poppy."

I pressed two fingers against my forehead and sighed. "I think I may be getting a metaphorical headache now." I reached into my cloak and pulled out my violin. "Care if I play? It helps me think."

"Are you taking requests?" Sebastian asked.

"I'm only playing it once," I warned them. They'd have me play "My Heart Will Go On" on repeat if they could. Reggie sat next to Sebastian, lacing their arms together, as I began. The song was effortless, having played it so much in my youth. I moved with the music and smiled. I didn't often play for a captive audience, and there was something about these ghosts who brought back the joy I used to get performing.

I had forgotten what friends were like in reality until I'd met them. Sure, I had memories of Eliza and Jake, and Sylvia was definitely the person I was closest to, but there was something about these ghosts. They were dead like me, they worked in the afterlife like me, but they'd cultivated new lives for themselves out of the wreckage of their human bodies. Maybe I could build a different life for myself.

I didn't know how yet. Reapers followed different rules

than ghosts, and the whole being related to every grim reaper was problematic on the dating front, but still. They had found ways to be happy. I finished the last note of the song, letting it echo through the quiet, then lowered my violin. I looked up and found the couch empty.

I turned to my right and found the front door open. Jake, his parents, Mina, and her dad peered into the apartment.

Chapter Twenty-Three

Jake

EVERYONE HAD HEARD the violin music coming from the floor below. Poppy and I could make excuses about being able to see each other, label it as a fluke or luck or something to do with our before-death attachment. There was no way to brush this off.

"What's going on?" Magnolia asked. "Who was playing that recording? Was that our Poppy?"

Our Poppy. Once you were loved by Magnolia Robinson, you were part of the family. "It wasn't a recording," I explained, then hesitated. "Poppy's here."

My stepmom gasped, her hands flying to her mouth.

"Where?" Dad asked.

Mina grabbed my hand and squeezed, warning me to keep quiet. "She's over by the television stand," she said.

Poppy, who was on the opposite side of the room, moved to the television stand, but kept her eyes glued to mine.

"How do you know that?" Jim asked.

Mina squeezed even harder and for a moment I worried she'd break a metacarpal bone. "Because I can see her. I recognized her from the pictures Jake and Eliza have shown me."

"What are you doing?" I mouthed.

"Covering your ass," she silently returned.

Dad and Magnolia leaned into the apartment, then exchanged a look. "Why don't I see her?" Magnolia asked.

Jim was staring at his daughter. "How long?"

"Since Mom's wedding," Mina said.

Jim looked like he just took a punch in the gut. "And now we all hear her."

How could everyone hear her but not see her? What did it mean?

Mina waved her arms, pushing everyone back with an invisible force. "My place. Last thing we need is Alan to come home and wonder why we're crowding his apartment."

My family and Jim walked ahead of us while Mina stayed behind, matching my pacing as we climbed the ornate spiral staircase. "You made things more complicated," I admonished. "But thank you."

"Dad won't want to put this in a report, ergo your name and 'grim reaper' won't be linked."

I paused and looked over at her, "Jim always writes reports."

"Not when his daughter may be in danger, like if she could see a reaper."

I shook my head. "I don't like it."

"You don't have to. I'm buying you time to figure this out and not lose your mentorship. You couldn't save me from myself, but I can protect you. Even if it's just this."

I stopped and pulled her into a quick hug. She squirmed

away. "We've hugged twice today, this is too many emotions for me."

"There's the Mina I know and love."

We started walking again. "Quit," she begged. "Walk away from the death threats. Come work with Carma and me."

"If I quit, I can't be Daisy's mentor, and we are back in this same mess," I reminded her.

"What if this case kills you, Jake? You're already getting death threats, and judging by how slow we're climbing the stairs, I can tell your leg is killing you."

I threw her a pointed glance. "If I can't be trusted to do my duty even when it's hard, then what was the point in taking the SHAP oath twelve years ago?"

She flinched. She had gone against the SHAP Code of Conduct by starting a relationship with Carma during an investigation where Carma was the target.

"I'm sorry. I didn't mean it," I tried.

The look she shot me made it clear she knew I didn't really mean the apology. "What would you have done? If Poppy had been the focus of a case?"

I was silent, my mind remembering the feel of her body against mine, the press of her lips, the way she said my name. I was a liar to say I'd do anything different than Mina. I had already kissed Poppy. If she were alive and in reach? I'd never let her go.

"So what now?" I asked, not answering her. She didn't need me to.

"I haven't heard of anyone hearing a grim reaper before. I think Dad's going to have to make some calls."

"If Jim makes calls, people will know Poppy's a reaper."

"SHAP can't hurt me like it can you, Jake. I'll take the hit on this one."

We reached the landing, and I grabbed her hand. "I want to argue with you, but I know you're right."

She squeezed my hand. "God knows you've saved my life enough to earn some payback."

"That favor has been returned multiple times."

She pointed her finger at me. "Don't you dare die on me, got it? If you can see Poppy because you're going to die soon and you don't tell me, I'll kill you myself."

I gave her a quick squeeze before she stepped back. "I promise. No dying."

She shook out her shoulders. "Okay. Time to go lie to my dad."

✕

"WOULD YOU LIKE to explain to me why our home was destroyed?" Sebastian asked when I trudged in the door to my condo.

The last several hours had been full of a lot of disbelieving gasps (Magnolia), vehement refusal to go into a safe house just in case (Dad), and silent conversations (Eliza and me, Mina and me, Mina and Carma, Sebastian and Reggie). Poppy had not returned to Mina's apartment, and I wished I could call her and check on her. She must be reeling, even more than me.

I hung my keys up on my key rack. I was so tired. Maybe I'd start with the glass in the kitchen first and then just deal with the rest tomorrow. I turned to the living room and froze. It was spotless.

The chairs were righted, the pillows and blankets returned to their usual position. I moved to the kitchen and saw it too had been restored. I turned to face Sebastian.

"If you inform Mina about this, I will deny it for all eternity," he warned. "And I will haunt you worse than I do now."

"All those years Mina complained you didn't help with housework. It was a lie."

He waved me off. "Stop being so overdramatic. I only do it when I need to. Unlike Reggie, I have no desire to do many human things like cleaning. I save my energy for my assignments."

"So you pitied me enough to clean."

"You've had a difficult day, as indicated by the state in which I found our lodgings."

"Thank you."

He nodded once. "Did you make headway with your family?"

I moved back to the door and toed off my shoes, making sure they were aligned on the small mat. "No. They agreed to let Mina install cameras tomorrow but they refuse to go into a safe house."

"How many threats have you received this week?"

Seven. "Three."

"How confident are you that you can see Poppy for some other reason than your imminent demise?"

Not at all. "One hundred percent." He studied me, and it didn't take an investigator to know all his time spent with

Mina meant he could smell a lie almost as well as my mom. "I'm going to bed."

He touched the brim of his hat. "Goodnight, Jake." And he disappeared.

I limped to my bedroom. *Please let me wake up tomorrow.*

Chapter Twenty-Four

Rule #35: Reapers are encouraged to review the activity boards, located at both the pier and in the barracks, and to join in daily events. Building a strong community is a must for a reaper.

— The Reaper Code of Ethics, official handbook

Poppy

WHENEVER I READ books where the main character did something stupid, I yelled at the pages, wondering how they couldn't see how they were messing everything up. I knew if I stopped to write down my actions over the past week and read them back to myself, I'd probably be disgusted. This knowledge didn't stop me from checking on Jake.

The room was dark, the alarm clock on his nightstand read 1:58 in pale white numbers. I listened to his even breathing, the sound reassuring. I didn't know what was happening, but it felt like we were careening toward something unchangeable. Devastating.

I knew I should've left. I definitely should not have walked over to the bed and pressed my hand to his chest to feel his heartbeat. I needed the reassurance that he was still alive, that there was still time to try to fix whatever was breaking.

I gasped when he grabbed my wrist and blinked awake.

"Poppy?" His words slurred with sleep, but I had no doubt he was alert. "Are you Edward Cullen-ing me again?"

I laughed once. "I guess I am. Sorry."

He released my wrist and shifted his legs, then patted the bed next to him. "What's wrong?"

I sat on the edge of the bed. "I just wanted to check in on you," I admitted.

"I've been worried about you too." He brushed his hand with mine.

I soaked in the warmth of his touch. "Hey, I forgot to tell you. All the people from the storage unit? They were recruited via social media." I told him the details of my conversation with the souls, and he reached for his phone and made notes.

"This just keeps getting worse." He set his phone down and sighed. "How are you holding up?"

I scrunched my face. "Dry heaved for a solid ten minutes after that."

He shifted his pillow so only half was behind his head, then fluffed it. "Take off your robe and come here."

I shouldn't. I needed to keep my distance. Doing this was only going to hurt more. I stood and took off my cloak, hanging it on a hook on the back of his door.

He lifted his blanket as I approached, and I slid beneath. He turned to his side and pulled me into his bare chest, resting his forehead against mine. He kissed the tip of my nose. "How was the rest of your shift after?"

"I hated it," I admitted. "But nothing tied to Vixen and

no scary half souls, so not so bad in the end." I looked into his eyes and finally felt like I was home. "Kiss me?"

He ran his fingers through my hair, and I sank deeper into the bed, his scent, his warmth. I raised my hand and trailed my fingertips over the stubble on his jaw. I leaned forward and lightly brushed his lips with mine.

His hand cradled my head as he kissed me back, our movements slow. We savored each other for long minutes. With a breathy laugh, he pulled back. "I wish we had just ignored our parents and been together. We missed so much," he admitted.

"Me, too. Do you ever wonder what it could've been like? If we hadn't waited?"

This time his laugh was full sound. "Sorry, I just imagined your dads or Magnolia finding us in bed like this as teenagers."

I covered my mouth and pressed my face against his firm chest. "Oh no, I can't even imagine." I giggled. "We both would've been dead. Probably literally."

"Definitely literally."

I lifted my head back up, bumping his nose with mine. "We're not teenagers now."

He stole another kiss. "No, we're not." *Kiss.* "But Poppy, what are we doing?" *Kiss.* "Is there any way this ends happy?"

I pressed my hand against his cheek, my fingers running around his ear to the back of his neck. "I don't know. Nothing since the moment you saw me makes sense. All I know is that I can't stop kissing you."

He gave a low growl and his mouth found mine again. These kisses weren't soft and sweet, but sinful. Age and I assume experience had made him more confident, more in control, more teasing. I was melting from the inside out.

If he had kissed me like this when I was sixteen, I would've grabbed his hand and stolen a car. I would've denied my birthright. I would've done anything and everything to stay in his arms.

I didn't need to breathe, but I couldn't stop myself from gasping as his hand skated down my body, his thumb stroking the side of my breast before gripping my hips and pulling me tight against his. I nipped his bottom lip when I felt him against me. God, I wished I was just a normal human. He moved against me, and my chest filled with flutters, but the human pleasure I would've experienced if I wasn't a high-end skeleton was missing.

"I have a confession," I breathed against his mouth.

"Hmm?"

"I can't have an orgasm. I'm not even sure I can actually have sex. Wasn't sure I could even kiss you until today."

He tilted his head back to study me in the dark. "My head's a little fuzzy...not sure I'm following. You can't have sex?"

I made a face. "I mean, I'm surrounded by my family and extended family on a floating death island, so I haven't actually *tried*, but I'm basically just a skeleton animated with magic. I can't even take off my clothes."

He groaned and buried his head in my shoulder. "Of all the things you've told me about being a reaper, that's got to be the most depressing."

"You're telling me. I finally get in your bed and I can't do anything about it."

He lifted his head and gave me a kiss. "Honestly? Kissing you is the best thing ever. It's enough."

I gave him a saucy smile. "I mean, just because I can't take off my clothes doesn't mean I can't take off *your* clothes. I can think of some fun places I can kiss."

He groaned and rolled over on me, pinning my arms to either side of my head. "As much," *kiss,* "as I'd like that—love that," *kiss,* "let's just keep it mouth kissing for now." *Kiss.* "And maybe neck." He nudged my chin with his nose and kissed down my jaw and behind my ear.

I let out a breathy laugh. "I'm not complaining."

He pulled back. "Wait…how can I even kiss you? If you're a skeleton, how do you feel so human right now?"

"You know how ghosts have to practice moving and interacting with objects?"

He chuckled. "Oh yes. It's Sebastian's best excuse to not help with chores."

I released a breathy laugh. "It's like that. The more familiar I am with something, the more I can interact with it as if I were still human. Like if I go to the library, I can literally rearrange the shelves. But if I go to a new bookstore, the books slip through my hands."

"And I'm familiar to you." It wasn't a question.

I kissed the corner of his mouth. "I knew you better than I knew myself. You're the thing I'm most familiar with."

His lips smiled against mine. "Good."

He kissed me again and I got lost in him, the heat and the pressure of him erasing years of longing and need and loneliness. When we finally separated, he rolled us over, laying me on his chest. I put my hand against his ribs where his heartbeat was the strongest. *Thud, thud, thud.* With each beat, I thanked the universe he was still alive.

He ran his fingers through my hair and I snuggled deeper into his arms. "How did we survive without each other?" I asked against his warm skin.

He let out a single laugh. "Well, technically, you didn't."

I sighed. "Touché."

He kissed the top of my head. "I don't know. I don't even know what the hell I'm going to do when you inevitably leave tonight."

I turned my head and left a long kiss on his chest. "I'm here now."

He squeezed me tighter. "What was it like? Dying?"

I lifted up, looking at him. "Jake…"

"I know we're purposely ignoring that the most likely reason I can see you is because my time is almost up."

"It might not be!" I argued.

"But it could be." He traced my eyebrow with his fingertips, then drifted over my cheekbone, my jaw, and my bottom lip. "God, I wish I had days, weeks, years to memorize you again. I forgot about the way your lip dips here." He traced my cupid's bow. "This scar from when you fell off the swing-set when we tried to see if we could go over the top." He traced the memory that blended in with my jaw.

He leaned up and kissed the skin next to my mouth. "This dimple you only get when you're really happy." His lips brushed my eyelids. "The way you pretended not to watch me."

"That obvious, huh?"

"I was watching you back."

I closed my eyes tight as he kissed me again and again. It was even better than a summer day by the pool, than the smell of the rain, than my favorite book. I was warm and content and at peace. For just this moment, I was as happy as I was at sixteen on summer vacation.

He laid us back down, one arm behind his head, one around me, and I rested my head back on his chest. I could talk about the dark times, but only if I knew he was still breathing, still living. "I was lucky," I whispered into his skin. "Reaper deaths are usually peaceful, as long as they come before the natural one. I just fell asleep and woke up on a boat."

"You hate boats."

"I still get motion sick."

His fingers playing with my hair paused. "Seriously? You can't have an orgasm but you can get seasick?"

"*Right?* It's bullshit." I traced the outline of his muscles with my fingers. "I get my own room. And no, it isn't any more organized than when I was a teenager."

"I'm not surprised."

"If anything ever happens to you, I'm going to be there. I promise." It wasn't a promise I could technically make, but I'd figure it out. I wouldn't let anyone else be by his side. No matter what I had to do.

"Then I have nothing to worry about."

"You trust me?"

"Completely." He kissed the top of my head.

"So, what have you been up to for the last, I dunno, twelve years?"

He chuckled. He told me stories about his life until his

voice faded, until his hand stilled, and he fell into sleep. I missed sleeping. It was a reset, a relief that I desperately needed.

A pull in my chest reminded me it was time to get back to work and all at once, my happiness vanished. If I could cry, I would've had tear trails down my cheeks as I kissed Jake softly and climbed out of bed. Every step away from his arms made me colder, and by the time I slipped the cloak over my arms, I was heavy with frost.

I walked through the door and came face to face with Sebastian.

"Do you know what you're doing?" he asked.

I looked back at the door. "All I know is that when I'm with him, it's the happiest I've ever been."

He nodded and bowed his head. "Then the turmoil's worth it."

"He's worth everything."

As I always did after my visit to the human realm, I pulled my hood up before attempting to walk through my usual portal. The gray mist around me felt heavy, as if it was judging me with how I'd spent my break. "You're just jealous," I grumbled, as if the mist were sentient and could possibly give a damn.

I raised my fingers to my lips, trying to hold on to the memory of Jake's mouth moving against mine. I closed my eyes for a moment and imagined what it would be like if I had stayed alive. If we had convinced our parents we were responsible enough to start a relationship.

I imagined the secret kisses and the late-night climbs through windows. Then as we grew up, vacations together, moving in together, getting married. Days and nights and days together. Silly fights, and hot-as-hell makeup sex, and doing dishes side by side. Endless adventures. Arguing about what we'd have for dinner or what movie we'd watch. Lazy Sundays curled up reading on the couch.

I covered my face with my hands, took a deep breath, and shook my head to clear it. That's not what happened. That wasn't what was going to happen. My brain had figured it out, and now my heart needed to listen.

With an expletive, I turned off my glamour and stomped through the portal door. Or at least I tried. It was like walking in wet concrete. My feet stopped moving and my hood came off. I raised my hands to replace it, startled when I saw they were still in human form. That was weird.

I paused and concentrated on removing my human form and turning back into a skeleton. When my hand was only a series of bones, I took another step forward and eased through the portal. I walked back to the human realm, then back to the reaper world with no hiccups. Maybe I just did it wrong the first time. I mean, I'd been doing it multiple times a day for twelve years, but my mind had been wandering.

The pull in my chest told me to get to the boat dock to meet Sylvia. With one last glance over my shoulder, I hurried to work.

To: G_Fletcher@unbelievablebodies.inc
From: B.Somerset@cmail.com

Fletcher,

I'm extremely disappointed with these trials and therefore am revoking approval. Please deliver the remaining un-

used product to the warehouse in Hayvenwood, Michigan, within 48 hours. When you arrive, we will discuss your future with the organization.

Sincerely,
Somerset

To: B.Somerset@cmail.com
From: G_Fletcher@unbelievablebodies.inc

Somerset,

I implore you to let me continue with the final two scheduled trials. I truly believe that if we adjust the dosing, we will correct the issue.

Fletcher

To: G_Fletcher@unbelievablebodies.inc
From: B.Somerset@cmail.com

Fletcher,

I'm not a pharmacist, but I'm interested to know how every test subject has died from a fentanyl overdose while trying our product—which should not contain any fentanyl—and how a dosing modification will prevent this?

Sincerely,
Somerset

To: B.Somerset@cmail.com
From: G_Fletcher@unbelievablebodies.inc

That's impossible. We haven't altered the pills in any way. We are clearly being sabotaged!

To: G_Fletcher@unbelievablebodies.inc
From: B.Somerset@cmail.com

Fletcher,

You'll forgive me for not believing you. I suggest you find the person who is sabotaging you and have them accompany you when you drop off the remaining product. This is your only warning. If you do not arrive at the Hayvenwood warehouse within your assigned time period, you will not like the outcome. And yes, this is a threat.

Sincerely,
Somerset

Chapter Twenty-Five

Jake

I HAD ONLY managed four broken-up hours of sleep, but I woke up happier and with more energy than I'd had in weeks, maybe even months. The sun seemed brighter, warmer. My leg pain was bearable enough to shower standing up.

I couldn't stop myself from smiling when I glanced at the bed, where I'd held Poppy in my arms for hours. I'd had a few different partners in my bed over the last decade, but no one had ever made me feel the way she did. It wasn't just nostalgia and secret kisses. I knew Poppy almost as well as I knew myself, even now.

Sure, years had passed, but she still loved with her whole soul, still wanted to help everyone she met. She was extremely loyal and never shied away from duty. Good god, and the way she kissed. As if there was nothing else in the universe that mattered but our lips pressed together.

I pressed my hand to my chest, trying to calm my racing heart. I needed to get my head on straight so I didn't do something ridiculous like giggle or blush in front of Sebastian. He didn't need to know I had a guest in my bed.

When I walked into the kitchen, he glanced at me from the living room. "I already know. You two weren't exactly quiet."

I winced. "You can't tell anyone."

He went back to leafing through a book. "I'm not going to. But I'll tell you the same thing I told Mina when she was falling for Carma: Tell your partner."

"Mina didn't tell me until it was basically too late," I pointed out.

"Not for lack of me trying. Inform Paris now before things get out of hand."

I flipped on the coffee pot. "She already knows about Poppy."

"Does she know you spend hours having romantic interludes with someone who's going to collect your soul soon?"

"Speculation."

"Just so."

"Why are you trying to ruin my good mood?" I grumbled, pulling a travel mug out of the cabinet and scooping in hot cocoa powder.

"I know it may seem out of sorts, but I do care about your well-being." He paused for a moment. "Has Poppy explained why she never shared that she was a reaper?"

I frowned at him. "She wasn't allowed."

Sebastian lifted a shoulder. "And you both always followed the rules until now?"

"What are you saying?"

He closed his book around his fingers, holding his place. "Maybe I'm incorrect in my assumptions, but if she was as close to you and Eliza as you claim, it seems rather unbelievable that she didn't tell you about being a reaper. Rather callous to leave you questioning what happened to her for twelve years."

I poured coffee into my cup, then a splash of cream, before screwing on the lid and spinning it between my hands to mix it up. "I can't wait until you fall in love someday. It's happened to Mina, Reggie, and now me. It's coming for you and you're going to lose that judgmental stance."

He just stared at me and turned a page. "I'm perfectly content with my life. I don't need another being infiltrating my routine and causing havoc."

I laughed. "If only our hearts were under our control." I grabbed my laptop bag and my gray cane, which I preferred for work. "If it were, I would definitely not be in love with a dead woman."

Sebastian sat up straighter. "In love with?"

I paused, my hand on the doorknob, replaying the words in my head. I hadn't meant to admit it out loud, but it was true. I had loved Poppy since we were kids.

Her death had not stopped my love—because what was grief, if not unrequited love?—but now that she was tangible, real, able to kiss me again, it had come back full force. "I've been in love with her for two decades. Not going to stop now."

He closed his book. "Jacob, I hold Poppy in very high esteem, but there is something very unsettling about this entire situation. I greatly dislike that she kept such a serious secret from you for so long."

"Have you even met Poppy in more than passing? You don't get to pass judgment on her until you actually know her."

He pursed his lips and opened back up his book. "Make sure Eliza knows I want to be moved to her house if something happens to you. I need to be able to check on Reggie and Mina."

"Eliza would never put up with your shit. You could just retire from SHAP and go stay with Mina and Carma."

"SHAP is the much-needed structure I need in my death. When every day is punctuated by the never-ending monotony of drifting aimlessly through space and time, it can destroy a person. Living or dead." He glanced up at me.

"Noted." I opened the door and looked back at him. "I hope you have a non-monotonous day."

"I hope you stay alive."

I SHOULD NEVER have said I was in a good mood out loud. It was like the universe wanted to challenge the very idea. It was the only explanation I had for the gunfight in the middle of Café Eleonora.

The café was a well-known SHAP hangout, the makeup of the customers at least sixty percent lethal agents any time day or night. Attacking any agent anywhere near the front door was a suicide mission, not to mention that SHAP was mere footsteps away. This, however, was not a deterrent for the really desperate.

I had barely walked through the doors of SHAP this morning when my phone pinged with the email from an unfamiliar address.

Jake,

Let's compromise. Meet 3:30pm at Café Eleonora. Come alone.

Fletcher

Fletcher. That's the name Poppy mentioned. Fletcher had been involved in the clinical trials. I had no plans to compromise and I definitely didn't arrive alone. Paris was wearing a borrowed branded apron and was refilling sugar containers at the table opposite me. Reggie sat across from me, watching the kitchen doors.

A man wearing a tight thermal, beanie over messy hair, and a cocky-as-hell smile walked up to Paris. "Hey beautiful. Can I buy you a coffee?"

"No thank you," Paris responded, not looking up at him.

"Just give me your number and I'll get out of your hair."

Reggie snorted. "Is this guy for real? He'd ghost you faster than me, and I *am* a ghost." By the man's lack of response to Reggie, it was obvious he was a full-blooded human.

She sighed. "I said no and I'm busy. Please leave."

I studied the tables around me, looking for the humans and any supernaturals who couldn't hold their own. A group of teens hovered around a phone, an awkward first date, a business meeting with warring laptops, a writers' group three coffees in, a dad reading to his kid. Two shape shifters, a werewolf, a handful of agents, and a gaggle of ghosts in the corner.

Thermal Guy leaned his hip against the table. "All I need are seven digits."

My jaw clenched. I hated nothing more than men who

couldn't take no for an answer. "She said no," I growled, turning to him.

I heard the soft snap of a tranquilizer gun a second before he grabbed his neck. Paris caught him as he started to sink to the ground, the fast-acting dart taking quick effect, then deposited him in an empty seat behind her without breaking a sweat. "He was annoying me," she defended.

Reggie stared at her wide-eyed. "Cuando crezca, quiero ser como usted," he said reverently. Paris tilted her head and Reggie translated. "When I grow up, I want to be like you."

"God help us if you're ever allowed to carry a tranq gun," I grumbled at him.

The bell over the door rang and two men—likely were-wolves by their stance and bulk—and a woman walked in. They didn't look around, just laser focused in on me.

"Told you to come alone," the woman said, glancing at Reggie.

"I did come alone. He was here when I got here," I explained. The woman put her hands on her hips which pulled her shirt tighter, revealing the outline of a holster and gun beneath the fabric. My stomach tightened. I didn't have a good feeling about this. "Reggie, go order me a pineapple juice on the rocks." Code for get the civilians out.

"Aye, aye captain." He disappeared.

The woman sat down. "So you're Jake."

I lifted a shoulder. "That's what they call me."

She pursed her lips, looking pointedly at my gray cane, which was balancing on the end of the table. I had activated the recording device in the handle before setting it down. "They say you're not only one of the best agents, but that you're also extremely attractive. I don't really see what all the fuss is about."

I leaned forward. "Well, that feeling is mutual. Judging people for using mobility devices just makes you a shitty person." I clicked the button on my watch to test if Fletcher was a supernatural creature.

She shrugged. "So does taking away something that saves people's lives."

"Venom does more harm than good."

In my peripheral vision, I saw the staff quietly moving through the crowd and asking the civilians to leave, probably under the guise of closing early. The SHAP crowd pretended to be finishing up, but their ears and eyes were pointed in our direction.

My watch buzzed and I glanced down. *Vampire-human hybrid unregistered.* My stomach dropped as realization dawned.

All vampire-human hybrids had been returned to full human or they were registered through SHAP's database. For her to be unregistered would mean she was made from oral venom but never part of the Thinner program, and that also meant there was probably more than just her. Which explained the influx of demons, who made good on their promises that they'd come visit if we didn't get the hybrids under control. After all, in their opinion, if vampires and vampire-human hybrids didn't follow the rules, why should they?

"What if I told you that I know where the main supply of Vixen is coming from?" Fletcher asked.

I lifted a shoulder in an effort to appear nonchalant. "I'd

say I'm not surprised as that's probably part of your job."

She leaned closer. "What if I also told you that I have eyes on everyone in your family right now? Your niece is in math, your sister is in her office with headphones on, your dad is in his car on I-75, and your mom is showing a house on Willow Street."

I lifted the corner of my mouth while clicking my watch button six times rapidly, dispatching an emergency SOS signal. "Wrong. My mom is dead."

"Well then, the rest of your family will soon join her."

"Unless?"

"We make a trade. I give you the location of the warehouse and leave your family—and you—alive. In exchange, our paths never cross again."

I crossed my arms and leaned back in my chair. "Why would I let you walk free?"

"You mean outside of saving your family? Because you want Vixen off the streets, and so do I. But for different reasons. Call it a mutual back scratching."

My watched buzzed three times, signaling that a team was on their way.

"I have a question," I started. "When you recruited for your clinical trials, did you only accept the dying to make yourself feel better if it didn't work?"

She hid her surprise, but not quickly enough. "Not all of them were dying. It's always good to have a control."

Poppy was right. Five terminal and one healthy soul. It would account for the shadow attack. "Yes, I suppose it is. Or to have control, which is why I'm assuming you're pushing for this deal."

She tilted her head to the side. "You're smart."

"But you're not, if you think I'm going to let someone who not only threatened me, but threatened my family, walk away."

She leaned across the table. "Ah, but you know that working with me is the best chance you have to close this case, and isn't that what you want to do the most? Close this case and move into a mentorship?"

I concentrated on not reacting. *How did she know about Daisy?* Daisy's powers were a closely guarded secret, and my requested transfer to be her mentor was only known by a handful of trusted people. I needed to break this down, needed to think like Mina.

One, Fletcher wanted the Vixen off the streets. Two, she knew about my job change. Three, she was an unregistered hybrid. I studied her for a moment, the faint smile, the cocky attitude, the unhurried perusal of the shop. She was confident she'd get what she wanted, which meant she had an ace up her sleeve.

As if Mina was sitting next to me whispering into my ear, the thought popped into my head. *Once you take Vixen off the streets, it'll all be in one place: the evidence room at SHAP headquarters.* Which wouldn't matter unless Fletcher had access to it. Sometimes the simplest—although most devastating—answers were right.

There was a leak at SHAP.

Which also meant she probably already knew I had sent out the SOS call, based on the smile she flashed me. I had seconds to come up with a plan. I looked around the room and took in the remaining crowd. Two shapeshifters, four ghosts, three werewolves (two were Fletcher's bodyguards and one was Eleonora), and six human agents, including me and Paris.

I caught Reggie's gaze and looked up at the sprinkler system. He returned a puzzled look but shifted closer. "I don't presume to know your age," I said to Fletcher, "But have you seen the cinematic classic *Titanic*?"

She frowned. "Like twenty years ago? I was a kid. Probably saw a few scenes."

I looked over her right shoulder at Reggie. "I don't know if you know this, but ghosts love that movie. I swear, if they could flood an entire room with a sprinkler and then float around on doors, they would."

Reggie's eyes widened as he looked up, spotting the sprinkler. He immediately disappeared and I inhaled slowly, trying to calm my heart rate. I couldn't get too excited yet. This plan could still fail catastrophically.

I had no doubt Paris and I could take Fletcher, but her werewolves posed an issue. I wouldn't have time to give the order to shoot them before they filled me with bullets. Not unless they were sufficiently distracted. Every werewolf I knew hated water, and I just had to hope these two were the same.

"I think you've had one too many concussions, Agent Robinson. You're not making sense, and quite frankly I'm bored with all this." She stood and pulled out her gun, leveling it at my heart. "You have five seconds to agree to a deal with me or die." She shrugged. "Either way, I win."

Paris broke character and grabbed her weapon. *Dammit.* I wanted to keep her presence hidden. I couldn't blame her.

Newbie Jake would've reacted in the same way.

Fletcher's werewolves drew their own weapons and trained them on Paris and me. "Ah, so you did bring company," Fletcher surmised. "Pity. Deal's off." The remaining agents drew their pieces and pointed them at Fletcher and her guards. "Uh-uh, not a good idea."

I raised my eyebrows in a silent reply.

"Because if I fail to call in the next ten minutes, my team's got orders to kill your family. Which means if you kill me, you're effectively killing them."

I pressed my lips together. I didn't have to kill her, just slow her down. "Put your weapons down," I ordered the room. I couldn't risk someone taking her out. Not yet. There were grumbles, but I heard the click of guns on tile.

Fletcher took a step back. "Maybe I'll kill your family, anyway. Just to send a message." She shifted her aim. "And I'll start with your pretty partner."

The sprinklers went off, dumping water all over us. Something hard slammed into me as I dove for Paris. A gunshot rang out, and moments later pain radiated through my left arm. We hit the ground so hard, I lost my breath. I rolled us over, shouting at the pain in my leg. A flash of purple faded into nothing.

The two werewolf guards were cowering from the water and the SHAP agents had taken them into custody. I looked around for Fletcher, but she was gone; the glass front door of the café was off its hinges. I hauled myself up with a growl and limped heavily toward a werewolf, holding my gun against its forehead.

"You have ten seconds to tell me where Fletcher's going

or I'll put a silver bullet in your brain," I threatened.

"Please, I have a family, too," he begged.

"Then you know I'm serious." I cocked the gun. "Nine. Eight. Seven—"

"We know where the main lab and warehouse are," the other one shouted.

I didn't move the gun but turned to him. "Where?"

"Hayvenwood, Michigan." *Hayvenwood.* If Fletcher wanted to take out the main lab, no doubt she'd be headed there soon.

SHAP vans rolled up, an armed team entering through the front door and the kitchen. The sprinklers were turned off, and I helped Paris off the floor while SHAP took the werewolves into custody. Paris twisted her soaking wet apron and did her best to tie it around my bicep as a tourniquet as Jim approached.

"Family's safe," he promised. "Security got Daisy. Eliza incapacitated her attacker and got word to your folks."

"Mina and Carma?" I prompted.

"Belphegor."

"We need to get him on payroll." I ran my right hand down my face, trying to wipe the dirty water out of my eyes. "Get my family to a safe house off SHAP radar." I gave him a long look, trying to silently communicate my suspicions about a mole.

He held my gaze and nodded. "See a medic."

I looked at Paris. "You okay?"

"Just bruised." She looked up at me. "I should've waited."

I nodded. "Your instincts will get stronger." We walked

out the door and I sat in the back of a SHAP ambulance as they attended to my arm.

"Got lucky," the medic said. "Only needed three stitches from that bullet."

Reggie appeared next to me, panicking. "You got shot!"

"Reg, buddy, I'm fine," I admitted.

He took a deep breath. "What if I hadn't been able to get the sprinklers on? What if Poppy hadn't been there?"

My head snapped to face him. "Poppy was here?" The flash of purple.

He nodded. "She redirected the bullet, mano. A second later and that would've hit your chest. You saved Paris; Poppy saved you."

"Holy shit." We sat in silence for a beat. Had Poppy just saved my life? Did that mean she really was here for my soul?

"What now?" Reggie asked.

"I go to Hayvenwood and try to finish this thing before it's too late."

Chapter Twenty-Six

Rule #12: A reaper is never allowed to leave their post during an assignment.

— The Reaper Code of Ethics, official handbook

Poppy

"YOU'RE REALLY QUIET tonight," Sylvia observed as we sat on top of a streetlight pole, waiting for an accident.

I shrugged. "Just…thinking."

"About Jake." It wasn't a question.

I stared down at the large traffic light swinging back and forth in the wind. "It made it bearable, knowing he was alive and happy."

"We haven't gotten to the point where we have to take the people we love across the river. We've been lucky."

Pain, dark as ink, spread through me. "I don't know that I can," I admitted. "How could I say a forever good-bye?"

She reached out and took my hand. "We'll figure it out, together." She sighed and then looked up at the rain-filled clouds. "I love the rain. I miss it."

"Me too." I missed everything that wasn't monotonous. The cloudless skies the color of cornflowers, the birds singing a musical song on a soft summer breeze. The smell of freshly cut grass and sunscreen. The sound of buzzing bees and the melody of an ice cream truck that played Christmas music in July. The dark clouds and thunderstorms, the flash of lightning, the taste of snowflakes on my tongue.

Something sharp tugged in my chest, and I pressed my hand there, trying to calm it. It tugged harder, physically jolting me. I threw my arms out, trying to maintain my balance. Sylvia grabbed my arm, steadying me, a touching gesture as literally nothing would've happened to me if I did fall.

"You okay?"

"Something...something's wrong." This wasn't a normal reaper pull. This was a gut-deep, something horrible is about to happen unless you stop it warning.

Jake. His name repeating louder and louder in my mind. Concentrating hard on Jake's energy, I pinpointed his location and disappeared.

"Poppy, wait!" Sylvia yelled as the sound of metal on metal filled the air. The accident we were waiting for had really bad timing.

When I appeared at Café Eleonora, I saw the gun leveled at Jake. No chance in hell. Jumping on his back as he tried to protect Paris, I shoved them both to the ground while shifting to my skeleton form. The bullet deflected off my bones and away from Jake's torso, shooting a hole into my cloak and slicing open some skin on Jake's arm. I paused only to make sure he was still alive, then disappeared. I had to get back to Sylvia.

When I returned to the scene of the accident, I heard my

sister's scream first. It chilled me to the bone. I had never heard her scream, at least not from true fear. A demon had launched itself at her and was going for her neck.

I pulled out my sword and dispatched the demon, before stepping in front of Sylvia. "Who's next?"

The accident was gruesome, but the surrounding demons were even more terrifying. Amon was there and judging from the way the other demons copied his pose, so were his buddies.

Sylvia stood in front of five souls, her scythe poised and at the ready. "Make their ears bleed," she demanded, then stepped next to me, taking my sword.

I yanked my violin out of my robe and immediately started playing a hymn.

The demons hissed and covered their ears, then took a step back. One of the souls, a young woman, started singing. The demons grew more agitated. The rest of the group tried to sing or hum along, even if they didn't know the tune. The less-invested demons opened up portals and disappeared, leaving only Amon and two friends.

"Let's go," Sylvia ordered.

Our group moved in sync, one slow step at a time. The demons shifted with us, but it was clear they were debating whether we were worth the effort. Amon grew bold and tried to snatch the young woman who had started singing first.

Sylvia cut off his arm. "Fuck this. Run."

So we ran. I lingered back, playing my violin so aggressively that one of the strings broke. It would've left a mark if I still had skin. I kept playing, ignoring the missing string, but my songs had lost a bit of their sting. They were gaining on us.

Anya jumped through the portal and into the human world, with a bucket of Styx River water in hand. She tossed it on the three remaining demons, who gave up the fight and melted back into the ground. Leaders from every religion that had ever existed were constantly doing rituals on the water, which demons did not like. "That was brilliant!" I shouted. I made a mental note to carry a vial of water with me at all times.

Sylvia shoved the humans through the veil, then shouted for Anya and me. We crossed over and leaped into the boat. I shoved off the bank as Anya took the helm.

I slid onto a bench, breathing hard, even though I didn't need to breathe. It was an emotional response. Anya regaled the humans with fantastical stories, her gift of imagination and soothing cadence eased the trip. If anyone noticed the way she scanned the banks more frequently, or that she was moving twice as fast as she normally did, they didn't say.

"You left me," Sylvia accused, barely above a whisper. "This shouldn't have happened."

"I'm sorry." I didn't know what else to say.

She shook her head. "You didn't just screw up. We almost lost souls tonight. And why? Where did you go?"

"He would've died."

She gripped the wooden bench seat so tight, it creaked. "You interfered?"

"I...maybe?" Jake hadn't been on my manifest, so was it technically interfering?

"Poppy..." There was so much censure in her tone that I didn't even need to wait for the seasickness to strike for my stomach to knot. "I'm going to have to report this."

My head jerked up. "Sylvia, you can't. They'll reassign me."

"I don't think that's a bad thing. You're in so deep, you can't see that you're drowning."

I grabbed her hand. "It's always been you and me. Please."

She jerked her hand away. "It has because you've always had my back. But if you were mere seconds later today..." She shook her head. "We get these big jobs because we're a team, and it's not fair for me to do them alone. I need to work with someone I can trust, and I'm sorry, Poppy, but that's not you right now."

My world tilted, and it had nothing to do with the rocking boat. My sister had dumped me. My own sister. *But you let her down.* If I had been a few seconds later... It didn't bear thinking about. Not all reapers made it back alive, and tonight I'd almost lost my sister. Because I had been distracted.

I had to save Jake's life.

Pain echoed in my chest. She was going to file formal paperwork. Our entire family would know that I messed up and never let me live it down. Plus, I would likely lose my coveted spot on a preferred shift. I would have to earn it back. It's not that I had much of a life—er, unlife—it was just that I lived by a schedule.

I knew what days and how long I'd have to work from now until eternity. I knew who the boat captains would be, which reapers I would cross paths with, and how many souls I would ferry on any day. I needed routine to keep from spiraling, like I had my first year here.

But hadn't that routine already been thrown off? Wasn't that why we were in this mess?

"Whatever you feel is best," I finally told my sister. I didn't have the energy to fight her. She was right. I had screwed up and now I had to face the consequences.

"Poppy," she sighed and turned away from me. "I just need some space."

Chapter Twenty-Seven

Jake

PARIS KNOCKED ON the door to my room at the SHAP medical facility. I motioned for her to come in. "Came with an update." She closed the door behind her and hit her watch, checking the room for hidden creatures.

"Please." I had been locked in here for two hours as they examined me. They had rotated heat and ice on my leg, and finally determined I had just bruised myself pretty good. No torn ligaments or sprains. Sadly, like a regular human emergency room, it took hours to escape.

She read her watch. "Clear. Okay, your family, Mina, and Carma are en route to a cabin Jim owns in Grand Haven. They'll arrive in a few hours."

I nodded. "I can't believe Mina agreed to go."

Paris grimaced. "Jim bribed her. Told her she and Carma could remodel."

I laughed. Mina hated remodeling, but this was on brand. "Good for her."

She smiled quickly but got back to business. "I already called your guy in Hayvenwood. Loren, the ex-HQ agent." HQ was to SHAP what the U.S. Navy SEALs were to the human military. "He's in. There's only one road from the highway into town, and they've got a drone watching for Fletcher."

"Did he know about the warehouse?"

"Not that he said, but no way to tell if it was a secure line."

I tapped my fingers against my thigh. "We're walking into a trap, aren't we?"

She nodded. "More than likely. But I don't see another option at this point."

"Okay." I swung my legs off the bed. "Get me out of here and out of these scrubs." I tugged at the too-tight shirt I had borrowed, since my clothes had been soaking wet.

She checked her watch. "I had Sebastian put together an overnight bag for you. It's in the car. We have a plane to catch."

"YOU SAID PLANE, Paris. Plane," I reiterated. "Why are we standing in front of a helicopter?" I wondered if Poppy would be able to find me if I died in a crash. Would she be able to track me outside of Applechester? Was she tied to me or the town? I wished there was a way to ask her.

She sighed. "Because if I said '*helicopter*', you would've been upset. Like you are right now."

"Why did you book a helicopter?"

"Because you wanted to keep SHAP out of it, and I had access to one. Can't fly under the radar on a plane."

"Planes are safer."

"There's not much difference."

"Not—not much difference?! There are an average of 7.28 crashes for every 100,000 hours of flight compared to—" The blades started whirling, cutting off my sentence and drowning out all other sound. I gestured to them to make my point.

Paris reached out and took my hand. "Remember to duck!"

Once we were harnessed in and put our headsets on, we were lifting off the ground. I kept my eyes closed. I had only passed out twice in my life—the first time when I got the news about Poppy, the second from blood loss—and I was not going to do it again. My heart was beating so fast, it probably could've powered our trip.

"You look like you're going to faint," Paris worried.

"If I do, leave me be until we land." I sighed.

"Get it together," Paris warned, pulling out a binder. "We need to get familiar with the town. I've shrank down some maps for us to study, along with the names and backgrounds of the people we'll be meeting. If I had a photo of them, I included it. We have just over two hours."

"When did you have time to do this?" I asked.

"You were busy sitting in the hospital. Plenty of time."

I flipped through the paper. "I know Eliza calls you an unfeeling robot, but you're fucking great at your job."

Paris's cheeks were red, and she deliberately avoided eye contact. "I appreciate the compliment on my work skills."

We were silent as we reviewed the information, and I was grateful for the distraction. Hayvenwood, Michigan, was fifteen miles northwest of St. Ignace in Michigan's Upper

Peninsula. Inhabited by a plethora of witches, shapeshifters, and ex-SHAP agents apparently. Maybe even a dragon.

And a warehouse of Vixen.

I looked up and found Paris staring out the window and not at her map. "Hey, you okay?" I asked.

She startled and turned to face me. "Just been a big day."

I studied her face, the pinch between her brows, the purse of her lips. "Care to elaborate?"

Her teeth worried her bottom lip for a moment. "I wasn't prepared for how…terrifying it is to worry if someone is going to live through the workday."

I nodded slowly. Her eyes moved to me and then back out the window, and I suspected this wasn't just about me. "To be fair, things aren't usually this volatile. This case is definitely baptism by fire."

"I can see why you want to leave and mentor your niece. This is exhausting."

"It definitely is."

She checked her watch. "Okay, enough feelings talk. Time for a pop quiz."

Chapter Twenty-Eight

Rule #61: If a reaper disobeys a direct order and endangers a) another reaper or b) a human soul, the reaper may be suspended.

— The Reaper Code of Ethics, official handbook

Poppy

THE PINK SLIP had arrived just before I slipped into my cloak for my next shift. Shoved under my door, because they couldn't bother knocking. I was suspended for one week, unless I wanted to appeal the ruling.

Appealing it was a fool's errand. I had left Sylvia during a large soul pickup, and we had been attacked by several demons. We almost lost souls. I deserved this suspension, and definitely one that was much longer than a week.

But a week suspension meant seven entire days away from the human world. Seven days when I couldn't protect Jake. After seeing how close he'd come to death today, I couldn't let that happen.

If only I could find out when and how he was scheduled to die. Then I could make sure I was there. Maybe stop it.

I needed to kiss him every day, every hour, until I couldn't. I needed to hold him in my arms, needed to hear him whisper my name in the dark. I needed to know how long we had left together.

I was going to have to get a look at the master list. It was as close to a suicide mission as a dead person could have. If I got caught, I'd definitely be put into detention, for years. Possibly even Isle of Exile. The only option was to not get caught.

First things first, I needed some help from my family. I just hoped if they ever found out, they'd forgive me. With my hood up, I navigated down the halls toward my dads' place. I knocked on their front door.

"Hello! Anyone home?" I called. They should both be on shift, and I was relieved when there was no response.

I turned the knob and slipped into the main room, then called out again. Still no answer. I dashed into their bedroom and threw open the closet. I grabbed one of the dark burgundy cloaks from the back of the closet and rolled it up underneath my own. I squatted down and pulled out their lockbox, grabbing the key taped to the side and opening it. They'd never been good at hiding keys.

I shifted through the documents and irreplaceable photos, and grabbed my dad's spare ID. Each reaper was issued two, in case one was damaged or lost. The second ID would cancel out the first, which would mean Dad would figure out what happened in a matter of hours.

He'd know it was me. I just hoped I'd be with Jake again by then, giving Dad time to cool down. As long as he didn't file formal paperwork, I'd be okay.

Mission complete, I slipped out of their room and took the long way back to mine. Likely no one saw me. This was the most popular shift for reapers, and I hadn't passed anyone in the hallway. My great aunt Vivian did like to spy on people through a peephole, but I kept my hood up and my head down so she couldn't catch a glimpse.

When I finally got back to my room, I pulled off my robe and slipped my dad's on and rolled the sleeves. I pulled a non-embellished, worn purple cloak over top and tucked Dad's ID card in my pocket. Finally, I shifted into my skeleton form.

Now, I just needed an excuse to go to city hall. I paced around the tiny room. *Think, think, think.* I stilled, remembering Caroline talking about getting a new manifest after her screen had cracked.

I pulled my manifest from my pocket, checked it again. Neither Jake nor any of Jake's family were listed yet. Time to move.

If Poppy from a month ago saw present-day Poppy, she wouldn't believe her eyes. But that Poppy hadn't known the fear of losing Jake for all eternity. She hadn't known how addictive his lips were, how warm his body was, how much she needed him.

Present-day Poppy? *Ha.* I didn't even flinch when I stepped outside, grabbed a rock twice the size of my hand, and smashed the manifest until the screen splintered and fizzled out. I threw the rock into the river and slipped the list back into my cloak. Now it was time to visit the city hall for the dead.

The building was long and wide, made of white brick and white mortar, giving it stodgy chic vibes. Dozens of reapers in robes weaved in and out of the hallways, wrapped up in work. I'd never had an office job when I was a human, but this seemed dismal.

I couldn't imagine going from a nine-to-five on Earth, then coming here and doing the same. Religion always portrayed the afterlife as restful. Maybe some people got a restful afterlife. Just not Grims.

I studied the map posted at the entrance. The technology desk was three doors down from the stairwell I needed. I would drop my manifest off, find an alcove to change out of my purple cloak, then access the restricted part of the building. I was the first to admit it wasn't a strong plan—Sylvia was much better at planning—but I was on my own for this.

When I approached the tech desk, a line of five reapers slouched ahead of me. I didn't recognize any of them, since I was usually on shift at this time. Even though the reaper in front of me was tapping their skeleton foot incessantly, a strange calm washed over me. There was a building map behind the desk, and I studied it. Counted the approximate steps between me and the restricted files room. Planned out different entrances and exits. When I reached the front, I was bouncing on the balls of my feet, ready to move.

"Problem?" The man behind the desk barked. He had only bothered to make his face human. He had my dad's bushing eyebrows, but otherwise looked like a complete stranger.

"Cracked screen?" I handed him my list.

His expression didn't change. He handed me a form and a pen. "Fill this out. A new device will arrive before your next shift."

"Next!" he yelled, dismissing me.

When I finished filling out the form, I placed it into the labeled basket, then made a show of looking around, as if I didn't know which way to go. With one final glance at the map, I turned the opposite way I came in and walked deeper into the building. Like offices I had seen on television, city hall had rows of artificial potted plants lining the hallways.

Fake plants provided the perfect cover for a change over. When the busy cross traffic slowed, I ducked behind a tall fern and pulled off both my cloaks, this time tucking the purple under the burgundy one. After straightening and smoothing the fabric, I merged into a line of people, then crossed the hallway when I reached the stairwell access door.

I swiped Dad's card, sending up a prayer of forgiveness. I didn't know if there was anyone listening to a reaper's prayers, but it was worth a shot. The light on the door went from red to green and I opened it and slipped inside. I paused and took a deep breath to steady my nerves, then rushed up two levels of stairs and into another hallway.

Two lefts and a right later, another set of stairs. Next, a series of hallways that felt like they would never end. After what felt like a thousand steps later, I was standing in front of the restricted records room. Within these walls was the list of every person who would die this year, including date and location. I swiped the card. Despite not having muscles, I was tense, waiting for the small red light on the lock to turn green.

The door buzzed a denial and stayed locked.

No. No, no, no. Not this close. I swiped again, but nothing happened. It was stupid to swipe a third time, but I did anyway, too desperate to be rational.

An alarm went off. *Shit.* Security appeared at both ends of the hall and walked toward me. I swiped a fourth time, fifth time, sixth time. "Keycard won't work," I said to the guards flanking me. "Oddest thing."

I may have gotten away with it if Dad didn't push through the group and stare at me, dumbfounded. He blinked twice before reaching out and taking the card from my hand and studying it, then looking back up at me. He didn't need to see my human face to know it was me. I could tell by his hurt and surprised expression as he tugged down my hood and sucked in a sharp breath as if I had punched him.

"I'm sorry, Dad," I whispered.

Chapter Twenty-Nine

Jake

ONE-HUNDRED-AND-SEVEN MINUTES AND forty-eight seconds later, we touched down in Hayvenwood, in a clearing with a spray-painted runway coated in dead leaves and light snow. I groaned. "I forgot winter has basically started here." I shivered, my thin long-sleeve shirt doing nothing to stop the wind.

Paris shook her head. "You knew we were coming to the UP."

"I forgot for a moment I lived in Michigan," I admitted. "I did get shot today."

"Flesh wound," she teased, even though her eyes were serious. She opened my duffle and grabbed a fleece. "Luckily, Sebastian thought ahead."

I smiled tightly. "Guess I'm going to have to be nice to him now."

A black SUV stopped in front of us, and a man with a tight buzz cut stepped out and nodded toward us. I gestured for Paris to take the lead. I was moving much slower.

"I'm Loren," he said.

Paris introduced herself, then me.

"Jake." I shook his hand. "Thank you for agreeing to help."

"I made my living out of hunting down impossible and terrible creatures. Anything I can do to help a fellow agent, I'm in." Loren gestured to the truck. "Get in. We'll meet the crew and go over the plan. My sister-in-law is going to try to feed you." He gestured to my leg. "She also makes a great pain-relieving cream with witch hazel. I'll grab you some."

"I'd appreciate that." Normally I hated when people gave me unsolicited advice for my chronic pain—no amount of yoga, kale, or meditation would help despite how many people suggested it—but Loren was former HQ. He'd no doubt known pain and seen his share of terrible injuries.

"Sorry if I overstepped. I know getting random suggestions must piss you off."

I lifted a shoulder. "Figured no one leaves HQ completely intact."

He gave a single laugh. "That's the truth."

I pulled myself into the passenger side and looked around the cab. "This was a SHAP vehicle, wasn't it?"

Loren nodded. "My brothers and I invested in it when we retired. We might be out of the hunting business, but that never stopped trouble from showing up on our doorstep."

He navigated the truck through a tiny downtown that was decorated for Halloween. Leaves hovered in the air and people waved at Loren from the sidewalk, as if we were in a romantic comedy instead of a rescue mission.

"Is it overstepping to ask why you retired?" I asked.

He glanced over and me, then back to the road. "It's a

story you already know too well. Spent every waking minute of my life doing missions to the detriment of myself and my family."

I nodded. I knew it *all* too well.

"Family trouble came here, I followed, reconnected with siblings and Raine—my now wife—and decided to stay. Don't regret my decision for a second."

He turned into the parking lot of a restaurant called Billy's Blues & BBQ. "My brothers and I bought this place and made a new life here." He pulled along the front curb and put the truck into park. "Now, I choose what missions I go on. For SHAP family, especially if there's a suspected internal leak? I'm all in. Let's catch these bastards."

He opened the truck door and climbed out. We followed, meeting him in front of a set of doors with a CLOSED FOR PRIVATE EVENT sign taped to the glass.

"This place will be our headquarters. We've already booked you rooms at the motel down the street, too," he explained as we followed him inside.

The bar was made of dark wood with bottles lining glass shelves behind it. The floor was large black and white tiles that led to a small stage with a baby grand piano. Flat-screen televisions hung over the bar and the walls held photos of the town in different seasons.

A buffet had been set up on top of the bar while a collection of people ladened with laptops and maps milled around pushed-together tables. Everyone looked at Loren when he walked in, straightening and hurriedly finishing sentences. It was clear he was the leader in this group, a roll he'd earned, not demanded.

A woman with white-blonde hair that faded to blue on the ends walked over, as gracefully as a dancer. Loren lit up from the inside out, and I knew she was his wife before she even said her name. "Hi, I'm Raine."

After we all exchanged names, Loren put his arm around her waist and kissed the side of her head.

We went deeper into the restaurant, meeting two men that were clearly Loren's brothers, Grayson and Fenton, and their wives, identical twins Hazel and Romi. The sisters both had dark hair with a silver streak—Hazel's was long and Romi's was shoulder length—and purple eyes. Hazel had a cherry blossom tattoo across her chest, making it easier to tell them apart.

Romi studied me for a long moment, then took one of my hands in both of hers. "You've touched death."

It wasn't a question, but an irrevocably true statement. "Yes."

"Rom, you're being freaky again," her twin said.

Romi blinked and released my hand. She laughed at herself and smiled, shaking her head. "Sorry. I was dead for a while. I get weird sometimes."

"Sometimes?" Hazel teased, but gave her a side hug, then turned to me. "You seem like the kind of person who can roll with weird."

"My roommate is the ghost of a Duke who died in the 1800s. I can roll with weird."

Hazel clapped once. "Excellent. Now sit and eat."

I looked at Paris. "We have a special diet in our group."

Fenton, Romi's partner, overheard and stuck his head out of the kitchen. "I can make almost anything." His blonde curls bounced with his enthusiasm and it was impossible not to be instantly charmed by him.

Paris bit her bottom lip, but then approached Fenton to speak to him. She handed him a sheet of paper and they started discussing meal options. I made a mental note to get a copy of the list.

"So," Grayson started, tucking his dark hair into a small low bun, then rotating his shoulders, ready to get down to business. "I hear you know a hybrid vampire?"

I nodded. "The daughter of the woman who ran Thinner."

"Is it true the venom can heal the body? Even as a hybrid?"

"Carma, the hybrid, fell off a ladder last week and broke her arm. She was completely healed twenty-four hours later."

Grayson let out a low whistle and shot Loren a look. "I can see why people are willing to die for this. Not full immortality, just enough to live your best human life."

Loren crossed his arms and looked down at his work boots for a long moment. "The moral implications are huge. Not just recreationally, but politically."

No one spoke for a long moment, taking in his words. I'd been so wrapped up in the minutia of the case, I hadn't dwelled on the big picture implications. "Which explains why we think this is a set up."

Loren's gray eyes moved to me. "So Paris mentioned." He gestured to the table. "Let's eat and talk details."

Fenton set a plate down in front of Paris, reviewing all the ingredients with her, and then joined the group as we filled our own plates. Paris and I shared everything we had learned about the warehouse and that we suspected someone inside SHAP to be involved. Once he finished eating, Loren lowered a large retractable screen and plugged in a laptop. "The closest theater is fifteen miles away, so we watch a lot of movies here," he explained.

I looked over at Paris, who was staring down at her half-eaten food. "Everything okay?" I asked.

She nodded, cleared her throat, then looked at Fenton. "I'm used to very bland food. This is wonderful, thanks."

I smiled. "Email me a list of foods you're allergic to, please. Just in case."

She blinked at me. "In case of what?"

"I dunno. Just feels like something I should have as a partner."

She nodded.

After a few more rounds of compliments to Fenton, who was an incredible cook, we focused on the screen. "This is an entire view of the town," Loren explained. "Can you think of any criteria to narrow it down?"

Paris held up a finger. "In the last month, our team has captured two dozen dealers and four distributors, along with nearly fifteen pounds combined of venom serum and a new venom powder we call Vixen. You only need about an ounce of venom to make a hybrid, which on average, an adult vampire below twenty-five years dead can produce three times a day. I estimate there would need to be ten vampires in or around the facility, plus the equipment to extract the venom and produce the powder. It would likely be a twenty-four-hour operation."

"Okay," Loren said. "Let's rule out campus housing, coops, freestanding retail stores, and restaurants that are currently operating." He began typing, and transparent gray boxes covered several areas over the town.

Paris leaned close and whispered, "Is it possible to have a crush on technology?"

"Are you blushing?" I teased, her cheeks going even darker at my comment.

"I just really enjoy algorithms, leave me alone," she shot back.

Loren finished inputting data and turned to us. "Anything else?"

"I'll double check," I offered, as I opened my phone and navigated to Carma's detailed report on the SHAP database. "Carma stated her mom had to find a *new source* last January, which she suspects meant new lab. Assuming a lab would take about a year to get up and running, I'd say look for property that sold within the last three to four years to start."

"I'm on it," Grayson said, typing into another laptop. "Hayvenwood's small. We don't do a lot of land sales here." He clicked a few more buttons, then looked at his brother. "Coordinates incoming."

Loren's computer pinged, and he started typing again. "Okay, the yellow highlights are the properties in question."

Fifteen yellow highlights appeared on the map. We could rule out six of them, as they fell within the gray boxes. "Okay, down to nine," I said. "Can we narrow down any further?"

Romi tapped her chin. "Building temp?"

Paris nodded. "Yes. The labs are probably running hot.

Can we cross check energy bills?"

The sounds of fingers flying over the keys filled me with hope. Were we really making headway? Could we get ahead of Fletcher?

Grayson clapped and let out a cheer. "These two properties have triple the amount of utilities used compared to the other seven. Incoming, bro."

Loren's computer dinged and he inputted the information. Two properties came up. He split his screen, then brought up street-level views. "Two's a good start."

Paris leaned forward. "Which utilities are they using more?"

Grayson checked his screen. "Left one, more electricity, right one more gas."

She nodded. "Start with the one using more gas. I bet the electricity one is a licensed grower." She gestured to the screen. "See? It's all fields, which would let them expand if they needed. The gas-high property is located along the tree line, offering more seclusion."

"That is why I picked you as my new partner," I said, matter-of-factly.

Her cheeks turned pink, but she smiled and nodded. "Thanks."

Loren stood. "Okay, let's get the drone out first and see if we can get a lay of the land before we move in."

Paris bit her lip at the word drone and practically hopped out of her chair. "I need to hear more about this drone."

My laugh turned into a sigh as I shifted my leg. I'd been sitting upright too long and would kill for a recliner.

"I have something that'll help with your pain," Hazel

promised.

"Only your physical pain, though," Romi added.

Hazel turned to face her. "Creepy. Again."

She smiled at me sadly. "I do hope I'm wrong."

I stared at her, all humor gone. "Me, too."

Chapter Thirty

Rule #52: A reaper who has disobeyed more than one rule may be subject to imprisonment, pending a formal investigation.

— The Reaper Code of Ethics, official handbook

Poppy

I F I HAD hair, I'd be pulling it out right now. The cell I'd been detained in prevented me from shifting into my human form. I had been stripped of my cloak, tagged with a barcode that would alert anyone with a scanner of my name, crimes, and arrest record, and was now a bare skeleton standing in an empty room that was about the size of a coffin. I couldn't stretch out fully in any direction. Worse yet, they had taken my sword and violin.

I wrapped my arms around myself, leaning my head against the back wall. It would've been worth it if I had found answers, if I had discovered a way to warn Jake, if I knew exactly how much time he had left. Instead, I'd swung and missed too early, and now I was benched before the final inning. I was so upset, I was using sports references. Daddy would've been so proud—for the sports references, not the whole stealing Dad's ID and ensuing subterfuge.

A tap on the door startled me and I straightened. There was the sound of scraping, then the door unlocked on a loud buzz. It slid open and my sister stood on the other side.

"Move!" she whispered. "Now! We don't have much time."

I was so used to following Sylvia's orders that I didn't stop to think about the consequences. I just grabbed her outstretched hand and let her pull me around the corner. I saw the keypad lock pried open, a cut wire hanging out.

"You hot-wired the door?" I whispered.

"Shush." She pulled off her purple cloak, leaving an identical one underneath. She handed me the top one.

I slipped into it, pulling the hood up. I looked like more of a visitor at first glance now that my skeleton wasn't hanging out. "Now what?"

She pointed at the door marked COUNSEL and took a step toward it.

I grabbed her arm and yanked her back. "Are you kidding me?!"

She rolled her eyes. "No. The Counsel is in session. We can sneak through the crowd."

I shook my head. "That is the dumbest thing I've ever heard."

Her hands gripped my arms. "They're going to banish you." She talked over my gasp. "They're counting stealing Dad's cloak and his ID as two separate charges, plus damaging your manifest, and they're counting each swipe of the card. Plus the suspension on top of it."

"How many charges?"

"Fourteen."

I swayed on my feet. Two meant suspension. Five meant relocation to maintaining the river duty, which was strenuous and tedious. But ten or more? That meant Isle of Exile. How could I be hit with fourteen charges?

"They know you went through the lists. At Sunday dinner," she said, as if reading my mind.

"How?" I didn't even bother denying it.

Her hands squeezed. "Because I reported it."

I shoved her away and took a step back. "You what?"

She tried to grab for me again, but I darted out of her grasp. "I was angry that you were being so stupid! I just wanted to teach you a lesson. I didn't realize—"

"That what? You'd get me exiled?" Betrayal burned a hole through my chest. If she hadn't reported the lists, I wouldn't be in danger of banishment. I ignored the voice in my head that told me it was my own fault for breaking basically every single code I could. "You're my sister. You're supposed to be on my side."

She covered my mouth with her hand and pulled me tight against the wall. I was pissed at her, but I wasn't stupid. We were perfectly still as I strained to hear voices emanating from further down the hall. It would only take a guard three seconds to realize I was no longer in my assigned room.

Sylvia cautiously removed her hand from over my mouth and whispered. "I'm sorry, I love you, argue with me after I get us out of here." She tugged me behind her.

If I'd had a heart, it would have been beating uncontrollably. Instead, it was as if a spring had taken its place, spiraling tighter and tighter. I worried that my skeleton might burst into shards at any moment.

We stayed low to the ground, close to the cell doors but below the windows so the other inmates couldn't easily spot us. We were fourteen feet away from the door when a guard rounded the corner and spotted us, blowing a warning whistle. Well, shit.

Sylvia grabbed my hand, ran for the door, and tore off the key-code panel. She sliced the two wires in a matter of seconds. The door unlocked and we were through before the guard had caught up with us. I gripped the handle and held the door shut as she repeated the process on the other side with the panel. This time she tied two wires together, then made a lock slide into place.

"Should I ask why you know how to do that?" I asked.

"Max." She looked around us, our antics not yet noticed in the bustling hallway, indicating a session had just let out. "Move."

We walked into the crowd as the alarm sounded that a prisoner was missing. There were cloaks of every color here, but there were still only about ten purple ones. They were going to catch us quickly if we didn't move fast.

Sylvia pulled us into an alcove that had a fake palm tree. She moved the pot away from the corner to reveal two tightly folded blue cloaks. I gaped at her.

She fit the blue one over her purple and I followed. I practically swam in mine, the sleeves double the length of my arms. If someone looked too closely, they'd know this was something borrowed. We didn't have time to worry about it.

"Move," she mouthed.

Despite the urge to run as fast as I could, I focused on keeping a steady pace as guards filled the hallway. "Get to your assigned spaces immediately!" a guard shouted.

The hallway was emptying, people veering off into offices and into the main Counsel room. "Do we have a plan?" I whispered, looping my arm through Sylvia's.

"Working on it."

I surreptitiously glanced around and then leaned my head closer. "It appears we only have two options. Risk seeing Dad or run."

Another guard narrowed their eyes at us as we passed, then fell into step a few feet behind us. "Dad will lose his spot on the Counsel if we get caught," she breathed.

I swallowed hard, a human reflex. I couldn't do that to Dad. He loved his job. I couldn't embarrass him. "Then I guess we're running. Straight through the exit door?"

Sylvia nodded. "Three...two...one..."

We took off at a dead run. My blue cloak was hiked up to my ankles, but I still wasn't moving fast enough. The guard behind us shouted and heavy footfalls were hot on our heels. I yanked off the blue fabric and tossed it behind me, nearly tripping the guard.

It wasn't enough. We needed a miracle to get us out of here.

"Find Anya!" Sylvia ordered, before yanking off both of her cloaks. "Have you been waiting for me this whole time?" she taunted, waving her arms and then rushing at the growing group of guards.

I wanted to scream, to turn around and grab her, but she had created just enough of a distraction to give me the upper hand. I wouldn't waste it. I pushed through the exit doors and made a hard left, hurrying into the foot traffic on the main road.

I slowed my pace, matching the speed of the reapers around me. The bell rang on top of the detention center and heads turned to look at the noise. "What's that mean?" someone next to me asked.

"I'm not sure," I lied. It was a primitive alert, rarely used. There wasn't a whole lot of serious crime and rule breaking in the afterlife. I, like always, was the exception.

"Dude, they're saying someone escaped lockup!" A reaper said a few rows behind me. "Boats aren't sailing in or out."

"Does that mean we get a shift off?" someone else asked.

"Risking thousands of souls for one reaper is a stupid idea, ethically speaking," a woman added.

That I agreed with. Allowing demons or other assorted monsters free access to human souls because they were after me—who had just been trying to look up a name on a computer—was a rude awakening about afterlife priorities. Maybe Sylvia could talk some sense into them.

As we approached the docks, the group turned in unison. The crowd morphed into a sort of line as guards asked each reaper to lower their hood. *Shit.* I had a skeleton with a barcode and a human face that was easily recognizable.

I turned around and pretended to wave at someone further back in the line—confusing a few people—then started shuffling back. "I'll come your way!" I called cheerfully to my fake friend.

When I was out of the line, I walked along the river's edge, pretending I was simply out for a stroll. I scanned the water, trying to figure out how I was supposed to find Anya when there were no boats going out. I was running out of time.

A rock the size of my fist hit my shin and I gasped, jumping back. It hadn't hurt, but it had startled me. Another rock followed the trajectory of the first, and I dodged out of the way before inching toward the bank and peering over the large boulders that guarded the river's edge.

Anya looked up and waved for me to jump down. My shoulders sagged in relief. I looked around, then navigated my way over the rocks, making the six-foot drop to the scrap of sandy riverbank below. "Ready for Plan B?" she asked.

"This is already Plan B? What was Plan A?"

"Plan A was to calmly and casually sail you to the human portal, shove you through, and hide you there until we got shit straightened out here."

That was a good plan. "So what's Plan B?"

"Hope we can frantically speed sail you to the human portal, shove you through, and hide you there until we get shit straightened out here."

I opened my mouth to argue, but I had no alternative ideas. "How do we do that?" I managed. "They've stopped the boats."

"They've only stopped the boats they can see."

I stared at her. "And you've discovered a cloak of invisibility?"

She shot me a look, not appreciating my sarcasm. "No, we're taking a canoe. We just have to walk it out a ways first." She gestured to the shore behind her at the small, two-person boat that some reapers used for fishing.

"How are we going to get down the river without someone seeing?"

"Hence the walk out."

I shook my head. "I'm not following."

"Underwater."

"The more you explain, the less I understand."

She huffed and pulled off her cloak, balling it up and shoving it behind a rock. "Cloak off." I replicated her movements, then met her at the boat. She shoved it out into the water, wading in up to her knees.

She flipped the boat over, so the bottom was facing up. "Now we just walk underwater for a bit. Watch out for the soul suckers. They like to chew on skeleton bones."

I shook my head. "Uh, I didn't finish my physics class in high school, but can confirm this is impossible."

She put her hand on her hip. "Do we really have time to stand here and discuss how the physics of the River Styx on this side of the divide, combined with intention, is different from the human world? Or do you want to get out of here before they find you and banish both of us?"

I ran into the water, splashing louder than was wise. "Let's move."

We walked until the water was up to our chins, then took our positions underneath the boat, hanging on to the sides. As Anya predicted, the boat followed us down as we continued to walk along the riverbed. My skeleton feet sank into the sand, nearly up to my ankle, as if it were trying to keep me from floating up.

It was unnerving, but the sand released me with every step. This close to the surface, the diffused ambient light allowed us to check for any creatures ready to latch on and not release. As we journeyed deeper and darker, we were relying on hope and luck.

A ghost mermaid pod swam by. Mermaids had been hunted to extinction on Earth and tended to stay far away from shore as a result. I was surprised they were hanging around the river's edge, although they may have just been doing a drive-by for the local gossip. They didn't bother the reapers, so the reapers didn't bother them. They were only a danger to souls that went for a swim.

The mermaids, like any soul-hunters, did much better near the human world portals, especially near the loading docks. At the beginning of the journey, souls would try anything to be reunited with their bodies, including jumping out and attempting to swim back to the human world. Wasn't a great idea. Without a reaper, souls couldn't break through the barrier back into the human world anyway, leaving them vulnerable.

Anya's steps slowed and stopped as we approached a drop off. It was as if someone used a ruler and drew a line bisecting the river. Two more steps and all remaining light dissolved into inky darkness. She turned toward me and released one side of the boat. She made a little hopping motion and pointed upward.

I nodded, understanding. She counted down with her fingers. Three...two...one. We both jumped while simultaneously doing our best to flip the boat over.

It would've worked perfectly if something hadn't grabbed my ankles and pulled me back down.

Chapter Thirty-One

Jake

THE SUN WAS low in the sky as we inched toward the trees that guarded the property. The branches were nearly devoid of leaves, and one more fall rainstorm would likely purge the rest. The drone had captured enough of the property and surrounding generators to confirm it was likely our target. The moment we set foot on the property, I *knew*.

While I hadn't gotten any dominant supernatural genes—like the supernatural genes manifesting in my niece—I still was sensitive to the unseen world around me. When Romi's arm went out in front of Hazel to stop her from stepping into the forest, I recognized the same warning in my gut.

"I don't like this," Romi said into our earpieces, voice low. "There's something not right with these woods. Don't go too deep."

"Roger," Loren said. "Let's do a perimeter sweep, but don't cross the boundary of these trees."

I scanned the ground with my flashlight, the thick blanket of leaves and mud making it almost impossible to see if there were any hidden access doors. Smart. I hit the ground with my cane before I took a step, making sure I wasn't about to fall into a trap.

When my cane snapped a wire, launching a leaf-filled net into the air and dangling from a tree, we all froze, waiting for an alarm or a response. A squeak of a door followed.

"Probably caught an animal again!" someone shouted.

"Get in the trees," Loren ordered.

Paris and I exchanged a look. She understood my silent communication. I couldn't use my leg to climb a tree. She quickly scanned the area and pointed to a tree three rows in. Further in than Romi had advised, but desperate times.

I moved as fast as I could over a slippery surface with a mud-covered cane, then hooked the handle around a low-hanging branch. Pushing off with only my right leg, I hopped up until my hands went around the branch and lifted myself up using my arms. I bit down on my tongue to keep from making a noise, even though I was pretty sure I'd torn my stitches.

Paris jumped onto the other side of the tree, climbing up as if she spent hours in trees every week. After making sure she was secure, I looked around. Everyone else had disappeared. Good.

The back door closed with a bang and a flashlight beam proceeded the shuffling of footsteps. A man, about six foot, with a beard and baggy clothing stepped into view. At first glance he looked almost harmless, but there was something about the way he moved. Smooth and light.

Like a hybrid.

I held my breath as he reached down and picked up a large stick, then poked at the trap. The leaves caught inside rained down, exposing the empty net. A twig snapped behind me and to the left and I bristled. The man stilled and tilted his head, the flashlight beam going across the trunk of the tree, barely missing the branch I laid on. "Fucking squirrels," the man grumbled.

His walkie-talkie bleeped and a woman's voice came through. "Need you in the lab."

He swore again and grabbed his device. "Gotta reset the trap first."

"Trap can wait. Vamp horde has arrived for milking."

More swearing. "Be right there." I didn't even breathe as he walked back to the house.

As soon as the door closed, I blew out a breath. "That sounds like confirmation."

"Agreed," Loren responded. "Let's get out of here."

Paris dropped to the ground as silent as a cat, then turned to me. She grabbed my cane as Loren moved in front of me. "I'll grab your waist."

No wonder this guy was HQ. He instinctively knew what a mission needed. "I'm not a lightweight."

"Neither am I." He winked.

I nearly laughed as I lowered myself by my arms and he grabbed my waist. I let go and landed on the ground without jarring my hip. "Thanks. Probably tore my stitches."

"I can resew them with my eyes closed."

I took my cane from Paris, who was staring wide-eyed between Loren and me. "What?"

"I'm not usually attracted to men," she blurted. "But men who work together without ego, I dunno, just hits different."

I winked at her. She stuck her tongue out at me, then turned on her heel, walking toward the tree line. I had to admit Loren was exactly the sort of person I'd be attracted to, if he wasn't married and I wasn't in love with Poppy.

"Will the three of you stop flirting and get moving?" Romi ordered. "I don't feel good."

Her words sobered us as we moved through the trees. I knew without asking that Romi not feeling good meant something other than physical discomfort. I could move fast with my cane, but I couldn't run. Especially on wet leaves and mud at dusk.

We shifted away from the house, toward the end of the property where we had parked the truck. Another snap of a branch and Romi froze, looking to her right as if she could see in the dark. "That's unfortunate."

"What?" Loren asked.

A growl emanated from just beyond the tree line. A wolf pushed through the withering leaves, his golden eyes level with mine. Werewolves were big, but I had yet to see one that was as tall as a truck.

Paris breathed an expletive.

"Get out of there!" Loren ordered.

"He's faster than us," Romi said. "Got your gun?"

I pulled out my handgun, the wolf growling at my movement. Would the bullet even slow him down? The wolf took another step toward us, moving slightly to the left. A second pair of eyes emerged from the darkness. Then a third.

"Anyone got dog treats?" I asked, taking a step back as the creatures moved closer.

"We don't have records of hostile wolf packs in Hayvenwood," Loren explained. "Whatever these creatures are, they aren't ours."

I released the safety on my gun. "I've got five rounds. I can maybe buy us some time."

"I've got six," Loren added. "We may make it."

"Eleven bullets and three wolves."

"I have three tranq darts and four bullets. Wolves this size probably need two darts and ten minutes each." Paris added. "And there are four wolves."

"Fuck," Loren spat. "Make that six. I've got two flanking me."

"These are some impressive guard dogs," Romi murmured.

"Is there any scenario here where we aren't dog food?" Paris asked.

"Yes," I said, taking a deep breath as the wolves circled us. There was still a small pathway forward. "On the count of three, you fucking run."

"This is a terrible plan," Paris warned.

"Give me your gun," I ordered. She hesitated and I grabbed it from her hand.

"Three…" I said.

"If we live through this, I'm going to kill you myself," Paris warned.

"Two…"

"Jake—" Loren interrupted.

"One…"

Chapter Thirty-Two

Rule #25: In the rare event of a lockdown, no reaper is allowed to exit Isle of Grim.

— The Reaper Code of Ethics, official handbook

Poppy

I WAS LUCKY that without working lungs, I couldn't drown. Of course, it wasn't drowning I was worried about. Water rushed around me as whatever had my ankle pulled me deeper. I frantically fought back against their hold, kicking and trying to lean down to pry off their grip.

I couldn't see at all, everything was black. My fingers glanced off the large hand and no amount of screaming or thrashing seemed to make a difference. My panic morphed into dread.

This was going to be bad. Like really bad. Maybe if Anya—no. There'd be no rescue. I was wanted and charged with banishment. No one was on their way to help me.

I hadn't wanted to be a reaper anymore, but not like this. My daydreams were of me ending up with Jake somehow, living the life we should've had. *Jake.* At least once I was snuffed of existence, I wouldn't miss him anymore. I closed my eyes and tried to think of every good memory we had shared.

The way his lips felt on mine, how warm I was in his arms, the sound of his laugh, the way his eyes glittered when he was happy. I let myself fall into the memories. At some point, I would either be dead or released long enough to fight back. I refused to live my last moments in fear and panic.

I wanted to live them in love.

My chest burned with emotions as we started to slow. I opened my eyes, preparing for my chance, only to see through the water. We were nearing the surface. *What was going on?*

Without warning, I was unceremoniously launched out of the water. I screamed when I broke the surface, then dropped like a dead weight onto a small shore. I sucked in another scream when something—no, someone—landed next to me.

Anya rose from the sand, stared at me wide-eyed and launched herself at me, hugging me hard. "Oh my god, oh my god."

"What happened?" I asked, completely confused. We separated and both turned to the water to find the pod of mermaids who had passed by us earlier.

"Thank you for the music," one of them said, and *poof*, they were gone.

My mouth opened and closed, but nothing came out.

"Music?" Anya asked.

"I played at the old pier," I explained, as I got to my feet and climbed up the bank, peering over the rocks. To my left was a portal to the human world, to my right, a boat dock with an empty boat. "They brought us to a portal."

Anya stood next to me. "Whoa. They saved your life."

I laughed in disbelief. "Wish they would've told me before I had to come to terms with my own death. Again."

She wrapped me in her arms. "Get out of here. I'll take the boat back." She stepped back but held onto my shoulders for a long moment, as if committing me to memory. "We'll figure it out, okay? We'll get you back."

I nodded. "I have complete faith."

And with one last hug, I took off running. I leaped through the door and tumbled into the human world, skidding across damp grass. I stood on shaking legs, then looked down at my hands and feet, making sure my human glamour was in place.

I was here. I'd made it. I looked back over my shoulder to make sure I wasn't being followed, then started running. I'd never been away from the reaper world for more than four hours, and definitely not without my cloak, sword, and violin before. I needed to find Jake and get to safety.

It was nearly dark, a full moon creeping over the horizon. Headlights washed over me, but no one could see a barefooted, soaking wet reaper running down the sidewalk. When I reached the ice cream shop, I made a hard left toward Jake's place. I concentrated hard on him, trying to latch on to his location so I could just appear there. I didn't feel him. No pulling in my chest, no unshakable certainty that he was alive and well.

I ran faster.

What if something had happened to him? What if while I was locked inside that coffin of a room, he had died? What if I missed saying good-bye? What if I was too late?

I launched myself in front of Jake's condo, pounding on the door as I crossed through the wall. "JAKE!" I screamed.

Sebastian and Reggie looked up at me from the floor, where they were lying on top of the couch cushions. I stopped, staring. Surely if something had happened to Jake they wouldn't be doing...whatever this was. "Where's Jake?"

"Poppy?" Sebastian sat up, pushing back his blond hair. "What are you doing here?"

"Got in trouble, banished, escaped, and so on. Where's Jake? Is he okay?"

"Sí, Esqueleto. He and Paris went to Hayvenwood up north. Got a lead on the case." He sat up and stared at me.

"Where's your cloak?" Sebastian asked. "What happened to you?"

"I tried to break into the main computer system to find out if Jake was on the master death list, got caught, put in jail, they took my cape and my sword and my violin, then I was banished, which means like the end of my existence, but my sister broke me out and after that, my cousin and a pod of merpeople got me to the other side of the River Styx without anyone noticing and I just tumbled through a portal." It all came out in one breath.

They both blinked at me, not moving for a long moment. "I don't even know how to respond to this," Sebastian admitted.

"What are you two doing?" I asked.

Reggie gestured to the television. "He's Jack and I'm Rose, but I make room for him on the door and create enough buoyancy by putting my life jacket underneath."

I looked at the screen to catch the scene in *Titanic* where Rose laid on the door singing to the night. "So much room on that door."

"Precisely," Sebastian added.

"How do I get to Hayvenwood?" I asked, turning back to them. "Can you take me?"

They both shook their heads in unison. "We can't go more than ten miles from our home base," Reggie explained.

"Can you just transport there?" Sebastian asked.

I lifted my shoulder. "I'm not sure. We always just appeared where we were working, or I concentrated on finding Jake and was able to just poof wherever he was. But I can't feel him. I don't know if something's wrong or if he's too far away."

Sebastian was already on his feet, pulling out a drawer on the coffee table. He tried to grab something from inside and grunted when it fell through his fingers. Reggie reached in and grabbed it for him, then unfolded it on the floor. A map of Michigan lay stretched out in front of us.

It had highlights and pen marks, and the creases of the map were worn. This had definitely been used over and over again. I knelt and started searching for the town. I wasn't sure if a map was going to help, but it couldn't hurt. "Where is it? Any ideas?"

"Somewhere near the Mackinac Bridge?" Reggie said. "I don't remember how far, but I know it's north."

I skimmed over the lower peninsula of Michigan and into the upper, reading and rereading the tiny letters, trying to find the name. "Why can't I find it?" I shouted, mostly to the map.

Sebastian's finger pointed at a tiny pencil dot with an H next to it. "This is probably it."

"I don't know if I can travel three hundred miles," I admitted. "I don't even know if I can travel three."

Reggie reached out and grabbed my hand. "You can stay with us until Jake gets back. Or we can go to Mina's place. She and Carma are in a safe house with Jake's family. We might be more protected there."

"I must admit," Sebastian added, "I don't know how we could protect you from other reapers. But we shall try."

I nodded. It would be nice to spend time with the two of them. I opened my mouth to agree when something familiar pulled at me. Not the reaper clock directing me to find a soul, but the same pull I had when Jake was in imminent danger.

I pressed my hand to my chest and looked at them wide-eyed. "He's in trouble. Jake's in trouble!" I stood, panicking. I closed my eyes and tried to pinpoint him, tried to find a connection to him, but it was like I was still underwater. There were too many miles between us. "*Argh*, this isn't working!"

Sebastian pushed to his feet. "Perhaps you need something of his to hold, something that connects you to him?"

"Yes!" I took off running down the hall, the ghosts right behind me. I jumped onto his bed and pressed my full hand against the poppy painting, the textures of the petals pressing into my palm. I closed my eyes and thought of the first time that I saw it, the way it made me feel like I was floating in the clouds yet anchored to home.

I thought of the way Jake whispered "kiss me," the way

his warm breath moved over my skin. Then I recalled his heartbeat. The strong, rhythmic sound that was the most beautiful music I had ever heard.

I locked on his position.

With a flicker, I was gone.

Chapter Thirty-Three

Jake

"I THOUGHT YOU said you had a plan?" Paris shouted after I shot at the red wolf, then grabbed her arm and started running. Well, quickly limping.

"The plan is running."

"I throw you over my shoulder on the count of three."

I took a step to the left as a red wolf eased closer, his hot, damp breath washing over me. There was no way these were regular werewolves. I clicked the button on my watch. "You won't be fast enough carrying me."

She shifted her stance, so we were shoulder to shoulder. "Well, I'm not leaving you here."

My watch buzzed and I risked glancing down. "What the…?"

"What?"

"It says werewolf and vampire hybrid? Wolf hybrids?"

"What do you mean wolf hybrid?" Paris asked.

I stared at the wolf directly in the eyes, silently challenging it. Just as I wanted, it let out a blood-curdling growl, exposing its teeth. And its vampire fangs.

"They're vampire-werewolf hybrids," I surmised. "They

must be milking wolves as well as humans."

The red wolf lunged at me, taking me to the ground with the force of a truck. My gun went flying and I lost my breath as the weight of its paw crashed down on my chest. I couldn't breathe. The wolf lowered its head and opened its jaws, and I closed my eyes. At least if I died right now, I'd get to see Poppy again. Just one last time.

Someone whistled and snapped their fingers, and the wolf hesitated, then looked to the side. With a grumble, it backed up, leaving me gasping for air. A spotlight shined directly onto my face.

"What are you doing here?"

I blinked and pushed myself up on my elbows to see the man who had checked the net waving an automatic weapon at me. "Just on an evening hike. Seems I crossed over into wolf territory."

"With two of your closest friends?"

"We're majoring in environmental sciences at Hayvenwood University?" Paris claimed, raising her voice and making everything sound like a question. "Our TA told us to go on a night hike?"

"This is private property. You're trespassing."

"Oh man," Loren said in a voice so much higher than his own I nearly didn't recognize it. "We're sorry, bud."

"If you're students," he asked, "why'd I hear gun fire?"

"My daddy always taught me to carry a gun in the woods," Paris explained. "Bears."

"We'll leave right away," Loren added.

"Afraid I can't let that happen." He motioned with his gun. "I need all three of you to put your guns on the ground and then stand slowly. These guys haven't had their evening meal yet, in case you were wondering."

Three of us? I dropped my gun on the ground. With one hand up, I reached for my cane while turning to the left. Romi was gone. I concentrated on keeping my face devoid of any thoughts or emotions, even though hope beat in my chest. Maybe she had a plan to get us out of this mess.

I reached out a hand to Paris and motioned for her to come to me. "It seems I tweaked my leg in the fall. Can you help me up?"

"Why are you hiking with a bad leg?" the man asked, suspicion coating his words.

"Doc says I gotta exercise it," I explained. "Didn't know I'd get pounced on by a large animal."

The man grunted in response but lowered his rifle. Paris ran over to me, pretending to fuss. "Give me your tranq gun," I whispered as she bent down low.

She shook her head once, her eyes wide. She shifted and I saw the handle of the gun peeking out from her side holster. She grabbed both of my wrists to help pull me up, making a big show of it. Then, as she released my right wrist, I grabbed the gun, shoved her behind me, and shot two tranquilizers into the man's neck, then used my cane to knock the weapon out of his hand.

He dropped the gun and fell to his knees, the formula working ten times as fast as commercially available tranquilizers. As a hybrid, it wouldn't last long, but it would buy us time.

"Run!" I ordered. The wolves were distracted by the man lying on the ground, and we got a few second head start.

"Jake!" Paris grabbed me around the waist and hauled me onto her shoulder then started running. "If we live through this, I'm going to kill you myself."

"You would've done the same thing if you had the shot!"

She grunted a response.

"How are you carrying me? I weigh twice as much as you."

"I'm more than just a pretty face!"

"Never said you weren't." She shifted me and stumbled but quickly righted herself. "You'd be twice as fast on your own."

"Not leaving you behind."

I looked up as the wolves snarled, the entire pack focused on our retreating forms. *Fuck.* "Hey, Loren?"

"Yeah?" he called from the left.

"Grab Paris and haul her out of here, okay?"

Paris's arms tightened. "What—"

I rolled out of her arms and Loren scooped her up in a nearly identical hold, then took off with Paris struggling and shouting at me. My vision blurred with the pain of hitting the ground, and I sucked in a deep breath, trying to clear it. I grabbed my cane, which Paris had dropped when I fell, and pulled out the knife. It was about half the size of a sword, and probably wouldn't do much against these monsters. But I was going to leave some marks on the way out.

The red one launched at me and I held the knife in one hand, the weighted end of the cane in the other, and aimed for its neck. A flash of pink shot in front of me, the knife gone from my hands. I stumbled back as step as Poppy appeared in front of me, knife raised as if it were her sword.

She wasn't wearing a robe and was in skeleton form. "Touch him and die," she warned at the wolves. The red wolf hit the ground only inches away from her, then backed up, growling. "I know a few demons who like the taste of dog."

I turned at the flash of headlights and squealing tires. A black truck with the window down cut through the woods and stopped dead only a few feet away. *Romi.*

"I got Loren and Paris, let's go!" she ordered.

I grabbed Poppy by the waist and hobbled to the truck. I shoved her in, then followed.

Romi pulled out of the woods, clipping the driver's side mirror on a low-hanging branch. When we made it to the main road, she glanced at me in the rearview mirror. "Ah, yes. You're death."

Poppy's head shot up from my chest and turned toward Romi. "You can see me?" she asked, shifting to her human form at the same time I questioned "You can see her?"

Romi bobbed her head, not really yes or no. "I can't see her physical form, with my human eyes, but I can see her with my mind."

Loren looked into the back seat, then back to Romi. "You've gotten even weirder since your whole trip to hell."

"Yeah, love you too," she shot back.

"Trip to hell?" Paris asked.

"It's a long story," Romi explained. "I'll tell you later."

Loren held up his hand and pointed at me and Poppy. "I'm not playing with death again." He pointed at Romi. "She gave me my first gray hair. I'm too young for gray hairs."

"She's not death," I explained. "She's a grim reaper."

Loren looked pained. "That's even worse. Why are you hanging out with a grim reaper?"

Poppy lifted her head and waved, laughing awkwardly. "Well, technically I've been suspended from my reaper duties and am currently on the run, so if we see any reapers, don't worry, they're more of a threat to me than they are to you."

"What?" I asked. "We need to talk about this."

"Later," she whispered.

I relayed what she said to the group.

"Surprisingly that doesn't make me feel better," Loren mumbled. "Fine, but if I'm going to die, make sure my wife knows it wasn't my fault. She'll do a séance just to give me an ass chewing."

Romi clucked her tongue. "I'm so telling Raine you said that."

"I'll return your Christmas present."

"You shouldn't piss off a witch," she whisper-yelled. "She could turn your dick into a cactus or something."

He laughed once. "Try something and see what Raine does."

Paris looked over at me. "I'm pissed at you. I had it under control. But since you lived, I guess we're fine."

I nodded once, seriously. "I'm sorry that I doubted you."

She nodded back. "Poppy, why were you able to stop the wolves?" She was looking at me when she asked it, since she was unable to see Poppy.

Poppy was pushing the knife back in the cane. "Wolves—werewolves—are terrified of reapers. We're viewed as the highest on the food chain. I can't take a werewolf's soul unless they're ready to die, but they're a superstitious group."

"Thank you," I whispered, before translating for Paris.

Paris looked around me, although more at the door than at Poppy. "Thank you, Poppy."

"Now that we seemingly have a secret weapon," Loren said, "we need to figure out our next plan."

It was going to be a long night.

Chapter Thirty-Four

Rule #6: It is absolutely imperative a reaper does not spend more than four hours away from Isle of Grim...

— The Reaper Code of Ethics, official handbook

Poppy

I HADN'T HAD to actively worry about time for twelve years, but the press of each hour, each minute, each second grew heavier as the four-hour mark of my escape encroached. Would something happen to me? Would it come and go without notice? Would it hurt?

I glanced at the clock again. One hour and eighteen minutes left. I turned back to Jake, checking that he was still okay. We had made it to Billy's in one piece and recounted the story for a worried Grayson, Hazel, Raine, and Fenton.

"I'm coming with you tomorrow," Grayson said. "I'm still a decent hunter."

"Should we call in a SHAP team?" Romi asked. "Even with the leak, it's risky without it."

Loren and I said *no* at the same time. "This will be in vain if they get the Vixen before we do," I explained. "It's us or nothing."

No one bothered to argue. Loren had restitched Jake's

bicep, and Hazel had slathered something on the wound and given him a tube of something else to help with his leg.

While they were twins, Hazel's powers seemed to concentrate on the holistic spells—including healing potions—whereas Romi's powers were more about reading spaces and people. And seeing death, apparently. I wanted to ask her if she could see Jake's death, if these were the final few hours I'd have with him. I wanted to ask what happened to her, how she and Fenton made it work while she was dead, but I didn't have the courage. Not with Jake having to translate.

After another hour of throwing out potential backup plans, Loren ran his hand down his face and blinked hard. "We should get some rest. I'm wiped. We'll meet at oh-eight-hundred tomorrow to finalize a plan."

"I checked you into the hotel," Hazel said. "We got two rooms since I wasn't sure if you wanted your own space."

"Thanks." Paris gave Jake a smile. "I think you need to talk to Poppy more than you do me."

He nodded.

Loren stood. "Come on, I'll give you a ride."

Without much fanfare, we stood, and I followed Jake to the truck. I wasn't used to walking everywhere, but it seemed appropriate right now. The night was chilly, and I missed my cloak. Without it I felt even colder, especially my bare feet. It wasn't that I could feel the pavement, but my body registered the impact of moving across the cool ground.

It only took five minutes to get to the motel and as Jake and I walked into the tired but clean motel room, I crossed the four-hour mark. I watched the clock intently as a full minute passed. I looked down at my hands, rotating and flexing them. Then I pressed my palms to my face in several different spots. I bounced up and down on the balls of my feet, relieved that my legs were holding steady.

Jake dropped a bag on a chair and turned to face me. "You okay?"

Another minute passed. No sharp tug in my chest.

"Yeah. Yeah, I'm okay." I gave him a small smile. "Just haven't been in the human world longer than four hours since I became a reaper. Glad to see nothing bad happened."

He walked over and gave me a tight hug and I relaxed into his chest. He kissed my forehead, then leaned back, tucking my hair behind my ear. "I need to clean up. Can you give me a few minutes? Then we'll talk."

I nodded, grateful for the small break to regroup. While he showered, I sat on the edge of one of the queen beds, trying to calm my nerves. My fingers itched to play the violin again, to take these emotions and channel them into something tangible.

My chest burned like I needed to cry. I had lost contact with my entire family barely four hours ago. In all my years dreaming about spending a whole day with Jake, I never thought about the opposite side of the wish. Would I ever get to apologize to my parents? Would I ever get to hug my sister again? Was I going to be stuck in this in-between forever?

And what about when something happened to Jake? Because as much as I wished he could live forever, he was human and very mortal. I pulled my knees up to my chest and rested my chin on them.

"You used to do that pose when you were too tired to

cry," Jake said.

I startled and looked up. He was wearing a towel low on his waist, his damp hair messy, his eyelashes darker than usual. I hadn't seen him bare-chested and in the light since I was human, and my mouth fell open.

"Whoa," I breathed. Gone was his lean teenage body, replaced by sculpted arms and wide shoulders. A tattoo over his left pec peeked out over a dusting of dark hair that spread over his chest and narrowed down into a trail that disappeared below the towel. "What's your tattoo say?"

The corner of his lips lifted. "I'm surprised you don't recognize it."

Eyes on his chest, I slid off the bed and walked over to him. The floor fell out from beneath me when I recognized the cursive letters from the secret notes I used to leave him in the treehouse. *Love you forever.* My eyes flew to his. "Jake…"

He put his hands on my waist and pulled me into him. Lowering his mouth to just above mine, he whispered. "My heart's always been yours, Poppy." He sealed the words with a kiss.

The moment his lips touched mine, I wrapped my arms around his neck, standing on my tiptoes to kiss him harder. I'd almost lost him, lost this. I tightened my grip and deepened the kiss. What if this was the last one? Or the next one?

Jake flinched and leaned back, breaking the kiss. "Sorry, need to try some of Hazel's cream. Sore."

I laughed off my desperation. "Yeah, sure. Of course."

He grabbed a pair of boxers and the cream and shuffled slowly to the bed. He sat down and put his legs through the boxers, pulled them up, and removed his towel. Then he slathered some of the cream on his hand and leaned on his right side, rubbing it into his left hip.

I walked over and knelt down in front of him, picking up the cream and putting some on my own hand. When he nodded his consent, I began rubbing into his calf and moving up to his knee. A strange cooling sensation covered my hands, and the smell of peppermint burned my nose. I frowned. I usually couldn't feel or smell objects in the human world. Jake had been the exception. It probably had something to do with it being a magic-based formula.

When we were done, Jake wiped his hands on his towel, and handed it to me to do the same. Then he reclined in the bed and I just stared. His body stretched out, clad only in boxers. I hadn't seen this much of Jake in twelve years. "God, you're beautiful," I whispered.

He smiled and patted the bed next to him. "Come here."

I hurried around to the other side of the bed, slipping in and resting my head on his chest. I closed my eyes and listened to his heartbeat, steady as always. "I missed this."

"Me, too." He wrapped his arm around me, his fingers playing with the end of my hair. "You said a lot of things back in the forest."

I nodded, kissing his chest, but didn't answer. I didn't want to ruin this moment with my story.

"Poppy, what happened?"

I was silent for a long moment, afraid to tell him and break this peace. "We can talk tomorrow, after your mission is done."

"I think we need to talk now, love." He leaned forward

and kissed the top of my head. "Tell me."

I blew out a long breath and told him, starting at the moment I left Sylvia to save his life and finishing at finding him in the woods. His heartbeat was no longer slow and steady but pounding hard, as if he was chasing someone. I pushed myself up to look at him. "Jake?"

He sat up. "You told me very specifically that me seeing you had nothing to do with me dying. Yet you risked your very existence to research that exact thing."

"I had to know!" I explained, choosing not to admit that just seeing him was already risking my entire existence. What was a little B&E on top of that? "What if I had been wrong? What if there was something I could do that would stop it? If only I had gotten into the main computer room—"

"Poppy!" he interrupted. "The most important thing to me is the people I love. I'm okay with not knowing when and how I will die. What I'm not okay with is you were almost banished from literal existence, and you lied to me about it! Just like you didn't trust me enough to tell me that you were a reaper."

It was as if a gunshot went off. All the ambient noise in the room went silent. The leftover drip of the showerhead, the whirl of the heater, the footsteps and closing doors of people in neighboring rooms. His accusation hung heavy between us, as if he had carved the words out of the air. "Jake…"

"Poppy, why didn't you tell me?"

"I couldn't."

"Couldn't? Or wouldn't?"

"Both. Neither. I wasn't allowed. And even if I was…"

"You still wouldn't have, would you?"

"No."

He swung his legs over the side of the bed, his back facing me. I wanted to reach over and wrap my arms around him, make him understand why I didn't, why I couldn't tell him.

"Why don't you trust me? I would have done anything—"

"Exactly. If you knew, you would have been obsessed with trying to stop it or coming with me."

He turned and looked at me over his shoulder. "Was coming with you an option?"

I shook my head. "No. Not for you."

He ran his hands through his hair, the aggravated sweeps leaving it sticking up in multiple directions. "Why not?"

"Because you deserved a long, happy, fulfilling life. Anyway, we weren't legally married, so the reapers wouldn't have invited you to join."

"Your parents weren't legally married, either. Same sex marriage wasn't recognized in Michigan until after you became a reaper. So try again."

"Your age."

"I was eighteen. Legally an adult. Next."

Dammit. He was right. "Okay yes, there are exceptions. There has to be paperwork filed stating you are in a committed relationship, and even if human laws don't recognize the union, reaper laws do. They don't discriminate."

"So what's the real reason?"

"Because I knew if I told you, you would do anything to come with me. And I couldn't let Eliza grow up without her big brother; I couldn't let your folks lose their son because of me. I couldn't carry the guilt of being the reason you weren't able to see your mom in the afterlife."

"You didn't even give me a choice!" he shouted.

I stood on the bed. "I never get the luxury of making choices, Jake! It's all I've ever wanted my entire existence is to make a goddamn choice about my own life! This was the only one I ever got to make."

My hair fell in front of my face and I tugged it back. "I've always known my endgame was being a reaper. I spent my life waiting for the call, and when it happened, I had to do a job I hated for literally eternity. You would hate it, too. But I had the choice to save your life and give you a peaceful afterlife."

"Poppy—"

"I will always and forever make the same choice. Even if it means giving you up. So I'm sorry that sixteen-year-old me didn't tell you because it made it hurt more, but I'm not sorry that you got to continue living your life and will get to be free in your afterlife. I'll never be sorry."

He stared at me, searching my face for a long moment. Then, he reached out, grabbed my knees, and pulled me down to the bed. He rolled on top of me, his hands lifting my arms over my head, and kissed me like it was our last kiss, like he wanted to permanently tattoo the feeling of it on my lips.

I arched into him, and he released my arms. I touched him everywhere I could reach, skating down his back, up his spine, over his broad shoulders. Jake's hands moved over my waist and his fingers went under my shirt to touch the sensitive skin of my stomach. We both stilled.

He lifted his head to look at me. "I thought you couldn't remove your clothing."

I looked down at his hand. "I've never been able to before. Maybe it's something to do with being in the human world so long." I lifted my arms and he slowly raised the shirt up, exposing human skin I hadn't seen in twelve years. I had refused to wear a bra—I wasn't going to wear underwire for eternity—yet I was still shocked when my bare breasts were exposed. With one more tug, the shirt was gone. He sucked in a sharp breath.

I raised my gaze to his and smiled. "Kiss me."

Jake's eyes went molten as his mouth moved directly to my right breast, his tongue licking circles around my nipple, then sucking me into his mouth. A spark of pleasure rioted through my body and I gasped in a breath. That hadn't happened since I was human. "Again, please," I begged.

His hand cradled and caressed my left breast while he savored the right, white-hot heat filling my chest and moving lower. He switched his adoration to my left breast, and I moaned, hands in both sides of his hair, holding him in place.

"I didn't know," I whispered, "I haven't been able to..." Then I was lost as his hips moved, his erection pressing against the spot where I needed him most.

His mouth moved back and forth, his hips pressed rhythmically into me, and I whispered his name as a wave of release washed over me. Not a full orgasm, but bliss nonetheless.

I bucked against him and rolled us over so I was straddling him. "I don't want you to hurt your leg."

He licked his lips, staring at me as if I was the most treasured woman in the world. "Fuck my leg." He sat up and captured my mouth in a searing kiss, his hands digging in my hair.

I dragged my lips away from his and kissed his jaw, underneath his chin, and the sensitive skin of his neck. He tilted his head back to give me better access, and I took full advantage. Sucking, nibbling, licking, tasting my way over his whole neck, his collarbone, and his chest. I pushed him back, so he was lying down as I worshipped his chest, his torso, then finally, I was pulling down his boxers.

I might not be able to properly orgasm, but I could do this for Jake. I could unravel him, make him forget everything he was worried about, if only for a few minutes. Make him say my name in that way no other person ever had. While I wasn't completely innocent, I had only done this a few times with Jake before I'd died. It was probably going to be more enthusiasm than skill, but I didn't care.

Enthusiasm and rhythm was all I needed.

God I had missed the feeling of him. I licked once, twice, and by the third time he was already groaning my name. He pulled my hair back, keeping it tight in his hands as I took him deeper into my mouth.

He gave over control, his body in my command as I wound him tighter and tighter. I was mesmerized by the way his abs tightened, how his breathing hitched, how he rasped out my name as if it were a benediction. It was only him and me in this moment, connected as close as we had ever been. Gone were the years that separated us, the fear of death, the anxiety about tomorrow.

It was just this, his molten eyes finally closing as the pressure built and released, his body arching and going taut beneath me, his cry of my name on his lips. My entire body throbbed with a wave of something I hadn't felt in so long, I couldn't name the emotion.

Then he was pulling me to him, kissing me as if it were our first kiss, last kiss, everything in between. "Poppy, Poppy, Poppy," he whispered. "I forgot how good you feel."

I snuggled against the curve of his shoulder. "I hope to remind you a few more times."

He laughed and kissed me again. "I love you," he admitted. "Always have."

I took his hand in mine and laced our fingers together. "Love you, too. Forever."

It was minutes or maybe hours or maybe days before he shifted. "Need to stretch," he murmured, his voice thick with sleep. I helped him do his routine, then took over foam rolling his tight muscles. "It's so much better when you do it."

"Good. You need to sleep well tonight."

When I finished, he patted the bed and closed his eyes. I kissed him softly and covered him with the blankets, then I pulled on my shirt. I wished I could sleep, pass the time until dawn instead of sitting here worrying about tomorrow. I closed my eyes and snuggled against him and thought about what it would be like if I was really a human.

This lasted an entire ten minutes before I gave up. I had too many thoughts in my head. What I needed was a book. What were the chances the hotel had a romance novel lying around?

Moving as silently as possible, I got up and opened the nightstand drawer. No takeout menus or motel literature. Only a Bible.

I sighed. Well, it was better than nothing. I cracked the curtain a little to let in the moonlight, just enough to make out the words on the page, then climbed back into bed next to Jake. I wasn't religious, but I was desperate. Anyway, learning how different people wrote about the afterlife was fascinating to me.

I lifted my hand to turn the page when it slid over my finger. "Ow," I whispered, then froze. *Ow?* I held my hand up to the moonlight, seeing a shallow cut over the skin, the first drop of blood rising.

I concentrated on dropping my human glamour, my hand changing back into a skeleton. I looked at it front and back, then pulled my skin back over it. The cut was gone. *What the hell?*

I closed the book and tossed it to the floor, and tucked my head into Jake's shoulder, looking at my hand out of the corner of my eye. I didn't know what was going on, but forget reading. I'd just hold Jake all night.

I stared at my hand until the sun poked through the curtains.

Chapter Thirty-Five

Jake

I RARELY HAD the opportunity to wake up with Poppy in my arms, this being only the fourth time in my entire life. The first three had been when we were camping with our families, and Poppy and I were stuffed into a tent with Eliza. Inevitably sometime in the night, we would gravitate toward each other. We'd always had to let go as soon as daybreak came.

Now there was complete freedom. The weight of her, the coolness of her body, the smile I felt against my skin, her lips on my chest. Her touch always made my head quiet. This, right here, was why every other relationship had failed. No one had ever made me feel the way Poppy did. She could slow down time and make the rest of the world disappear.

Poppy was my person. Well, my reaper.

I didn't know how this story would end, but right now I couldn't be bothered to think about it. Not when her lips were moving down my body again. Not when her mouth and hands woke me up better than any coffee or alarm clock in the world.

After she'd made stars appear behind my eyes, I hurried

to get dressed, impressed that despite the long day yesterday and the physical activity with Poppy, my leg was only moderately sore. I stretched and then Poppy helped me put more of Hazel's cream on my leg. By the time I had slipped into jeans, my body felt better than it had in weeks.

I checked out my bullet wound and was impressed that it no longer stung when I moved my arm. "Hazel's creams are magic," I admitted. "I don't feel like I've been hit by a bus this morning."

Poppy clapped her hands. "Excellent." She gave me a deep kiss, and I had to admit, she was magic, too.

A knock sounded, and I opened the door to find Paris. "Loren's here."

I nodded and grabbed my fleece. I looked over my shoulder at Poppy. "You coming?"

"Is it okay if I do?"

"Of course." Truth be told, I wanted her in my sight. I still wasn't convinced that she wasn't going to disappear forever when my back was turned. There was a warning deep in my gut, one I couldn't quite vocalize, that knew this wasn't over yet. That a banished Poppy didn't mean she could just stay with me until the end of my human life...unless that end was today.

I shook my head to clear it. I had to be sharp and focused. I could worry about Poppy and me tomorrow. Hopefully, tomorrow.

"You're limping less today," Paris noted.

"Hazel's creams are amazing. I'm going to have to buy several to take home."

Paris made a sound in the back of her throat.

"What?"

"You have the tendency to push yourself to your breaking point. Hopefully, with a little less pain, you'll rest better and not use it as an excuse to push even harder."

Poppy snapped her fingers. "I like her."

I sighed, not bothering to argue. I knew I did. "You're so reserved at times, I wondered why you chose field work," I told Paris. "But the way you read people is astonishing." We started walking again. "You remind me of Eliza sometimes."

She laughed. "Don't tell her you said that."

"Are we going to ever talk about that?"

"Nope."

"I have some theories," Poppy mumbled.

"Me too," I whispered back.

We climbed into Loren's truck and headed into town, to a small diner called Eggs 'n Oinks. Hazel, Romi, Raine, Fenton, and Grayson were already there, waiting at pulled-together tables in the back of the restaurant. Romi touched an empty chair next to her and said, "Poppy, come sit near me."

My chest ached at the gesture of inclusion. I took a seat on Poppy's other side, so I could translate if needed. The group told us about Hayvenwood, the history and the lore. After we ordered, we got down to business.

Loren looked at his watch, then back up at us. He was a natural-born leader, and I could see why he was on the elite team. I was happy to defer to him for this mission. His knowledge of the town and geographical challenges were unrivaled.

"I also have some new knowledge about yesterday," he

explained, sucking down the rest of his coffee. "Talked to a werewolf friend. He used to work at Billy's and is part of the only registered werewolf pack in Hayvenwood. Said they've been keeping an eye on the aggressive wolves, which showed up in January and have been multiplying."

Paris and I exchanged a long look. *January*. When the former weight-loss company Thinner had launched. When rogue vampires first appeared. When oral venom—a distribution form previously thought unattainable—hit the market.

"This wasn't about only human hybrids," I concluded. "This is bigger."

Loren nodded. "The question is why? Is it ego to see how many creatures they can crossbreed? Or is there a bigger purpose behind it?"

"We've been shutting down Vixen circles for three months. Hopefully someone will talk in exchange for leniency."

"What's your gut say?" Loren asked, looking from me to Paris.

I looked at Paris, too. Despite us only working together for a short time, I trusted her completely. "I want it to be ego," she said. "But my gut says this is bigger."

I nodded. "I agree. At the hearing for Lucinda Nicks, she said there was a supernatural crime syndicate behind everything. I don't think she's wrong, but I don't think that's all of it. Someone's trying to create a hybrid army. The question is, why?"

"Supernaturals haven't liked SHAP for decades," Loren offered. "That's nothing new."

"But they're not just focusing on creating hybrids," Paris reminded. "One of our victims had said whatever they took was supposed to cure them. Maybe hybrids aren't the focus there, but then what's the missing piece?"

Poppy tapped the table in front of her. "They're trying to start an empire," she offered.

I stared at her for a long moment, the unspoken fear in my stomach solidifying. I set my coffee cup back on the table and swallowed hard. She was right. "Whoever's behind this would be able to create a near-invincible army and also promise to cure any ailment. Together? They could create a near-undefeatable community."

Grayson let out a low whistle. "And become exceedingly wealthy in the process."

Loren ran a hand down his face, Raine and Hazel exchanged a long look, and Romi put her hand on the back of Poppy's chair. My hand squeezed Poppy's and I looked at Paris. "We have to get this right today."

"I'm all in, partner," Paris promised. She looked around the table. "Last night didn't go as expected and we know they have the upper hand."

"I've been working on that," Loren said, and picked up his phone. "And it looks like we have some backup meeting us here in an hour. They were there last night." He gave Paris and me a long gaze. "Couldn't talk to them until they were home this morning."

"Is it enough?" I asked.

"You've got me, too," Poppy added.

I turned to face her. "Poppy—"

She shook her head. "I can help. We know the hybrids

are afraid of me. I go in first and—"

"You can't take on an entire pack of hybrids alone."

She raised her eyebrows. "I mean, I did it last night."

"Then what? If we had the numbers, we would be unstoppable. But with only a handful of us? The risk is still too high."

"Then you need quality over quantity. Ask them how many other supernatural people they know who may be willing to help!"

"And how can we trust them?"

Romi cleared her throat. "Jake, please translate for us."

"We're not going to do it," I warned. "Poppy says quality over quantity."

"And?" Romi prompted.

I frowned my disapproval. "She suggested I ask you how many other supernatural people might help. I am concerned about the wrong people finding out."

"A valid concern," Loren confirmed. "But there are those in town whom I would trust with my life."

Romi and Hazel exchanged a long look.

Raine smiled and nodded at them. "You know I'm in."

Grayson crossed his arms. "Not a chance in hell, woman."

Hazel just smiled and tilted her head at him. "If you wanted a wife who obeyed your every command, you shouldn't have married me."

"What?" Loren asked, looking between them, then pointing at Raine. "No. You are not going after Mordecai. Fen, back me up."

Fenton sat back in his chair, calmly sipping his hot chocolate. He shook his head. "No can do, Lucy. One, I am not an idiot. I'm siding with my wife on this. Two, I happened to think she's right."

"Until a dragon eats her."

"She's not going to eat us," Hazel said. "She only eats people who assume she's male based on her name."

"Allegedly," Grayson grumbled.

"Hybrids don't have anything on a dragon," Fenton chimed in.

"Dragon?" Paris breathed, her hand reaching out and capturing my forearm. "The rumors are true?"

Romi nodded. "She's hard to find, but I spent a lot of time exploring this place when I was a ghost. With the Hayvenwood pack and a dragon for backup, we won't need SHAP."

I grabbed my coffee and gulped down the remaining overly sweet brew, frowning at the taste. I hadn't mixed well enough. "Let's go find ourselves a dragon."

BY THE TIME we paid our bill, the alpha wolf of the Hayvenwood pack, August, was waiting in the parking lot in human form. They were lean but toned, with a low ponytail and tanned skin, dressed in a tank top, jeans, and boots, despite the cold and cutting wind. August looked up from where they were leaning against a car, piercing dark eyes locked on Poppy. They shifted, their jaw clenching and shoulders tightening.

"Reaper," they hissed. "I can't see them but I know

they're here."

"She's on the team," I explained. "Not here for any souls."

"Forgive me for not believing her lies." They turned and grabbed their door handle, but Loren stepped forward and put his hand on the door.

"I'm calling in my favor," Loren said. "Last year, when you were being hunted, my brothers and I were the ones who protected the pack until the poachers were caught. You said you owed me. This is payback."

The air went electric. August froze, closing their eyes. Their hand dropped from the handle and turned. They lifted their chin, squared their shoulders, opened their eyes, and nodded. "I don't renege on promises."

Loren was close enough to August that their noses almost touched. "Neither do I. And I promise you, this reaper won't hurt you or the pack." Loren stuck out his hand, and August shook.

When they let go, Loren stepped back and nodded. "We're going back into the woods today. We need protection."

August studied the group, then looked back at Loren. "Those messed up wolves aren't the only thing you need to be afraid of. The creatures that come out of that place aren't normal."

"We know." Loren confirmed. "The plan is to get the evidence we need to take them down."

"Can't do it with just my pack. You got back up?" They crossed their arms. "Besides the reaper?"

Loren shook his head. "Can't trust backup."

"We're going to find Mordecai," Romi added.

August scoffed. "No one just *finds Mordecai*. She finds you."

Romi tilted her head and studied August. "Except you, right?"

They shook their head. "Maybe. But it's still not smart."

"Get the dragon and I'll owe you," Loren added. Judging by August's stunned face, I surmised that Loren bestowing a favor meant a great deal.

August blink hard a few times, swore, and ran a hand over the back of their neck. "I need two hours. Pack sleeps during the day and they're hard to wake up early." They sighed. "And then I'll see if I can find Mordecai."

"Done," Loren promised. "Stay in contact."

August nodded, then turned and opened their car door before pausing. "If you make this compound disappear? Slate's clean. Some of my pack went missing when they moved in. My guess? Failed experiments."

"Two hours," Loren reiterated.

TWO HOURS SOMEHOW felt like minutes and years at the same time. We set up shop at Billy's again, checking and triple-checking detailed maps and satellite imaging to make sure we knew all the ways into and out of the woods. Earpieces and bulletproof vests were distributed, and weapons were checked and double-checked.

Every breath was an eternity as we stared at Loren's cell sitting on the table. Exactly two hours after August left, the text came. "We're a go," Loren said.

Fenton, Raine, and Hazel stayed at Billy's, running home base, doing preliminary surveillance with the drone, and communicating with us via earpiece, while Loren, Grayson, Romi, Paris, Poppy, and I piled into the truck. We drove to the edge of town, a half mile away from the compound, and pulled close to the tree line.

A reddish-brown wolf emerged, walking up to Loren's window and lowering its head. "August," Loren explained. "Ready?"

The tension in the car ratcheted to ten. "Ready," we each confirmed.

Loren lifted his hand and the wolf moved. Shifting the truck into gear, we followed it into the woods, tree branches scraping the sides of the vehicle. I could make out the roofline of the lab when Loren slammed on the brakes.

I jerked forward in my seat, my arms going out to keep Poppy, Paris, and Romi safe. In front of us in a small clearing, a pack of werewolves paced back and forth, snapping at the hybrids on the opposite end of the clearing. Grayson swore.

"Why is Grayson using that tone?" Hazel asked into the earpiece.

"We've been delayed," I responded. "Nine werewolves, six hybrids."

"What if we back out?" Grayson asked. "Go around the main entrance at full speed?"

"That's not going to work," Paris explained.

I turned around to see another three hybrids creeping down the trail behind us. They were the size of black bears and hitting one would severely damage the truck.

"Oh shit," Hazel said. "We have a problem."

"We never liked things easy," Grayson sighed. "What, babe?"

"Drone spotted Fletcher," she replied.

"She just pulled up to the warehouse," Fenton added. "I don't know how she got to town without us seeing her."

I straightened in my seat, anticipation burning beneath my skin. "You get the sample, I get Fletcher."

"Sample first, Fletcher second," Loren argued, voice tight with concentration. "She won't talk. Sample will go farther."

"She's after my family!" I argued. Poppy squeezed my hand in support.

"Doesn't matter right now anyway," Romi explained. "We're trapped."

Poppy squeezed my hand one more time and then let go, giving me a quick kiss. "No, we're not."

"Poppy!" I yelled but she opened the back door and jumped out.

"I'm assuming that was Poppy exiting the car?" Romi asked.

I moved to follow her, and Paris put her arm out to block me. "She's already dead. You're not."

"I can't let her do this alone," I argued.

"If you get out of this truck, I'll shoot you myself," my partner promised. "Don't let your emotions screw you up this close to the end of the mission. She's got this."

I stopped fighting her and instead leaned through the middle console and watched as Poppy walked toward the hybrids without hesitation. The Hayvenwood pack whimpered and stepped back, giving her a wide birth. The hybrids barked and snapped at her.

Poppy stood perfectly still as a gray hybrid wolf charged her. Right before the collision, Poppy raised her right hand, as if to pet the creature. The creature took two steps back, dancing on its paws back and forth but not getting closer. Three more hybrids ran out from behind the truck and she spun around and raised her other hand.

"They're not running," I exclaimed. "Why aren't they running like yesterday?"

"I don't know," Paris said.

The Hayvenwood pack scurried between Poppy and the hybrids.

"I need to get her out of there!"

Just then, a hybrid ran into the side of the truck, cracking the back window and jolting us to the side. A second one slammed into the opposite side.

"This isn't ideal," Paris said, leveling her pistol at one of the wolves. "I'll tranq them." She pulled the trigger as another blow landed, causing her to drop her gun.

A large shadow blocked out the sun for a moment, nearly as dark as an eclipse, and when the sun reemerged, every creature in the field had frozen.

"Mordecai's here," Romi breathed, reverently.

In a blur of black iridescent streaks, the hybrids closest to Poppy disappeared. Only a breath later, the two wolves destroying Loren's truck vanished. The remaining hybrids ran for the trees as Mordecai landed in the clearing, next to August.

We all sucked in a breath as the giant four-legged creature—slender with bat-like wings and white eyes—nuzzled August, nodded to Poppy, then launched herself into the air. Her iridescent dark purple scales glittered in the afternoon sun as she released a burst of sound that was a cross between a bassoon and a chainsaw before she disappeared into the clouds.

"That's the coolest thing to ever happen to me," Grayson whispered.

"I'd be mad at you since our wedding was literally three weeks ago," Hazel responded, "but I would say the same thing. Romi, I need a detailed play-by-play later."

"Got it, Zee."

August trotted up to Poppy and bowed their head, then ran in front of the truck, looked at Loren, and started running. "We're moving!" Loren warned.

Paris opened the door and yelled for Poppy, who dove in.

"She's in!" I confirmed.

Loren hit the gas. This time, neither August nor Loren went slow. It was probably a moot point anyway. Hybrids running through the trees would explain any loud noises until they heard the motor.

"Fletcher is exiting the building," Fenton said. "She's standing next to a white Escalade, license plate Charlie, Zulu 1-5-8 Tango. She has two large suitcases and two bodyguards with her." Fenton described the men we had arrested in Café Eleonora.

Paris turned to me. "Looks like our leak at SHAP let them go."

"They're either not super loyal to her or this is a trap," I offered.

"I always think everything's a trap," Grayson said.

I nodded. "Good call."

Before the final clearing to the driveway, we stopped and parked. "Did a perimeter check with the drone. We're clear for exterior foot traffic and visible traps," Fenton. "Through the windows, I've counted four other people inside in the lab and one in the bathroom. Fletcher climbed in the passenger seat of the truck. You get the sample. Raine and Hazel are taking over drone duty. I'm going after Fletcher." We heard car keys clinking in the background.

"Stop at the yellow light on Crooks and Main," Romi warned. "Love you."

"God you're creepy," Hazel said. "Fenton's out the door. Raine's got him on speakerphone to listen in. I'm following Fletcher with the drone. Her truck just did a U-turn and is speeding away from the compound. No one else has come in or out."

"Paris, Jake, and I will take the lab," Loren ordered. "Grayson, bathroom. Romi, you and Poppy eyes on perimeter."

"Copy that," I said, and the others agreed.

"Be careful, team," he added.

Poppy pressed her lips to mine hard, and then at Loren's hand signal, we all exited the car, closing the doors gently. Romi and Poppy headed off deeper into the woods, while the rest of us inched closer to the warehouse.

"Ready on my signal. Three…two…"

Romi screamed and I turned to look over my shoulder at her running out of the woods and toward us. She was waving her arms, but I couldn't hear what she was saying.

Not over the sound of the building exploding.

I TACKLED LOREN as the explosion shook the ground, a wave of heat washing over us. Feedback filled our earpieces. "ROLL CALL!" I shouted.

"Paris safe!"

"Grayson mostly safe," he said. "Just a little shrapnel."

"Romi safe! I think Poppy's still with me."

"Loren safe."

"What happened?" Hazel asked, voice high.

"Explosion." I rolled off Loren and pushed myself up.

I surveyed the wreckage. Scorch marks stopped a foot away from us, debris littering the ground mere inches away. Had we been a few steps closer…

"JAKE!"

I turned to find Poppy running at me. I scooped her up in my arms as she wrapped herself around me. "I'm okay," I promised.

"I can't lose you."

"You're not going to. I'm okay." I lowered her to the ground as Grayson and Paris moved into view.

"It's a brutal explosion, man," Grayson said. "Not even sure a vampire could survive that."

Fire truck sirens filled the air.

"We going on record or escaping?" I asked.

"Our emergency team is well briefed on weird," Loren said. "Let's hope there's something in this mess that can help."

"I need to get out of here before the reapers come," Poppy warned.

I relayed her concern to the group and Romi lifted her hand. "Keys!" Loren tossed them to her. "I'll be back to pick you guys up. We'll head to Billy's."

Poppy gave me a quick kiss and ran after Romi.

Chapter Thirty-Six

Rule #11: It is imperative that a reaper remember to change into comfortable clothing that they do not mind spending eternity in before their human expiration date. Once dead, the clothing cannot be removed.

– The Reaper Code of Ethics, official handbook

Poppy

MY ANXIETY DIDN'T die down until the team was back at the bar, debriefing us. There were several bodies—human presenting and wolf presenting alike—but any drug stock was burned up. Fenton had attempted to chase Fletcher in his truck, but he'd lost her as she vanished into the woods. Apparently we weren't the only ones who could drive through forests.

It had been a bittersweet ending and everyone was exhausted. Even me, somehow. After a late dinner, we went back to the motel.

"Come shower with me," Jake said.

I surprised even myself by shaking my head. "I think I need a minute?" I admitted.

He kissed me softly and nodded. "Take all the time you need."

I waited until he closed the door and turned the shower on, then sat down in an armchair and covered my face with my hands. Today had been so much. Too much. My brain and body weren't used to this much Earth and I was wrecked.

While dismal, gray, and boring, the reaper world was quiet and cool. Outside of my jail break, it was always a safe space, a home. I'd never appreciated that until now.

I had forgotten that the energy in this world was constant, overwhelming. Or maybe it had just increased over the last twelve years. With a long sigh I stood and stretched, reaching under my shirt to scratch my stomach.

I froze. I'd forgotten I could remove my shirt.

Cautiously, I pulled it over my head and brushed my hands over my body from shoulder to hip. Then I tugged at my leggings. They came away from my body and I saw my black underwear underneath. I pulled them off and folded them, setting them on the chair.

I walked over to the mirror and sink outside of the bathroom and stared at the body I hadn't seen in twelve years. It was both what I remembered and somehow not. The scar from my appendix surgery at fifteen was still there, as was the mole just above my belly button. Age had brought me a rounder stomach, creases underneath my breasts, new stretch marks, and a dusting of age spots. I had said goodbye to my thigh gap a long time ago.

I smiled at the woman in the mirror. As a teenager, I had been awkward and unsure of my body. As an adult, I was happy with the way I looked and the way my body had grown.

I turned on the water at the sink and ran my hands under it, then splashed some onto my face. It felt like it should feel wet, but my hands were dry as if I was washing them with gloves on. I turned the sink off and walked back to the bed, sitting on the edge.

The bathroom door opened and I stared at the sight of Jake in a towel. Good lord, my man was breathtaking.

Jake stopped short, staring at me. "How? I thought…you said…" He swallowed hard.

"I guess the longer I'm on this side, the less restricted I am." I should be terrified that something was very obviously happening to me that shouldn't be, but right now I wasn't going to think about it.

His mouth hung open.

I bit my bottom lip. The way he was looking at me made my entire body warm. He made me feel like I was the only person on Earth.

The entire day fell away. The entire week. Right now, it was him and me alone in this room. "Jake? Kiss me. Everywhere."

His mouth sealed on mine before the words were completely out of my mouth. This wasn't some tender exploration, but years and years of pent-up need. We had never gone *all the way* as teens, Jake wanting to wait until I was eighteen so our parents didn't kill us. Now, we were both over eighteen, completely alone behind a locked door, and with zero family around. And I was able to take my pants off.

I wasn't going to let anything stop us tonight. After all, what was the worst thing that could happen? I was already technically dead. I wasn't going to die again.

His arm went tight around my waist and he tossed me to the center of the bed. He pulled off his towel and dove in beside me, pulling my body against his.

I gasped at the feel of his warm skin touching every inch of mine. Our mouths collided again. Long strokes of his tongue against mine stoked a fire low in my abdomen, a feeling I hadn't had since I was alive.

He shifted to his back and licked his lips. "Bring those hips here and hang on to the headboard. Let's see if I can make you fly."

My entire body twinged with a jolt of pleasure as I climbed up his body. His hands gripped my hips with purpose, moving me directly over his face. With his eyes locked on mine, he pulled me down to his lips. He moaned and I cried out as the wet heat of his mouth moved over my most sensitive flesh.

His tongue tasted me, savored me and *oh my god* I couldn't believe I had forgotten how amazing he made me feel. Gone were the timid strokes of a young man who knew we would pay hell if we got caught, who was as inexperienced as me.

There was no hesitation now. "Tell me what you want," he breathed into me.

"You, right there," I returned.

He groaned as his arms wrapped around my legs and he arched up to somehow give me more pressure, slipping his tongue deep inside of me, then around my sensitive nub. The pleasure grew tighter in my stomach, and I moaned, my hands gripping the headboard until it creaked.

"Please don't stop," I pleaded. "Yes, perfect, don't you dare stop." I didn't even know what I was saying, my pleas lost to the fog of pleasure.

I thought I'd known what I'd been missing all these years, thought that the novels I read had somehow captured what it had been like in Jake's arms. Not even close. He groaned and I felt it throughout my entire body. I closed my eyes, my head falling back. It was too much. My legs trembled and I sucked in air through my mouth, somehow needing the breath.

He began moving his tongue in a steady rhythm, me grinding down on him and him gripping me tighter. Oh god, I didn't even care if I couldn't orgasm, this was the most amazing feeling I'd ever had in my entire life. I forced my eyes open and looked down into his, the blue so dark, they were nearly midnight. He was entirely focused on me. With a wink, he applied just a little more pressure with his tongue.

I screamed.

Every muscle in my body tightened and then splintered apart. It was a tidal wave, and I was drowning. It was sunshine and starlight and lingering kisses and whispered I love yous and everything that I had held in my heart, times a thousand.

Minutes and days and decades without him didn't exist in this moment. Memories of witnessing hundreds of thousands of deaths were pushed completely from my mind. I was simultaneously falling and flying with his arms around me, and a laugh of pure elation escaped.

He smiled against me. "God, you're so beautiful when you come."

"Jake," I whispered as I floated back down to earth, my arms too much like jelly to hold myself up.

He moved me to his chest, taking my weight. "I will never get tired of doing that," he whispered against my lips. "You were made for me, Poppy."

"You were made for me." I kissed him long and deep, until the fire reignited and I arched into him, needing more.

"I'm not done with you yet," he said against my mouth. "Get back up here."

"Compromise," I whispered, turning my body around so my mouth could taste him, too.

As we moved together, hot mouths and shallow breaths and desperate pleas, he added one finger and then two, and I fell apart a second time, his name a prayer on my lips.

"Jake, I need you," I gasped. "Please."

"Give me one more orgasm, love, and I'll make your wish come true," he teased, returning his mouth to me.

He didn't need to ask me twice. Just imagining what he'd feel like, combined with the way he moved his fingers and tongue, sent me spiraling a third time. My body was still throbbing with aftershocks, when I pulled away and spun around, my mouth crashing against his again. "Make love to me. Hurry."

He laughed softly and put both of his hands on the side of my face. "Are you sure?"

"Jacob Robinson, shut up and stop wasting time before another emergency or something happens!"

He laughed into my neck, wrapping his arms around my shoulders. He was damp with sweat and I loved it. "God, I love you." He kissed me softly, as if to remind me that I was precious to him. "Do we need to talk about birth control? I get tested annually, and all my results came back negative."

"You're the only person I've been intimate with, and not since I was sixteen." I kissed him again, moving so we were so, so close.

"Birth control?"

I pulled back and raised my eyebrows. "I haven't had a period in twelve years. I don't even have ovaries."

"Are you sure you're ready?"

"Jake. Please make love to me for the first time."

He smiled and stroked his hand through my hair, then kissed me. "I forgot you're new to this."

"While we were waiting for me to turn eighteen, I had to inconveniently die."

"It was extremely poor timing," he agreed and kissed me again. "It'll be easier for you to be on top." Another kiss, this one on my neck. "Wrap your hand around me and guide me, Poppy," he whispered.

I sat up and he followed me, his mouth staying against mine. "Jake," I breathed as I shifted and slowly welcomed him inside of me. There was pressure that eased into pleasure. Our lips together, mouths opening, gasping for air.

"Holy shit." He laid his forehead against the crook of my neck, lifting his hips up once. "Good god, if I knew this was what you'd feel like, I would've risked anything to have you back then." He dragged his lips up my neck, his hands digging into my hair. "Move please, love. Please."

I experimented with different ways to move my hips, each moan from me and groan from Jake reverberating throughout my entire body. An inferno stoked by lips and hands and desperate whispers burned in the space between us. He wrapped me tighter in his arms, my chest pressed against his as he took over, his tongue in my mouth moving in rhythm with his hips.

The pleasure built deeper, stronger than before. I was drowning in a wave, a tropical storm, a hurricane. Jake's hand moved between us, his fingers finding my sensitive bud and stroking with purpose. My vision blurred.

"I love you," I cried, the words the only thought left in the universe.

"Poppy," he whispered back. "My heart's always been yours." He rotated his hips. "Come for me, love."

Each one of his words crashed into me and I detonated. In the history of my existence, there would forever be a line marking the before and after. Jake had always been a part of me, and me of him, but this was more. This was *everything*.

His entire body tensed and he growled my name, his release sending me back into bliss. I was already drowning and this sunk me straight to the bottom of the ocean. It was more divine than the most beautiful music, than my favorite book, than any of the thousands of daydreams I had conjured. It was more emotion than I had felt in twelve years.

A white-hot knot tightened in my chest and a sob burst from my throat.

Jake pressed his mouth to mine as something wet cascaded down my face. "Hey, hey," he pulled back. "Why the tears?"

"That was everything."

He kissed me again. "It was. It really was."

Then his words sank in. *Why the tears?* I broke the kiss

and pressed my hands to my cheeks. I pulled them back and saw them glistening with wet. But how? I couldn't cry. Of course I also couldn't orgasm or have sex until about twenty minutes ago.

I looked up at him, then showed him my palms. "Jake, what's happening to me?"

His thumbs stroked my cheeks, wiping them dry. "I don't know, but I'm right here, okay? I'm by your side."

A twinge in my chest sucked all the air from my lungs. I gripped Jake's shoulder, my eyes going wide. I sucked in a breath, then another, the twinge repeating.

"Poppy? What's wrong?" One hand covered mine on my chest while the other rested on my neck.

"I don't know," I managed, gasping for another breath. Was I dying? *Again*?

Jake's fingers stroked my neck, but he stilled when he moved over my pulse point. His eyes widened. "I think we need to talk to Romi."

I pressed my pointer and middle finger against the other side of my neck. Faintly, like the flutter of butterfly wings, a beat brushed against my fingers.

A heartbeat.

ROMI AND FENTON lived in a small ranch style home on the edge of town, a few miles away from the motel. Without hesitation, Fenton had come and picked us up, keeping the conversation light. He talked about the remodel he did, since Romi had been in a wheelchair for several months due to an injury, and how the wide doorways really made the house seem bigger. When we pulled into the gravel driveway, every light in the house was burning bright in welcome.

Romi met us at the door, holding it wide open. She smiled and gestured for us to come in, as if midnight was a perfectly normal time to have people over. After a quiet conversation with Fenton, who hurried out of the room as if on a mission, she joined us in the living room.

"Wow, the widened doorways make this place seem bigger," I commented, admiring the space. Everything was bright white and ornate, from the wood paneling to the white-on-white curtains with embroidered designs.

"They really do," Romi replied.

My gaze snapped to hers. "You can hear me?"

She nodded. "I'm glad you called me."

Fenton came back into the room and handed Romi a sweatshirt, a pair of tennis shoes that looked new, and a pair of thick socks. She kissed him and he stroked her cheekbone with his thumb, a touch that silently spoke such intimate words, I had to look away. He retreated to the kitchen, where he put a kettle on the stove.

She sat on the edge of the coffee table directly in front of me. "Poppy, I can see you."

"What?" Jake said looking between me and Romi, then at Fenton. "Can you see her?"

Fenton turned around and nodded. "I thought it best I waited to share the news until you were here."

"These are for you to change into. I'm sure you're tired of wearing the outfit you died in. I know I was." Romi put the clothes in my lap. "What's happening? Tell me everything."

"You can see me?" I repeated staring down at the clothes. "I…" I looked at her. "I don't know."

"Start from the moment you became a reaper."

She took my hand in hers while I explained the night I died, waking up as a reaper, and finished with the heartbeat. I released her hand, took two of her fingers, and pressed them against the pulse point in my wrist.

Her purple eyes searched mine. "Ah, I see."

Fenton brought over four mugs and a teapot on a tray and set it next to Romi, along with some small pastries, then took a chair on the other side of the room, showing his support but giving us space.

"Do you want to try eating or drinking anything?" Romi asked.

"I'm scared," I whispered.

"Then we'll wait."

"What's going on?" Jake asked, looking between us.

Romi looked at me and I nodded, giving her permission to explain it. "I don't exactly know the details without more research, but I have two guesses."

She picked up a mug and filled it, offering it to Jake. "Sip on this. It's a family recipe and will calm you." Reluctantly, he released my hand and took the cup. She poured another one for Fenton, who stood and retrieved it before returning to his seat.

She took both of my hands. "The first idea is that the power source that keeps you all in their reaper state is directly tied to the island. Reapers likely need constant renewal of their magic, which is why you had to return daily and possibly why your shifts were broken up the way they were. Galinda, Loren's friend and a SHAP agent, might know more." She smiled sheepishly. "I'm still learning about the supernatural myself."

I squeezed her hands. "And the second?"

"I think that maybe you weren't supposed to be a reaper."

Jake sat up, setting his cup back on the coffee table. "What do you mean?"

"The seasickness, the inability to remove souls from the body yourself, the desperate feelings of not belonging, they all point to a mismatch. It's possible when you transitioned, your heart and your soul and your love for Jake prevented you from assimilating fully. Maybe being away from the reaper magic is allowing your body to reverse the process."

"I'm becoming human again?" I whispered, the words sounding like the punchline to a bad joke, but they were also everything I ever dreamed.

"It's only a guess," she clarified. "But it would explain everything you've told me." She looked at Jake. "If you give me twenty minutes, I'll pack a bag and we can hit the road tonight. I think it's best if we immediately see a SHAP doctor. I know that there's a leak, but is there a physician you trust?"

Jake nodded. "Paris had one on her team."

"Can you get a non-SHAP helicopter?" Fenton asked.

"I'll make some calls."

Fenton looked at his watch. "I'll get Loren's truck just in case they can't do a night run." He looked at me. "Are you comfortable with that?"

My stomach rolled. "Is it possible to be motion sick while sitting still?" I had always struggled with seasickness, although I could usually tolerate the backseat of a truck if we weren't on twisty roads.

Jake kissed my cheek. "You always did feel sick before a long trip." He squeezed my hand. "It'll be okay."

Fenton nodded, then stood. "I'll call my brothers and pack a cooler and some coffee. We can grab your stuff at the motel on the way out."

"I'll call Paris," Jake said.

Romi patted the pile on my lap. "See if the shoes fit. If not, we'll find you a pair that do." She stood. "I'm going to go pack and call Hazel to let her know I'll be out of town for a few days."

"You really don't need to," I said too fast. "It's too much of an inconvenience."

She put her hands on my shoulders. "No, it's not. You don't have to go through this alone." She released me and hurried into the bedroom.

I turned to Jake, silently staring into his storm-cloud eyes. He stared at me back, our silent wishes and prayers and hope too precious, too fragile to say out loud. Was it possible? Could it be possible?

Maybe I would get my happily-ever-after—no—*our* happily-ever-after.

Chapter Thirty-Seven
Jake

FENTON AND ROMI had us packed and ready to go within thirty minutes, as promised. Paris confirmed the next helicopter wouldn't be available for ten more hours, so we piled in the truck. Fenton took first shift driving with Poppy in the front seat. Paris was strapped into the trunk, a make-shift bench seat made of couch cushions and a harness, while Romi and I occupied the middle. I wished I could sleep, but I was too worried, too hopeful, too much in disbelief.

Could Poppy finally have the chance to live a normal human life? Well, as normal as one can be after being dead for twelve years. Could it mean that we'd be together for as many years as she had left? Was this the reason I could see her? Because somehow she had begun to change back?

Paris had gasped in surprise at the sight of Poppy when we had picked her up, but like a good agent, she took it all in stride, and then immediately fell asleep in the back. I was restless after an hour, wishing she was awake so we could talk about the case. Four and a half more hours seemed like an eternity in the dark.

My leg didn't love sitting upright this long without

breaks to stretch, but we all agreed that we'd try to make only one stop, to get gas when we reached a more populated town about ninety minutes outside of Applechester. The long stretches of forest that hugged both sides of the road only diverged into small towns shut up for the night, and they were too risky. With Fletcher still at large, and us likely now on her radar, we were taking extra precautions.

"Romi?" Poppy asked. "Can you tell me your story? From the beginning?"

She nodded. "Of course." Romi was great at storytelling and the restlessness settled. Poppy asked question after question, and Fenton filled in parts that Romi missed.

"Could that happen to me?" Poppy said. "Where I have to be in the hospital for a long time?"

Romi reached out and took her hand. "I don't think so. You seem to be doing okay right now, which is a good sign! And your death wasn't violent like mine."

"Also, you didn't have to climb out of hell," Fenton added.

"That's a solid point," Poppy concluded.

We drove on, Romi's conversation leading her to share the stories about her twin and their best friend Raine. I eventually pulled out my crochet, using the dashboard light and touch as my guide. It wasn't going to be perfect, but at least it lowered my anxiety.

I watched Poppy laugh and gasp and cry, her face silhouetted in the same dashboard glow. She was so beautiful, so confident in her emotions. I could feel her hope filling the cab, as if she was on the verge of having everything she ever wanted.

It was going to be interesting explaining her presence to my family, and I worried about how she would handle not seeing hers again for a long time, but I couldn't do anything about that right now. All we had to do was keep going.

"Um…" Poppy turned around in her chair. "I think I have to go to the bathroom?"

"Think?" I prompted.

"Well, it's been awhile, but I think that's what this pressure is?"

"Romi," Fenton said. "Any feelings, good or bad, about this exit?"

She closed her eyes and tilted her head to the side. "Hard to tell. Possibly neutral." She gave us a sad smile. "I'm still working on feeling out new places. I'm pretty decent at Hayvenwood, but the further we get away, the less intense I feel things."

"We just need to travel more," Fenton added. "But we've been so busy getting the bar up and running." He took the next exit with a rest stop and pulled into the nearly empty parking lot.

Two semi-trucks were in the back of the lot, idling for the night. Two dim streetlights illuminated the sidewalk in front of the building, which immediately dipped into shadow.

"I'll do a perimeter check," I said, reaching for the door.

"We'll go together," Paris said, sounding completely awake.

I startled and looked back at her. "You were passed the hell out!"

"It's a talent." She lifted a shoulder. "Now come on, I

have to pee, too."

The two of us climbed out, weapons and flashlights in our hands. We went in opposite directions around the building, then met back at the front entrance.

"All clear," Paris confirmed, "but unsettling. Let's move quick."

"All clear," I echoed. "And agreed."

We moved as a group to and from the building, and then returned to the highway without incident. Paris, who was more awake now than any of us, took over driving. Romi and Fenton took the back, and I laid down in the middle seat, exhausted enough to close my eyes, and drifted into a light sleep.

I WOKE WHEN the truck stopped moving, my body stiff and sore from lying down while buckled in. I pushed myself upright and saw we were at a gas station. That meant only ninety more minutes to go. Paris grabbed her purse, but I called her name. "I need to stretch my legs. I've got it."

"I'll come out with you," Poppy said. "I'm getting stiff, which is a new feeling for me!"

"Do not envy you relearning what hurts," Paris added.

We slipped out the door and I squinted at the blinding florescent lights illuminating the twenty-four-hour gas station. "Cash," I told Poppy. "Don't know if we're being tracked."

She nodded and bounced alongside me as we walked into the small convenience store, where the cashier sat on a stool behind a partition. Despite being a small town, the station was right off the highway, likely making it an easy target for robberies.

"Thirty on pump three," I said, dropping the bills into the small opening at the counter.

The cashier looked up when he handed me my receipt, his brow furrowed. "Not again."

"What do you mean?"

He gestured behind me. "Some weirdo wearing a purple cloak has been in here for the last three nights. That woman you came in with is talking to her. I'd get her away from the freak show, man."

My blood ran cold. Purple cloak. I spun around to see Poppy talking to...air. I ran over to her. "Who are you talking to? Are you okay?"

She looked up at me, eyes huge. "Sylvia," she whispered.

"Let's go." I grabbed her hand and kept her behind me as we hurried out the door.

"Call your loved ones!" Poppy yelled to the cashier, who gave her a strange look. "If he can see Sylvia, it means he's about to die," she whispered.

I should've had Paris pull the truck around. I should've called them from inside the store. I should've tried for the helicopter after all. Romi opened her car door and jumped out, shouting as she ran toward us. But I couldn't hear her.

Not over the sound of the explosion. Déjà vu.

As if in slow motion, Poppy screamed. "No!" She tackled me from behind seconds before a wave of heat and debris swallowed us whole. All the oxygen disappeared, and I sucked in a lungful of smoke, choking until my eyes watered.

"Poppy?" I wheezed. "Poppy, are you okay?" I went into another coughing fit.

Someone grabbed me by the shoulders, hauled me to my feet, and pressed a gun to my head. In my career as a SHAP agent, I'd had a gun pressed to my head enough times to not panic immediately. I tried to suck in a calming breath, still shaking with silent coughs.

"Stop," my attacker ordered.

Fletcher. I could tell by the voice. "Can't order an involuntarily reflex to stop for your convenience," I shot back, pissed off, coughing through the entire thing. She'd likely killed the attendant who was only doing his job, and for what? To come after me? "You didn't have to blow up *another* building."

"What can I say? I like being theatrical." She turned us around, to face the spot where she pulled me from. Romi and Fenton were crouched over Poppy, while Paris held a gun pointed at Fletcher in one hand and her cell in the other. Loren was next to her, gun trained on whoever was behind us. "Speaking of drama, we should talk about your girlfriend."

My gaze went to Poppy again. Fenton tore off his coat and bundled it under her head. Then Romi shifted, and I saw it. The blood on her hands. Poppy's blood.

"Poppy!" I cried out, trying to shove away from Fletcher, but she was a hybrid and stronger than any human.

"Calm down, Prince Charming, she'll be fine."

I scanned Poppy's body and saw a giant shard of curling metal that had caught her side. It wouldn't have hurt a reaper, but it would kill a human. I was going to lose her again. My knees buckled.

"How very sweet though," Fletcher cooed, lifting me off the ground with one arm. "She'll die saving the man she loved. Had she been a few inches to your right, you'd be bleeding out right now instead of her. Of course, that would've deprived me of this."

I stilled, realization dawning. Maybe I hadn't seen Poppy because she was coming for my soul. Maybe she saw me because I killed her. "What do you want?"

"Your life for hers. I give her the venom, she turns into a hybrid and miraculously heals. You die and get off my back. I have a plan, and you keep getting in my way."

"Let me guess…gathering up as much Vixen as you can and selling it to the highest bidder. It's why you were cutting the venom with fentanyl, wasn't it? To skim off the top and keep as much as possible?"

"You're good, I'll give you that." She leaned even closer and said into my ear. "You know what? Maybe I'll take your partner, too. Seems she's just as skilled."

"Me and me alone," I shot back. "And Paris will drop the case, and make sure it's not reopened." I held my partner's gaze even as she shook her head no. "Paris, promise you'll let the case drop."

"Jake, I can't do that," she protested.

"You can't work if you're dead," I warned. I knew she'd never give up this case, not when it took so many innocent people. But I just needed her to agree so we could help Poppy.

She clenched her jaw and lowered her phone to her pocket, putting both hands on her gun. "Fine. I promise.

But if she makes one wrong move…"

"I wouldn't do that if I were you," Fletcher said. "I've got my boys with me. And they'll tear you apart with their teeth before you could blink. Also it's really hard to kill me."

Paris raised one eyebrow in challenge, but kept her mouth shut.

"Jake!" Poppy called, her voice barely above a whisper.

"I'm here, love," I promised. "If I give you something to make you better, would you take it?"

"I—" she wheezed, "I don't know."

My eyes were glued to the puddle of blood next to her. There was no way that she'd survive this. I'd seen enough of life and death and everything in between to know when a miracle was needed. "Love, listen. This would turn you into a half vampire, okay? But you'd still be half human. You can heal and still live a wonderful life."

"She's losing consciousness," Fenton said, looking over his shoulder at me. "This decision's got to be yours."

"It can't be," I admitted. "The only thing she wanted was to make a decision about her own life. I can't make that for her."

"She won't have a life soon!" Fenton returned.

"She'll go back to being a reaper, right, Sylvia?" I asked, knowing Sylvia was here. "That's why you were here, wasn't it? To take her and the station attendant."

"Jake," Loren called. "Look at me." It took all my strength to tear my gaze away from Poppy and look at him. "She made her decision. She gave her life to save yours. Either way, her human life is over. She's either going back to being a reaper or she's going to be a hybrid."

My eyes stung as my heart cracked in half, knowing there was nothing I could do to save her delicate human body. Why couldn't she have waited just one more day to turn human?

"If she goes back to being a reaper," Paris added, "all of this, everything you two fought for is over, forever. And I'm pretty sure Fletcher's gonna kill you anyway."

I felt her arms move in what was probably a shrug. "She's not wrong. This is an Academy Award winning speech—"

"But you can give her a chance," Paris interrupted, ignoring Fletcher. "She's still partially human as a hybrid and maybe they can reverse the venom. If it's not laced with fentanyl. She can still live a wonderful life. And a life would've been her choice. I just met her, but I'd bet my own on it."

"I've got a shot," Loren said, holding his gun level. "Bet we can get the venom and take out the trash."

One of Fletcher's wolves moved into my sightline with a gun on Poppy. "Go ahead and try. Your reaper's not coming back with a bullet through her skull," Fletcher warned.

I sank in defeat, running every scenario through my head and all of them ending with someone I cared about dead. "Take care of her, okay?" I asked Paris.

"With all of me," she swore.

I swallowed hard, my mouth dry and my eyes wet. "Fletcher, you have a deal. Me for the venom. Straight, non-diluted, no-fentanyl venom."

"Pleasure doing business with you," Fletcher said. "Bring the pill!" she called.

I heard a door open and one of the werewolves sauntered

over, stopping just outside of my field of vision. I wondered if I managed an escape if I could take them. Chances were slim.

"Give it to the one covered in blood," Fletcher ordered and started dragging me backward. "If you keep your word, I'll never see you again. If I do see you, I'll kill you on sight, no questions asked. Then I'll go after everyone you've ever loved."

The werewolf tossed a pill bottle to Romi who caught it midair then turned around to walk back with me. I knew if I didn't make a break for it while in this parking lot, I was a dead man. But I didn't want to struggle until they'd dosed Poppy.

"Paris," Romi called, then gave her a nod. She grabbed something from behind her back. "Jake, duck!"

I shoved Fletcher's arm with all my strength and threw my head back, my skull making contact with her nose. She hissed at the pain. I didn't care that she'd heal almost immediately, I only cared about distracting her.

Three gunshots rang out. A burst of fire burned across my temple and forehead, my vision going hazy. Fletcher's hold disappeared and I plummeted to the ground.

I was turned over, Paris looming over me. She ripped off her sweatshirt and pressed it against my forehead. I hissed at the pressure. "You scared me, you asshole," she shouted. "It's just a graze."

"Poppy!" I shouted, or maybe whispered. My ears were ringing from the shot. I forced myself to sit up on my elbows and looked over at her pale, still body.

Chapter Thirty-Eight

Rule #100: A reaper may not barter, promise, compromise, or offer a choice to a soul they've come to collect.

— The Reaper Code of Ethics, official handbook

Poppy

I T WAS WILD staring down at my own body. "Can I be a reaper without a body?" I asked.

Sylvia put her arm around my shoulders. "I'd reunite you, and we would pull the metal out. Your body would transition as soon as we crossed back over."

I nodded, swallowing hard. "I can't believe I got to be human again for a little while."

"Was it worth it?" she asked.

I pressed my fingers to my lips. "It was worth everything."

She pulled back and examined my face. "You and Jake totally had sex, didn't you?"

My mouth fell open. "I don't kiss and tell."

"Means yes," she said. "Was it great?"

I just smiled.

"Good. You deserve it."

I frowned. "Wait, how are you here? And can I even go back?"

"I'm here because your name popped up on Daniel's manifest, and he raised hell that I should be the one to come get you since we're partners." She turned to me and took my hands in hers. "And you're not automatically banished upon reentry. Our parents were able to appeal to the Counsel and"—she straightened her shoulders—"I'm going to apply to Counsel and see if we can change a few things."

My eyes widened. "You? Sylvia Bethany Grim? Running for Counsel?"

She shook my arms. "Yes, you dork. I don't think that people younger than twenty-five should become reapers. I think we should have visitation rights with people in the afterlife, although I'll admit I'm not sure how that'd work. And I believe we should reconsider Isle of Exile."

I released her hands and threw my arms around her. "I love you."

She grumbled but hugged me back begrudgingly. "Love you, too." She pulled back and put her hands on my shoulders. "I'd love you by my side."

I nodded. "Of course." Neither of us missed how my voice cracked. I hadn't been ready to leave the human world again, but if I could help no other reaper experience what I did, then it would have to be enough.

"I think, though, that I can wait a few decades before that happens. Change takes time, you know."

I frowned. "What do you mean?"

She nodded back to my still body. "If I put you back in your body and they give you that pill, you'll turn into a hybrid vampire. You'll have a really long life and I'll be waiting for you on the other side, okay?"

"And if I don't want that?" I asked.

"Then I take your soul and your body before they put that pill in your mouth. But you can never come back. They'll remove you permanently from traveler duty. You'll never see any of them again, including Jake. It's your choice."

My choice. I finally got to make a choice. "Will our family be mad if I stayed?" *Will you?*

She smiled a sad smile. "Mad? No. But we'll miss you. Terribly. You're my best friend, you know."

"You're mine, too." My voice was full of tears I couldn't shed.

"I knew you'd want to stay." She winked at me.

I startled. "How'd you know they'd be able to save me?"

She smirked and shook her head. "Because Jake would do anything to save you, and this couldn't be the end of your story." She bobbed her head. "And I may have had a few ghost friends keeping me updated about where the closest Vixen was. There was some in the gas station if we needed, although I didn't expect Fletcher to blow it up."

"The guy in there!" I looked around for him. "Is he still alive?"

Sylvia waved her hand. "A shapeshifter friend doing me a favor. He's fine."

I looked back at her wide-eyed. "You're not allowed to interfere like this."

"You're not the only person who would do anything for the people they loved. I'll be okay. But you must go back right now if you're staying. Go before it's too late."

I wrapped her in one last hug. "Thank you. Love you."

"Yeah, yeah." She hugged me back. "See you in like seventy or so years. It'll go by in a blink." She kissed my forehead. "Bye, Poppy." She shoved me backward.

I opened my eyes, already screaming as I resettled into my body. The pain was so white hot, it was cold. I held out a shaking hand and Romi dropped a capsule into it. I tossed it into my mouth and tried to swallow but nearly choked.

I closed my eyes and with the last of my energy, I chewed on it, the powder spilling into my mouth and burning my tongue. I kept trying to swallow it down when a bottle of water was gently pushed against my lips. I gargled and choked, but finally swallowed.

My body jolted as something warm spread over me. *Please don't let me die again.* I heard Romi say something about removing the metal, and then I felt them tugging at my middle. It was like being stabbed repeatedly with a knife, but suddenly, it was gone.

I opened my eyes to find Jake kneeling next to me, blood dripping down his face, holding my hand against his heartbeat. "Poppy," he whispered.

"I chose you," I admitted with a smile, my voice stronger than I anticipated.

He kissed the back of my hand. "Thank god."

I reached up and touched the wound on his forehead. "Just a scratch," he promised. "Romi, Paris, and Loren have perfect aim, although I have no idea how they simultaneously killed the wolves and Fletcher."

Paris let out a single laugh. "We were assigned to take

out hybrid vampires. I carried the bullets that would kill them. Don't know how Romi did it."

Romi blew the hair out of her face. "Fenton and I may be pacifists in general, but we've literally been to hell and back. I always carry magic bullets that will kill almost every supernatural creature."

Jake's eyes widened. "I'm going to need some of those."

"After you stop bleeding," she promised.

We all looked up as the ambulance, human police, and firefighters arrived at the same time. Jake helped me sit up and I looked down at my blood-soaked clothes. I lifted my shirt away from my torso, revealing only a shallow cut.

"We get another chance," I whispered.

"We do," Jake said back, kissing me softly.

Something appeared on the ground next to him and I was startled to find my violin and a stack of letters weaved through the strings. The top one read TO POPPY, LOVE DAD. And for the second time in twelve years, I burst into tears.

Chapter Thirty-Nine

Jake

AFTER A GRUELING forty-eight hours, including a blood transfusion, Poppy was finally sleeping. While they couldn't reverse all the effects of Vixen, she was now mostly human. She tolerated eating small amounts and was sleeping for a few hours at a time, but when she got a paper cut on a magazine, she healed within a few hours.

"Maybe it's the venom, or maybe I'm still part reaper?" she'd suggested.

"As long as you're happy and safe, that's the only thing that matters," I returned.

The steady beeping of Poppy's heart monitor lulled me into sleep in a chair next to her bed. A touch on my shoulder had me drawing my weapon and leveling it before I even opened my eyes.

"Just me," Paris whispered, her hands in the air. She reached out and pressed her hand down on my arm, lowering the gun. "Fenton and Romi are going to take over. It's time."

I put my gun away and scrubbed my hands down my face, every inch of me aching and exhausted, despite being euphoric that Poppy was okay. I turned my head to check on her. She was sleeping on her side facing me, her hands balled up into fists in front of her. I reached over and unballed her fists, smoothing out her fingers. She let out a small breath but didn't wake.

I pushed myself to standing, my joints creaking and popping. I was stiff from neglecting to do my exercises and forgoing ice and heat, but all my focus had been on Poppy. Paris turned and exited the room and I limped after her.

Fenton and Romi were waiting in the hall. "We're here as long as you need," Romi said.

Fenton agreed. "Get some food and rest. We're well versed in long hospital vigils."

"Text or call when she wakes up," I directed. "And if she needs anything. Or—"

Romi hugged me tight. I fell silent. "We will. Promise. It's okay." She released me and then gripped my shoulders. "You only have to do this once. After that, it's done."

I released a breath. "Thanks."

When we got to Paris's car—I was far too tired to drive—she reached into the back and grabbed a lunchbox and set it on my lap. "Ice packs for your leg. Eat the food because I'm guessing you haven't eaten today."

I opened my mouth to argue but she was right. I couldn't remember the last time I ate. Breakfast yesterday? Dinner the night before?

The loud sound my stomach made confirmed her accusation. I plopped the ice pack on my leg and opened a glass storage container to reveal a pasta salad. Using the fork in the bag, I took a bite, then paused. "This is different."

"Gluten free pasta," Paris explained. "And garlic oil since I can't use regular garlic. Oh, and nutritional yeast instead of parmesan since I can't have dairy."

I took another bite. "The texture's a bit off, but it's good."

"Eh," she shrugged. "You're just really hungry. It's tolerable."

"Fair." I had finished the pasta and the granola bar she'd included by the time we pulled up to Blackburn House.

She unbuckled her seatbelt and turned to face me. "Are we sure?"

I nodded. "We have to tell him and this is the safest place I could think of."

"Even with the ghosts?"

"Especially with the ghosts."

Mina was waiting for us at the door and immediately wrapped me in a tight hug. When she pulled back, her fingertips grazed my forehead near the bandage. "Stop trying to die on me."

"It's on my to-do list," I promised. Now that Fletcher was dead, Mina, Carma, and my family had been released from protective custody. "Your dad here yet?"

She gave Paris a brief hug. "Yeah. We're in the front room."

I tried not to think about how long of a walk it was from the porch to the front room. On a good day, it was just down the hall and to the right. But today, it seemed like miles. Usually, I kept quiet, just dealt with the situation without expressing my needs.

Whether it was just sheer exhaustion or a lesson I learned

from Poppy about asking for what I needed, I said, "Grab the rolling chair."

Mina smiled and pushed the door open wider, revealing a computer chair. "Let's roll."

I groaned at the pun but moved inside and took a seat. "Thanks. Don't dump me out."

"Not until after the meeting," she promised. "We plan to get a few wheelchairs to keep on the property for guests. Carma's already working on plans to expand the doorways in the rooms and redesign the bathrooms on the main floor so they're all accessible."

When we moved into the front room, everyone turned to face us, quiet anticipation filling the space. Carma was seated on a black, low-backed sofa, while Jim and Eliza occupied two white armchairs. Eyes on the floor, Paris moved to a matching chaise, opposite the semi-circle from Eliza. The chaise had a skull carved into a decorative wooden piece on the front that was very Carma.

Sebastian and Reggie appeared next to my chair. "There are no other spirits inside," Reggie confirmed.

"I detected no additional supernaturals on the exterior as well," Sebastian added.

I nodded. "Good. Let me know if that changes."

"How's Poppy?" Carma asked.

I gave a brief rundown as Mina passed around cups of coffee and tea, before sitting next to Carma. "I'd like to press pause on the Poppy discussion for a moment and explain why we're here while it's safe." I shot a questioning look to Sebastian and Reggie, who both nodded that we were still in the clear.

I leaned forward and set my mug down on the glass table in the center of our group and rested my elbows lightly on my legs. "Jim, Paris and I believe there is a leak at SHAP."

All eyes studied Jim, who had his ankle resting on his opposite knee and his fingers tented in front of him. "How certain?"

"I would bet my life on it, sir."

He looked at Paris. "And you?"

She handed him a sheet of notebook paper. "I made notes of every occurrence that we believe indicates someone is a double agent."

Jim studied the list for a long moment before handing it back to Paris. "Destroy this." He stood, put his hands in his pockets, and moved to a bank of windows overlooking the side lawn. The trees lining the property line were splashes of orange, yellow, and brown against the thick gray clouds. Unlike Hayvenwood, Applechester was just reaching its peak color season. I'd have to take Poppy on a long drive through the woods.

Jim didn't speak for a long time and we remained silent, giving him space to consider his options. My phone buzzed with a text.

Romi: *Poppy's awake and told me to tell you that if you don't take a nap and eat a decent meal before you come back, she will make you watch 27 Dresses again*

I pressed my lips together to keep from laughing. She and Eliza had that movie memorized.

Me: *Tell her I need to catch her up on a lot of movies*

Romi: *She says you just evaded promising to eat and nap*

Me: *I promise. Tell her I don't want to waste time on a movie I've seen 100000 times when we can watch a new one*

I tucked my phone back in my pocket, then stilled. I had always been waiting for the *next* thing. The next clue, the next mission, the next promotion. But if the last forty-eight hours had taught me anything, it was that there may not be a next time and I needed to make *this* time count. The decision crystalized in front of me so clearly, I nearly reached my hand out to touch it.

The antique grandfather clock in the corner ticked a steady rhythm, but instead of the sound twisting my anxiety tighter at the waste of time, it merely reminded me to take in the moment. I looked around the room. To the corner where Poppy and I used to meet near the old bar. To the crown molding I helped Carma and Mina replace. To the spot under the newly repaired chandelier where I danced the chicken dance with my niece. To the hallway outside the door where I first caught a glimpse of Poppy's cloak.

There were so many powerful memories contained within these walls, and so many more I wanted to make. Now there would be one more. I opened my mouth to speak, but Jim turned around first.

"Here's the plan. Jake and Paris—"

"Excuse me, Jim," I interrupted, "but please consider this my resignation as an active field agent. I will be starting my role as mentor to Daisy, even without SHAP's backing, effective immediately."

Eliza's head shot up, Mina gasped, and Reggie and Sebastian elbowed each other. Paris gave me a discreet thumbs up. Jim stared at me for a long moment. He didn't ask me if I was sure; he trusted me and knew me well enough to know this decision was final. Instead, he nodded and I swore, for a single moment, he stopped frowning. That was almost the equivalent of a smile.

"You will be sorely missed," he said, then turned to Paris and Eliza. "You two will be partners. Figure it out. Here's the plan…"

Chapter Forty

Poppy's Human Rule #1: Live with my whole heart

Poppy

BEING HUMAN AGAIN was startling. Well, mostly human. When the venom mixed with my reaper magic, it had a strange reaction. I had a heartbeat, functioning lungs, a stomach that still loved chocolate, and could now smell, feel, and taste things in the human realm.

I could no longer drop my human glamour, but I could heal faster than an average human. Thank god. I had already broken my nose and three fingers trying to remember that I could no longer walk through walls. That was going to take some getting used to.

Everything was brighter, louder, sharper than I remembered, and with that came sensory overload. Humans were never quiet—hell, neither were ghosts—and I wasn't used to constant company. While I had spent the last twelve years wishing to be around humans, I had taken my solitude for granted.

The night that Jake took me back to his place and found everyone we knew waiting in his living room, I had a panic attack. I didn't miss those at all. He had cleared everyone out—including Sebastian—and gone to run errands to give me some alone time.

I sat on the couch for a long time, too overwhelmed to move, until my heart rate had settled. Then, I took off running and slid across the wood floor in my socks. I laughed. It felt like how I used to glide across the earth as a reaper.

I stood in the center of the bedroom, staring at the violin case on the dresser. When I was overwhelmed back home— well, my reaper home—I'd play to the water and Isle of Exile. It made sense that if the music helped me then, it would help me now.

But feelings didn't always make sense, and I couldn't bring myself to touch the case. On the other side of that bow, there wasn't my sister or my family. There was just a gaping hole in my life that I didn't know how to navigate around. I had gotten what I always wanted—to be human again with Jake—but every dream comes with collateral damage, and this was truly a life for a life. My reaper life for my human life.

I pressed my lips together and took a deep breath. No, a life for a life wasn't right. I didn't give up my reaper life, I'd just postponed it for a while.

The realization eased the tightness in my chest, and I turned and walked into the bathroom, then started the shower, filling the room up with steam before stepping in. Showers were quickly becoming my new favorite thing. I had spent so long being cold and the water heated me from the outside in. It was almost like standing in the sunlight.

I marveled at my reddened skin and the way my nose

prickled at the fresh-smelling soap. I luxuriated in the way the running water blocked out all other sound. When I stepped out and grabbed a towel, I watched the goosebumps run across my skin. I had showered while I was in the medical center, but it had been quick and perfunctory. This had been at my pace and I'd been completely alone. My body felt a million times lighter.

There was just one problem: I didn't have any clean clothes. I had spent the last two weeks in a hospital gown and scrub pants, since Romi's clothes were destroyed. I still had the pink shirt and leggings that were packed in Jake's bag, but my entire body bristled at the thought of putting them back on. That outfit was important to me, but represented another time, another person.

With a towel wrapped around my hair and another around my body, I exited the bathroom and found stacks of folded clothes on the bed with a hair drier, hair products, nail polish remover, and a manicure kit. At the end of the bed was a pair of noise-canceling headphones. A note sat on top of the box.

POPPY,

I FIGURED YOU'D NEED A FEW THINGS FOR YOUR FIRST NIGHT IN YOUR NEW HOME.
ROMI

I turned around expecting to see Jake, but the bedroom door was closed, allowing me some privacy. I dressed in the softest black joggers and a purple HAYVENWOOD, MICHIGAN hoodie—it was hard to leave the purple behind—then dried my hair and pulled it up into a messy bun. I removed the chipped nail polish on my fingers and toes, then slipped my feet into some cozy slippers. I took three deep breaths before I opened the door and slid out of the bedroom.

Jake was in the living room, watching a sports show on mute. He looked up when he saw me and shut off the television but waited for me to speak.

I smoothed my hand down the front of my sweatshirt. "Everything fits."

"Good." He nodded his head toward the couch.

When I moved next to him, he grabbed a soft, fluffy blanket from the back of the couch. "Mina and Carma said this is the softest blanket they've ever felt, and Eliza sent us some soup and fresh bread for dinner."

Whatever was holding me together snapped at the generosity of the people in Jake's life and the tears I thought had dissipated came back. I cried into the blanket as Jake held me, his strength and his body heat my anchor as my head spun with emotions.

"What can I do to support you?" he asked, his lips against my forehead.

"Just overwhelmed," I managed.

"I'm right here."

When my sobs had turned into sniffles, he handed me a box of tissues and went to heat up dinner. He returned to the couch with a mug of homemade tomato soup and a chunk of warm, crusty bread. I peeled the bread apart, dipping the crust into the soup and then ate my way to the middle. It took me forty minutes to finish—Jake reheated my soup twice—but I wanted to savor the tangy sweetness of the soup with the sourdough bread. It had been the best meal I'd ever had, although to be fair I had said that about all my meals for the last two weeks.

"I have one more surprise," Jake admitted.

He brought back a black box from the kitchen and opened the lid. The sweet smell of chocolate washed over me and my mouth watered. "My favorite," I whispered, recognizing the box from a local chocolate shop. I reached out and ran my fingers along the edge of the container that housed a dozen chocolates.

"I know." He smiled.

It had been over a decade, but the truffles looked the same. My hand hovered, unable to decide. "I don't know how to pick."

"The brownie truffle was always your favorite," he reminded me. "Maybe start there?"

I nodded and scooped the brownie truffle out of the box and then held it close to my nose, inhaling the magical chocolate scent. It was sweet and floral, rich and decadent. It smelled how happy felt. I inhaled again, trying to memorize it. "I really missed chocolate."

Jake laughed. "Why am I not surprised?"

I smiled at him and then closed my eyes, lifting the treat to my lips and taking a small bite. Unlike the bland hospital food or the comforting soup, the truffle was a sharp cut through my taste buds. The chocolate coated my tongue, making my mouth tingle.

I moaned and then took another bite, trying to balance my desire to savor the morsel with shoving the entire thing into my mouth. I rolled the chocolate around on my tongue before swallowing. When I finished the last bite and sucked the remnants off my finger, I opened my eyes to find Jake staring at my mouth.

"Are you going to have any chocolate?" I asked.

"Yes. Immediately." Then he brought his mouth to mine and kissed me.

I thought nothing could taste better than chocolate but kissing Jake while my mouth still tasted like chocolate made my head swim. I swear kissing him as a human was ten times more incredible than kissing him as a reaper. His lips, his tongue, the feel of his five o'clock shadow stoked a fire low in my stomach.

I growled and fisted his sweatshirt, pulling him closer to me and deepening the kiss.

Jake broke away, his chest heaving. "I know you're still getting used to everything. We don't have to—"

I pressed my finger to his lips to quiet him. "I want to know how you feel now that I'm human. I bet you're better than chocolate."

"I'll take that bet."

He didn't take the bet lightly. In between feeding me three more truffles, he undressed me and made love to me, my skin practically glowing from the euphoria his hands and mouth and body caused. It was absolutely the best day of my new human life. Although, I had a feeling I would have a lot more best days, as long as we were together.

IT TOOK JAKE and me three days—most of which was spent

in bed relearning and savoring each other—to resurface and see everyone. We had stopped by Eliza's first. She and I laid on the couch with our heads together, catching up for six hours. Magnolia and Morris stopped by, and Magnolia got so emotional, she cried. I was pretty sure the last time she'd cried was when she gave birth, and Morris joked it was only because Eliza messed up her schedule.

Once the missing persons case Jake filed twelve years ago was closed, and I got a new license, passport, and voter registration card, real life pushed through. I missed my family, especially Sylvia, desperately. Not enough to regret my choice. Knowing they were waiting for me on the other side was enough. Before bed, I always took a half an hour to write down everything that happened during the day. When Jake asked why, I said, "I want to give us all something to talk about at family dinner."

Sometimes though, on the days when I missed them so much my entire body hurt, I reread their letters. They were full of suggestions of things to do as a human—from trying new food to sky diving to visiting old family friends in every corner of the globe. I traced the words with my fingers, memorizing every line. When I'd admitted to Jake that I was concerned my tearstains would wash the words away, he scanned them and he framed the original ones, hanging them on the wall next to his mom's letter.

The nightmares came as no surprise. Years of witnessing so many deaths haunted me. Loren had texted Jake the number to a therapist who dealt with supernatural issues, and the SHAP physician had prescribed some antianxiety medication to help. It was weird opening up to a stranger about my reaper life, but the last two video calls had gone well.

We spent Halloween at Blackburn House handing out candy and books to kids and adults alike. Carma had helped me find a purple cloak and painted my face like a skeleton. Weirdly, it made me feel less homesick. The next day, on Día de Todos los Santos, I went with Reggie and his family to the park.

I listened to stories of Reggie's human life, then shared a few funny stories of our adventures together, at his brother Alan's insistence. While their Applechester family rolled with the fact that I had been dead only a month ago, the people visiting from out of town shied away. But the best part of the whole day was seeing Lola open up to Reggie. Kids were great at adapting to weird—or in this case, dead.

"You know what sucks?" Reggie said later that night, as his head leaned on—well through—my shoulder, "I can't hug you anymore."

"That really does suck. But it's only for a few more decades. Promise."

At his request, I played the violin for the first time since becoming human. My fingers ached from my lack of callouses, but I kept going until Reggie's neighbors knocked on the walls. It was still hard, each slide of the bow somehow cutting and healing at the same time, but I figured new memories would make the old ones easier.

The next day, I strung twinkle lights wrapped in white sheer fabric around my bedroom, then resumed practicing. I couldn't see the real fairy lights from my strings anymore, but this helped. Jake just smiled and told me I could decorate however I wanted as long as it made me happy.

Then, one day, being human wasn't so hard anymore.

By the time the first snowflakes hovered in the air, two weeks before Thanksgiving, I finally felt ready to take on family dinner at the Robinsons'. While I was getting more and more comfortable being human every day, I was still nervous.

Jake grabbed my hand on the front porch. "You're going to be fine."

"Yeah, they actually like you," Paris mumbled.

"You saved my life, Paris," Jake said. "My folks love you already."

"It's not your folks I'm worried about. It's my new partner." She tugged at the neck of her sweater as if it were choking her.

I reached out and took Paris's hand, who looked shocked. "Eliza can hold grudges. Don't worry, I'll run interference."

Tonight, Magnolia insisted on having a big celebration dinner. I was back, Paris had saved Jake's life—and Magnolia had yet to meet Paris which was thoroughly unacceptable in her opinion—and Jake had finally formally received his promotion from field agent to mentor. I was guessing by the delicious smells outside the front door, Magnolia had outdone herself.

Jake had sent her a copy of Paris's food restrictions and fingers crossed she'd taken the message to heart. If not, I would make her something myself and as I was still messing up peanut butter and jelly sandwiches, no one wanted that. I hadn't needed to cook much as a teen, between my big family and Eliza's love of cooking, and I had a lot to learn.

We joined Magnolia and Morris in the dining room, where they were setting out food. Eliza, Mina, and Carma were playing a video game with Daisy, and by the looks of it, Daisy was kicking their butts. I smiled, the sound of little girl laughter filling the room.

"Perfect timing," Magnolia said, rushing over to greet Jake and me, then spending a solid four minutes fawning over Paris. Paris turned so pink I was worried she'd pass out.

Just before I intervened, Morris stepped in and called, "Let's eat!"

After Eliza got Daisy cleaned up, we all sat down, making sure Paris and Eliza were at opposite ends of the table. Unfortunately, that put Paris next to Magnolia, who was a hurricane force today. Magnolia set a full plate of food down in front of Paris and started going through every ingredient and how it was prepared. Paris looked taken aback, but her smile was genuine. "I appreciate it. Thank you."

"Of course, dear. You saved my son's life; you're family now," Magnolia promised.

I didn't miss Eliza sucking down most of her wine glass. Mina elbowed her, and Eliza shot her a look. Then Eliza turned to me. "Poppy, how are you settling in?"

I shrugged and shook my head, still in disbelief. "Still trying to figure out life again, but god, am I grateful to be back. Now, I just have to figure out work."

Carma reached over and touched my wrist. "You remember how you told me you loved weddings?"

"I definitely do."

"Come plan events with us. You can even help us remodel if you want. I pay well." She leaned over and stage whispered, "I'm loaded."

I smiled. "That would be amazing, thank you. The only job I've ever had was walking the neighborhood dogs, so this will be fun!"

"Don't discount your last twelve years as a reaper," Jake added. "You had to stick to a schedule, save souls from literal demons, and work with your entire family, so we know you can do group projects."

I laughed. God, I loved this man. I leaned over and gave him a quick kiss. "You make a very good point." I turned to Carma. "I can't provide references, but I promise to do my best."

Carma smiled. "Deal. We can talk about a start date after dinner."

Magnolia leaned back in her chair, wine glass in her hand, smiling over the group of people at the table. Morris watched her, his eyebrows raised. "Wife, why that look?"

She gestured around the table with her glass. "Our family keeps growing and I'm very content." She eyed me. "For now. I still want more grandkids."

Jake lifted my hand and kissed the back. We weren't sure if we wanted to become parents, but it wasn't a discussion for the dinner table and definitely not anyone else's business. I loved Magnolia, but I knew how to hold my own around a nosy family.

Eliza laughed. "Thank god I got that out of the way eight years ago." She mussed Daisy's hair.

Daisy looked at me. "You used to be a grim reaper?"

I nodded. "I was."

She frowned, serious. "When my daddy died, did you help him cross over?"

I looked at Eliza, then back at Daisy. I only knew Ben from my brief visits to check on Eliza, and I definitely would've remembered coming for his soul. I just couldn't bring myself to say no outright. Not with Daisy's big blue eyes locked on me. "I don't always remember people's names, but I can try. Do you have a picture of him?"

Eliza opened her purse and handed me a funeral card she kept in her wallet.

BENJAMIN DYLAN SOMERSET, 1988-2020

*Somerset...Somerset...*I studied his face, trying to place him. I recognized Daisy in the slant of his nose and his smile, but I didn't recognize him. "I don't think it was me. I'm sorry," I said, handing the photo back to Eliza.

Daisy shrugged. "That's okay."

"You know," Magnolia said. "When your parents first told us about you being a reaper, we didn't want you and Jake together. There was just too much risk with not knowing when you'd get the call. But seeing you both together as adults? I'm just really happy."

My fork clattered to my plate as the entire table went silent.

Jake looked at his dad and then his stepmom as if they were strangers. "You knew?"

Eliza stood. "I cannot believe—" She closed her eyes for a moment. "We have searched for any trace of Poppy for half of our lives." She slapped her hand against her chest. "I watched *my brother* lose the love of his life and have no answers. He spent the last *twelve years* solving nearly impossible cases, making sure victims' families had answers so they didn't suffer like he did. Like we both did. And you both *knew?*"

Magnolia set her glass down and crossed her arms. "And now Poppy's back. This is all water under the bridge."

My eyes stung, my throat burned, my chest was tight. My heart was beating so hard in my ears, I couldn't hear any more conversation. Jake's hand slipped into mine and squeezed. His was shaking, too.

Eliza grabbed Daisy's hand and walked out of the house.

Epilogue

T HE CLOCK ON the mantel chimed midnight, yanking him from his concentration. He sighed and stretched, his back aching from a day spent in front of his laptop. The only light coming into the room was the moon, which was nearly full. A smile touched his lips, a memory of his daughter dressing up in a wolf costume for the Founders Festival and howling at the cardboard moon hung at the entrance gate. He wished he could've kept that picture of her.

He stretched his neck and blew out another breath, chasing away the memory. His computer dinged with a new email.

To: B.Somerset@cmail.com
From: undisclosed sender

Somerset,
Fletcher has been terminated. You've been reassigned.
Meet me tomorrow 13:00 hours.

The End

Don't miss the next book in the Love Me Dead series, *Dearly Departed*!

Join Tule Publishing's newsletter for more great reads and weekly deals!

Acknowledgements

First and foremost, to my readers: Thank you for spending your time and money on this book! The amount of love you give me is astounding, and I strive every day to deserve you. I hope that my words bring you comfort and joy…and maybe a few tears.

Big thanks to Mr. Heather and our families, who have navigated this journey with me. (Don't worry non-evil-stepmom, Magnolia is NOT modeled after you, hehe. Love you!!)

To my Tule team—especially my editor Sinclair—who believed in this book even when I struggled. Y'all are awesome and I'm so thankful for you.

Huge thanks to Janna Bonikowski and Elyssa Man for being the cohesive part of my brain. Big thanks to my alpha reader Sarah Estep, and to Erika Cooper for your notes. All the love to my sensitivity readers and Hayvenwood fact-checkers Jenna Walsh and Amber Young. To my translator Andrea Véliz García: thank you for all your brain space and heavy lifting. To my beta and ARC readers (especially my sister Kate) you're a gift I will never take for granted.

All the love to Jen Luerssen and Liz Lincoln for running sprints with me until our fingers cramped. You're the reason I finished. A shoutout to my fellow authors Dana, Stacey, Fortune, Jadesola, Christina, Shelly, Aliza, Sage, MK, Jem, and Joanne. To Lucie, Misty, and Mathew for your support. To Katie VG, who is one of the most giving and wonderful humans I know.

My Tacos, my Dolls (especially Jen and Bailey), and my Fantoms (especially the *snackladies* and *sister wives*), I love you and treasure you. To Eliza and Ci—my partners in chaos—life has been a wild adventure with you, and I can't wait to see what's next.

To the band Nicotine Dolls—whose music, stories, and pancake recipes have been instrumental in helping me write—I'm so glad to know you. Love you guys (and Phil)!

And last but never least, to the friends who have always believed in me, who are the first to cheer me on, who help physically or virtually when I'm struggling, who are only one message away, who send memes/TT/reels/tweets whenever they think of me: I'm so lucky. I love and appreciate you more than you'll ever know. Wishing you all laughter and good books.

Love,
H

If you enjoyed *Grim and Bear It*,
you'll love the next book in the...

Love Me Dead series

Book 1: *Blood Thinners*

Book 2: *Grim and Bear It*
View the series here!

Book 3: *Dearly Departed*
Coming in September 2022

Available now at your favorite online retailer!

About the Author

Bold, Breathtaking, Badass Romance.

When she's not pretending to be a rock star with purple hair, award-winning author Heather Novak is crafting sex positive romance novels to make you swoon! After her rare disease tried to kill her, Heather mutated into a superhero whose greatest power is writing stories that you can't put down.

Heather tries to save the world (like her late mama taught her) from her home near Detroit, Michigan, where she lives with Mr. Heather and a collection of musical instruments. She identifies as part of the LGBTQ+ community and believes Black Lives Matter.

Thank you for reading

Grim and Bear It

If you enjoyed this book, you can find more from all our great authors at TulePublishing.com, or from your favorite online retailer.

TULE
PUBLISHING